GO BACK

EMILY WAGNER

Cover artwork design copyright © 2025 by Niki Lenhart
nikilen-designs.com

Published by Water Dragon Publishing
waterdragonpublishing.com

ISBN 978-1-967547-17-3 (Trade Paperback)

FIRST EDITION

10 9 8 7 6 5 4 3 2 1

For Chris
My muse, forever missed ...

GO BACK

PART ONE

TIME'S UP

Blow it up.
There's nowhere else to go.
Don't you know?
Memories fade.
Fade away …

– Tech Junkies

"The end of technology began so innocently. Tech Shabbats, cell phone sleeping bags, social media detoxes; we all wanted to live without it for a little while — even me. It felt … freeing. But we never imagined our lives without it permanently. Like an unrestrained virus, Go Back swept into our lives, latching onto our greatest fears and turning us against ourselves."

– Grimes, S.
They're Taking Our Tech
[News Underground Opinion Piece]

1

SARAH

I T BEGAN LIKE A BARELY BURNING FLAME with embers nearly invisible to the naked eye. Then, the flames fanned out, singing more and more people, until it became a blizzard of societal change.

We couldn't stop it.

I never thought people would give up their tech, but they did. I did.

Some did it willingly. Others, including myself, were forced. Everyone remembers their location when we first learned the news. I was at a concert at the Elephant Ear in downtown Austin, Texas. I'd been working twenty-eight days straight, and I needed a break. Music had always been my solace, and as I rounded the corner of the club's dark abyss, the low, pulsing beat thumped against my chest. I'd always loved that sense of anticipation right before a show, when you can feel the music before hearing it, and this night was no different.

Before I entered the concert womb, a goth woman with a septum piercing and a raven tattoo on the left side of her long neck had asked, "Checking any tech?" I had always wanted a tattoo and envied her ability to ignore the permanence of it. I could never decide what to get. Plus, the pain factor. I had been too scared of the IV sedation process, so they had to put me under to get my wisdom teeth out.

As I nodded, the goth woman snatched my cell phone from my hand and placed it inside its numbered slot. Like an idiot, I had forgotten to leave it at home. They no longer allowed us to take photos or videos at live events. Artists said it helped with fan engagement and prevented live streaming. No live streaming equaled more people at shows.

Personally, I hated the rule. I needed my phone as a periscope. Being only 5'1" had its disadvantages.

The Elephant Ear had several stages in three different rooms. I headed into the medium-sized room—the one that hosted regional acts; hence, no VIP lounge—only a bar and some three-level aluminum bleachers against one wall for the few fans who wanted to sit during an eardrum-blasting performance.

No more than fifty feet in front of those bleachers, bodies thrashed freely in the heat of the mosh pit and bounced to the pounding music. I decided to go in. What did I have to lose? I longed for human connection, which I hadn't had for some time—because of, you know, work, but I didn't feel like talking. The black metal railings just managed to keep me and the other moshers upright. sound waves rattled my ribcage. The smell of smuggled smoke I'd have to scrub off at home filled my nostrils. Every few minutes, someone jumped, and either surfed or landed head-first on the floor.

Clinging to the rail, I craned my neck to the right to get a better look at the lead singer. That's when I noticed a man standing center-stage, right hand wrapped around a brown beer bottle. His thin red, plaid shirt looked to have been washed a thousand times. He glanced back and nodded. Was that approval of me or of the band? I had never excelled at deciphering the intentions of men. Plus, meeting a potential significant other "in-person" instead of on a dating app was so Gen-X.

As the opening act ended, the noise died down, and the next act started setting up, I stood there, deciding bar, band, or boy, when I noticed he stood next to me.

"Good crowd," he said in a sarcastic tone.

"Yeah," I said, trying not to sound too shocked that he had started the conversation. "You seen these guys before?" He couldn't have been much older than me, maybe early thirties, but his aquamarine eyes looked like they'd seen much more than three decades. His smooth, wide hand grasped his beer bottle.

"I've seen them live like eight times at least." He squinted and looked off to the left in thought. "So much I get in free now. Crazy."

"Wow," I said. "That's cool." He nodded, almost like I'd embarrassed him. "My name's Sarah."

"Chris. Nice to meet you," he added and took the last gulp of his beer. "Want one?"

"Yeah. Sure."

He hailed a server, and ordered me an Amstel Light, himself an IPA with a lizard on the label. When the next band started up, Chris bobbed his head up and down to the music. I chuckled and joined along. Something about him transported me back a decade, to a time when others' opinions couldn't sway my decisions. We laughed and sang along with the band, standing together as the crowd swelled around us. If only we'd had our phones to take selfies.

In between songs we yelled commentary.

"It's so loud," I said with cupped hands to amplify my voice.

"Did you see that guy?" Chris yelled back, and a guy leaned back into the crowd from the stage, but no one caught him.

"Ouch," Chris said, smiling.

The sensation of temporarily escaping the outside world, even for a brief period, was immensely enjoyable. Go Back attempted to strip us of our immediate connection, but in instances like these, I didn't find it bothersome. The crowd thinned, but Chris and I stood next to each other, our beers long gone. Despite looking tired, he still had the post-show buzz and probably wanted to stay up due to the ringing in his ears.

After I picked my cell phone up at the entrance, we made our way out into the open air to the ride share pick up point. No one drove anymore. Too many texting and driving accidents only added to the GB's public health threat initiative.

"Thank you for protecting me back there," I said, realizing we had just finished our first date.

"Don't worry about it," Chris said, then asked, "So, what do you do? Professional concert-goer?"

"Worse. A journalist." We both chuckled.

Journalists had become the bottom feeders of American society. Ever since the early 21st century when politicians decried us as the Fake News, we never recovered.

"But," I said, "I'm not like an excellent journalist or anything. My writing focuses on topics such as the latest tech craze or the new zoo baby. Basically, I answer the phone a lot."

Chris smiled. "Don't sell yourself short," he said and looked down to kick at gravel. "At least you have a job. I got laid off last week. The I.T. sector is crap now." His hand ran his hand through his dark, wavy hair. It almost brushed his shoulders. The wind also gave it a more tousled appearance. I kept trying to push away the feelings of desire, not only for him, but for how things used to be. Boy meets girl. Boy asks for girl's number. Boy takes a girl out on a date. They sleep together and never see each other again or hold out and make it last.

But now things were so much more complicated.

Rideshares came and went, and the last rest of the crowd shuffled to their cars or rides, leaving Chris and I in our long, drawn out, awkward goodbye. The warm Central Texas air brushed against my face and ruffled my hair. I held up my phone to order my ride through its smart app, "Mira, I need transport for one at 223 Smith Street outside of the Elephant Ear Club." Last time I ordered a ride, it took an hour because Mira couldn't hear me over the background noise.

Chris cleared his throat, looked down. "Want to grab some coffee?" he asked, revealing a perfect smile minus a crooked upper eye tooth. I couldn't see any reason not to.

•   •   •

The lights inside the 24-hour coffee bar were too bright, so we opted to sit outside where the whoosh of vehicles and the Metro filled the air. I'd been there many times after shows and usually ordered something like a hot toddy to warm my throat worn scratchy from all the concert singing and cheering. This time I stuck with some iced tea with lemon.

"It's nice outside," I said and wondered why I had. The air gave the sensation of snuggling with a warm blanket in a sauna.

"Really, now?" Chris nodded. Damn, I couldn't get over those blue eyes. "So, where are you from?"

"Here. Attended Northwestern, though."

"Oh! Ivy League!"

"It's not Ivy League! And you mentioned you're in IT ... or were ... sorry. So, you're no slouch yourself," I said.

Chris looked away for a moment and stroked his chin. His hands looked strong and smooth. "I'm self-taught. Never went to college. Or, well, I did for a semester. Community college. Just didn't work out for me."

"Don't sell yourself short," I said with a smile.

"I see what you did there. Well, what do you do when you're not investigating?"

Some loud teenagers walked by, their voices bleeding together in a cacophony. Then my phone buzzed, and a message appeared.

❗ EMERGENCY ALERT

This weekend, the United States government, in cooperation with the Go Back movement, will begin a cell phone restriction initiative. Officers will be assigned to enforce the initiative, which lasts from 8:00pm to 6:00am each day for all citizens. The purpose of the enforcement is to extend the life of the devices due to a shortage of Rare Eare Elements, as well as ensure public safety following the disclosure of elevated health risks of cell phone tech, including brain cancer. More information is available at whitehouse.gov/news.

Chris smiled at me. "Well, isn't that grand?"

I let out a loud sigh. "You know about the rumors, right?"

He nodded, then shrugged. "We'll see."

Yes, we will.

"Anyway, I enjoy going to shows, reading, hiking around Enchanted Rock, hanging with my sister when she's in a good mood."

"Ha! Same! I love Enchanted Rock. You know it's haunted, right?" Chris's eyes lit up like a teenager. I noticed some scruff on his square chin, also a few freckles on his slender nose.

We chatted for about another hour about random things like growing up and a little about the show, favorite foods. Chris drank at least three decaf lattes.

"Well, I'd better get going. Thanks for the drinks," I said, pushing aside thoughts of the impending technological apocalypse.

We walked to the patio exit. Chris leaned down to unhook the gate latch. Our arms brushed against each other, and I felt the tingle of new romance like static pulling on my arm hair.

"Yeah. Nice to meet you." He looked down and shuffled his feet.

Seconds later, my ride share arrived. "Hit me up on the socials, before it's too late," I told him over my shoulder.

2

OLIVIA

THE FLUORESCENT LIGHTING in the Go Back recycling facility bounced off the steel vats filled with melted down tech. Ed and I stood next to one labeled *SIM Cards Only*. Ed rapped his fingernails against the vat, creating an echo that seemed to bounce off every wall. I crossed my arms, irritated.

"Hey, did you hear the news?" Ed asked.

Of course I did. Two hours ago, my phone had blasted the message about tech restrictions so loudly, it couldn't be ignored. "Yeah, and you're aware that this is just the start."

"Wonder if the tech restrictions apply to us, too," he said with a not-so-charming chuckle. It was his "I'm uncertain about what to do, so I'll attempt to laugh it off" chuckle.

"Laughing it off won't work today, Ed," I scolded. "Of course, the restrictions don't apply to us." However, I couldn't be certain.

As we got back to the tedious of work pulling SIM cards out of their slots, I glanced over at him and thought back to our first meeting. We were innocent GB recruits who would soon discover the reality of what we had signed up for. I joined Go Back after my time in the military because I wanted to make a difference. Our job was to dismantle cell phones to preserve rare earth minerals. GB labeled it as an economic preservation, but it truly amounted to a power grab. As a recruit, I'd asked my superior, "Why don't we just turn off the fucking phones if we don't want people to use them?"

She laughed in my face. I later learned GB and the government weren't preserving the rare earths at all. They were keeping the best and selling the rest to other countries affected by China's ban on exporting rare earths.

Immediately after discovering this, I rushed to Ed. Anger flushed my face, and I couldn't refrain from rocking back and forth. "So, we're lying to everyone about how horrible cell phones are, and we're out there stealing them and dismantling them to make money off the minerals? All at the expense of citizens?"

"Pretty fucked up. Surprised you were unaware."

Without looking at me, he slid open the back of an old Samsung flip phone to reveal the square SIM card. He pinched it out and tossed it onto the conveyor belt that led to the inside of the vat. I remember wondering at the time if he knew more than I did.

"Of course I didn't know," I had replied, "otherwise I would never have signed up for this!"

"I hate it, too," Ed said. "But what can we do? We signed an irrevocable contract. If we break it, we're on the other side. They'd be hunting us."

"What the hell do you mean, hunting us?"

Ed was stoic at the time. His eyes didn't even blink.

"You are aware! Tell me!" I yelled.

"Shh, okay. I talked with someone over in development; the ones in charge of building the detoxes —"

"And ...?"

"And, she said, rumor is, the government is going to force people into the centers, at least the people who won't give up their phones." Ed's tanned forehead wrinkled; his dark eyes pierced through mine. He looked as serious as he did when he first asked me to team up.

"That can't happen," I said. *Not in the United States of America.*

"Well, I, for one, want to find out if it's true," Ed had said.

"Me, too."

•   •   •

After that, we did some digging. We went through dozens and dozens of files and found blueprints and plans and made our decision.

We were getting out of here.

We made contacts on the outside during our tech runs.

We created the Garden.

•　　•　　•

The lunch bell chimed, and I stared at the square yellow button on the backside of the silver vat to activate the eye scanning software. I caught the sound of a whoosh and paused. The vat reminded me of an oil tanker. I saw my reflection in it and noticed my dreadlocks looking frizzy. They seemed to mirror the craziness of the moment.

Ed and I stepped outside of the room and took off our heat-protective suits. We always joked how the getup made us look like demoted astronauts relegated to remain on Earth.

The GB Center was a nondescript brick building on the outside. Yet, within its walls existed a multitude of tunnel-like corridors and brightly lit communal zones, with the most sizable area known as "The Commons." A phone with a red panic button was positioned nearby, exclusively for internal calls. No access to the outside world. They only gave upper-level GB access to communications with our other facilities. And only they understood the full details surrounding them. I only heard of one time that someone pushed the panic button, not in the commons, but in their barracks. We never found out who did it or why, or what happened to them afterwards.

Ed and I found a table and sat down. Others streamed in as well, but Ed and I kept a low profile and didn't make eye contact.

"We'll be busy soon," Ed said in a low voice. "Lots more tech coming in once the next alert goes down."

I put my hand over my mouth, propped my head up and gave the subtlest of head nods.

"You seem distracted. What's up?" Ed asked.

Truth is, I was, but didn't want to let on. "I'm just thinking back to the beginning and how we got here," I said, pointing at our table. No one else sat near us, and the ones who sat elsewhere stared at their i-watches, looking at stupid GB approved videos, so

I felt comfortable speaking. If any other GB got wind, we'd get a sanction. No bad speech!

I continued, "I'm working on it. We'll get the tech back. I'm still trying to contact Isobel. The Garden is almost ready. We've added twelve new recruits this month."

"Right," Ed said as he gulped down the rest of his coffee. "I'm going to head back to the dorm and encrypt some messages. I'll meet you back at the end of break."

3

SARAH

I'D BEEN DIGGING INTO the Go Back movement for some time. The investigation led me to Rob Klein, a former Political Science professor and local GB expert. He agreed to meet in his office, but only if I did not record him or use any tech during the interview. He mentioned the permanence of technology was permanent, thus the necessity of pen and paper.

His office looked to be about eight-by-eight, with a wall of jam-packed bookcases behind an executive-style desk. Papers, manila folders, and random office supplies swarmed its surface, leaving little room for me to rest my reporter notebook, so I held it in my lap.

Mr. Klein locked the door and drew the blinds before he sat behind the desk. Frail and likely in his early 60's, he had gray, thinning, buzz-cut hair. Black metal bifocals adorned the tip of his nose.

He told me about the beginning of Go Back—an anti-tech group that had been around for a while but never had a leader. About five years ago, a guy named Dr. James Mason and his wife Lucinda became the unofficial leaders of the so-called New Luddites, or NLs, as people called them.

I was aware of the Luddites, but unfamiliar with the Masons.

"It all started back in the 80's. The NL's flew under the radar. No one was familiar with them," Klein said.

"That's about when the Internet started. I remember my parents talking about it."

"Yeah, the Masons and their NL minions infiltrated the government. They lobbied lawmakers to abandon new technology. They said it destroyed progress and would cause the society to collapse."

"Ha, that's a good one," I said. "In what way can technology impede progress? Makes no sense."

Klein's expression shifted "It does if you think about it. The Masons said tech would lead to a bigger gap between the rich and the poor, and that computers would replace people."

"Hm. I have talked to some people who got fired because their job became automated. I didn't think too much of it."

My hand cramped with all the writing.

"They blamed everything on tech," he said with a cough. "The NLs said people weren't able to keep up with technological advances, that people never slowed down enough to become fully sound, so to speak. They claimed tech led to a mental breakdown of sorts."

"Addiction," I interrupted.

"Yes. The NL's ran for office, not on an anti-tech platform, but on a mental health one. They won more and more and pushed their agenda once they got on the inside. People took stock in it. You got all that?"

I'd better. "So, what does that have to do with Go Back? We are unaware of the NLs nowadays."

"The NLs got violent. They started pelting people with paint at tech shops, held sit-ins at the Facebook and Google headquarters. They set up camp and engaged in hunger strikes, even bringing their kids."

"I remember seeing that on the news in college. Thought little of it." But maybe I should have

The professor continued despite my perspiring forehead. I shifted in the chair. "The Parkers didn't like it, and the NLs split into two factions, the NLs, which faded away, and the Go Back group, which was headed up by a guy named Sven Palhert. Have I got you up to speed?"

"Yes, very much so." I thanked him for his time.

After the interview, I transcribed all my notes into the Mira app, which typed it into my word processing system.

And so began my obsession with weeding out Go Back. I had decent information, but still, no one inside Go Back would provide me with any real details of their operation.

•   •   •

After that interview, we started getting calls about missing cell phones.

"Hello, News Underground. Sarah Grimes speaking."

"Hi. I can't find my cell phone. I've searched all over."

"How are you calling me?"

"I'm calling from my office phone."

"When's the last time you saw it?" I asked.

"Earlier today. I took a quick break, left it at my desk, and now it's gone." She breathed so loud, I had to hold the receiver away from my ear.

"Did you ask around at work?" I asked.

"Of course I did, but nobody knew about it. Afterward, I contacted my provider and asked if they could trace it, but they couldn't. Same thing happened to a friend of a friend. Please help me."

I wrote her name down like all the others and called every cell phone provider in the area. Most told me they'd gotten more than usual reports of people losing their phones. The police informed me that verifying matters like this was impossible, and individuals could only report their phones as stolen.

"Ma'am," the police dispatcher told me. "We are aware of those reports, too, but there is no way for us to figure out if —"

"So, we're both getting the calls? Can you at least confirm if the city or state is doing some sort of tech roundup?"

"No ma'am, I cannot."

•   •   •

After my shift ended, my assignment editor, Deb, invited me to coffee. I would have gone straight home, but recent rolling brownouts had me aspiring to be anywhere but home in this heat.

Plus, I'd been meaning to talk to her about all the calls I'd been getting about missing phones.

News Underground was on the second floor of a mixed-use building. Often, we grabbed coffee or food on the first floor, which was retail. The coffee shop smelled like roasted hazelnut mixed with s'mores. I took a deep breath and scanned the menu.

"How've you been?" Deb asked moments after we sat down.

"I'm good," I said with a slight smile. *Cut the small talk, Deb. I wanted to get the truth, like how can we get information on what Go Back is up to? I'd even go undercover.*

Behind Deb's head, a TV played a clip of last night's Saturday Night Live. Pete Davidson played President Gibson talking about the tech and the trade war with China. Gibson's Press Secretary, played by Leonardo Di Caprio, opened a huge cabinet filled with cell phones and tablets. They all landed on his head and spilled on the floor. I smiled and shook my head.

"Earth to Sarah ..." Deb said.

"Oh sorry, these skits are silly, but true."

"Yeah," Deb said, sipping her cappuccino. "Gibson is ready to sign Declaration 466-92. The tech recycling bill?"

"Yes. I am aware. Oh, and I've been wanting to tell you about these tips I've been getting. People say their phones are missing. I believe there is more to it than just chance." I felt more frustrated than ever, as crushed as the ground up coffee beans used to make my hazelnut latte. I had to convince her to let me write the story about Go Back, but I needed an official source.

"Alright, my apologies. Let's refrain from discussing work." It felt like minutes passed before she made small talk. "So, you getting used to it here down South? You've lived here in Austin for what, six months?"

Well, at least she pretended to care. "I'm from Austin, but I moved away for school." I stopped talking because she wasn't listening. During my pause, I looked around and noticed most people in the coffee shop held their devices. Nothing new, but many had looks of despair. Their fingers fluttered like hummingbird wings on the screen, tapping. That prompted me to check my phone.

I noticed a friend request from a Chris Cameron. A closer inspection revealed that the person was indeed Chris from Elephant Ear.

My heart quickened as I clicked the profile.

Chris Cameron

274 posts 348 followers 575 following

"Go confidently in the direction of your dreams! Live the life you've imagined."

~ Henry David Thoreau

IT guy, part-time guitar player, Digital Garbage recycler. Music-lover.

Witty and cute. I clicked *Approve* and slid my phone into my pocket.

"Shit, Sarah. Shit, shit, shit." Deb raised her voice and zapped me out of my trance. But before the glow wore off, my pocket vibrated. The text revealed a message. The baristas had stopped working, checking their devices, and mumbles filled the air.

I looked up at the TV monitors. President Gibson appeared in a live news conference. The ticker at the bottom of the screen read: *Gibson signs Emergency Declaration 466-92 after Mountain Pass mine announces closure. Tech draft begins soon.*

I read it again and blinked several times, trying to process what I'd seen.

"We should go," I said.

4

SARAH

W HEN I WAS LITTLE, I wanted to possess extraordinary powers. Once I assisted a kid at school after someone stole his lunch money. I ended up writing a letter to my teacher with all the evidence laid out about the suspect, a boy a grade above us, who always got in trouble. He ended up confessing and serving a three-day detention.

I experienced a sense of invincibility.

As I grew, I settled on journalism as my chosen career. I could expose politicians, reveal extortions and scams. Unfortunately, my dreams of catching the bad guy never happened. I ended up writing about festivals and street closures.

Until Go Back.

•   •   •

**GLOBAL STOCKS PLUMMET
AFTER GIBSON SIGNS EMERGENCY DECLARATION**

July 20, 2035

New York (CNN Business) President Ronald Gibson sent shivers through global markets on Thursday. Stocks plunged after he signed an emergency declaration following the closure of the Mountain Pass Mine. The Shanghai composite plunged 6.6%. The Stoxx Europe 600 index dropped about 2%. That sets US markets up for a bumpy start. The Dow Jones closed down 1,850 points.

•   •   •

I received my number a week after that declaration. It meant I had six weeks to turn in my tech for recycling. The fine print said we'd get another form of tech back, but the newer technology like smart phones, and any devices with Rare-earth elements (REE) like flat screen TVs and certain light bulbs and the like "had to be recycled now to gather the valuable minerals our great country needs for its economic prosperity."

Besides the recycling declaration, President Gibson also declared a national health emergency because of increasing anxiety attacks and so-called tech addiction overwhelming mental health facilities. As people gave up their tech, they became agitated. Gibson said he'd partnered with the Go Back movement, which offered to build detox centers.

At work, Deb asked me, "Any intel on GB?"

Suddenly, she wanted my help with something other than fluff? Perhaps our current hard news reporter's absence was due to paternity leave. I guess I'd seize this opportunity.

"We're getting several calls a day from folks saying they're being recruited to work for them, but not sure if they're legit. Also, lots of protest groups calling themselves the Anti-Backers are calling, too."

"Anti-Backers?"

"Those are the people against Go Back. Oh, and get this, Go Back supporters call themselves, Backers, and they're calling the Anti-Backers 'Fascists'. Can you fathom that? But I have no leads. Every time I call the GB headquarters, they refer me to Human Resources, and HR always refers me back to headquarters. I can't get a physical address or—"

"Some shady shit going down," Deb said, her voice muffled a bit as if she didn't want anyone else to hear. She walked away shaking her head. My desk phone rang.

"News Underground, Sarah Grimes speaking."

"Hello. Yes, I need to report a story." The woman's voice on the other end sounded rattled, but firm. Low and raspy. The caller ID read "Unknown."

I listened as she told me she worked for Go Back—at a recycling facility. At that point I started typing to try to get her every word. She told me the Go Back movement would stop at nothing to take all of our tech for themselves, killing if they had too.

I tried to get her name, but all she would give me was L.P. "Does that stand for something? Your initials?" I asked. Silence. "Listen, if you can't talk on record, help me out. Who else can I talk to and what should I ask to get the information you're telling me?" I heard breathing. Thankfully, that meant she was still there.

"No one will talk. But I have proof. I can send you some files. Do you have a Dropbox?" she said.

"Yes. Send it to … you got a pen?" Silence filled the line. I was worried she'd hung up. But if I held my breath, I still heard hers.

"Yes," she said.

"Email is sgrimes@numail.com."

She repeated it back to me, then said, "Ok, I'll encrypt it and send you instructions how to access audio file of Go Back telling the team about their plan to take all the tech and use it to sell on the black market, and back to China and Africa. Big tech is in on it, too. I also have internal memos of upcoming raids."

I pulled in a deep breath, released it, and blurted, "This is great!" I rubbed my sweaty palms on my pants. "Please, can we meet. You don't have to go on record. You don't—" I heard a dial tone and with it felt desperation. I pinched my lips together and grimaced. I still wondered about her motive, but knew I had what we called a "golden source" or someone who has major insider information.

Moments later, I received an email notification. I opened the attachment and found a schedule of all the upcoming raids. Upon closer inspection I saw the GB seal in the lower righthand corner. Bingo. Of course, I called GB to get its official response which was:

"The Go Back Movement does not condone violence at any level. Our detox facilities are voluntary and in response to President Gibson's public health threat declaration. Evidence proves that tech addiction is real. If you need help, please contact us at 1-855-TechLes."

My fingers shook at the thought of putting it all out there, but if what she said was true, people needed to know.

And so, my first article of substance with News Underground began.

POLITICS
THEY'RE TAKING OUR TECH
How the GB went from tech recycling to detox centers
By Sarah Grimes

The Centers are not spas.

The roundups are real.

Our tech is not coming back.

A source, who would only speak on condition of anonymity, confirmed the rumors to News Underground by phone.

When asked how she knows this, the source responded, "Because I work for GB."

When asked where and in what capacity, she said, "No comment."

The source claims Go Back orchestrated the recent public health tech threat and is hoarding tech for themselves, as are other government workers, like military—even as high as President Gibson.

"They're (sic) taking our tech for themselves. They recycle what they can't use, but they're keeping the very best. We've given up everything and now they have it all just to further their own agenda."

News Underground contacted many sources for this story, including the Austin Police Department and the FBI. APD police chief Janet Hines tells us, "We have been gathering some technologies according to Dec 466-92. Those include smart phones and some common 'smart' household items like Alexas, Miras, Siri machines. However, we have no knowledge about forced detoxes."

The Go Back Movement has gained momentum in recent years ..."

While discussing edits, Deb told me, "We rarely use unnamed sources, Sarah, but this Golden Source is too good to pass up. Excellent work."

I didn't have the heart to tell her it was just dumb luck. I was the one who answered the tip line.

5

SARAH

OUTSIDE THE NEWS UNDERGROUND BUILDING, Mira, my digital assistant, read my vitals in my ear.

Heart rate 95, blood pressure 107 over 90, steps 1652. I really needed to hit the treadmill to meet my step count. Oh, who was I kidding? I did not have the energy for that.

People on their devices passed by me, not even looking up—tech zombies we jokingly called them. Self-driving ride shares zipped by, holo-boards flashed warning messages about tech addiction and promoted GB Centers. The ads showed people in white robes sipping tea, like they were having the time of their lives. Lottery numbers flashed. So did reminders of the upcoming tech lottery.

Estimated screen time was up to eight hours a day. GB filled the news feeds with stories about child neglect, or even death, over tech use. It seemed no one comprehended how to navigate the world without GPS or social media. No one remembered their own loved one's phone numbers.

Ride share approaching. ETA 4 minutes, 38 seconds, Mira chirped.

A shiny black van appeared in four minutes. I swiped Mira over the pay portal and hopped onto a plush gray seat.

"Mira, Play Iron Ghost," I said into my wrist. Seconds later, grungy guitar riffs filled my ears.

The eight other passengers all kept their heads down. Small talk did not exist anymore. Still, sometimes those kinds of conversations were the only time I would have talked to someone else.

Seventeen minutes into the ride, my name flashed on a screen and my phone buzzed, letting me know I was home just in case I fell asleep.

Up five concrete steps, I turned to face my iris recognition. The opaque glass door clicked and I pushed it open. Immediately, my automatic air freshener hit my nose—the scent of jasmine with a hint of lilac. I plopped my bag on the couch and headed to the fridge to grab a beer. As soon as I popped it open, Mira vibrated, and my sister Liz's hologram appeared.

"Sarah, what have you done? I can't believe you wrote that."

I belted out a quick, high-pitched laugh. "You mean to tell me you read my article, Liz?

"Very funny, Sarah."

I paced the kitchen, stepping precisely into every square of grey tile. Pacing tended to calm my mind. "It's my job, Liz. Remember freedom of the press? Plus, people need to know that GB is evil."

"Yeah, well, you scared the shit out of Mom. She thinks you're making yourself a target."

We got quiet. I glanced out my kitchen window right over my stainless-steel sink filled with several used coffee cups. As usual, I could see neighboring windows. Most were dark, but the one I always looked into seemed brighter than usual. I could see the TV on. It looked like the late-night news. Suddenly, a silhouette appeared. I turned to pace the other way.

"Is it really true?" Liz continued. Her eyes shone bright green in the hologram against her neon yellow shirt. "I'm scared—"

"Okay. Take a breath. Just do what you're told. Hopefully, my source is wrong, and it's just a draft and that means not everyone will have to give up their tech," I didn't want to tell her I already got drafted. I switched off the holo feature out of frustration.

"That's not what your article said." Liz's voice called out. "I need to see your face. Put me back on!" I switched back.

"Liz, look at me. It's going to be fine. I love you. Talk to you soon, okay?"

"Sarah, please—"

I ended the call and put my wrist near each of my appliances to read their capacity and usage reminders to take my mind off the whole conversation.

Dishwasher: 40% loaded

Waste Chute: 90% full/recycling capacity met

I pinched my right index, middle finger, and thumb together and apart, and my discarded recyclables rumbled. The sound of loud voices and a megaphone overpowered the recycling noise. I glanced out of my windows, but saw nothing. Curious, I left my apartment. I opted for the moving sidewalk to make my trip faster. Moving past old, distinguished houses mixed with newer so-called pod-homes that resemble college dorms, I saw a brilliant sunset which revealed a portrait of magenta cirrus clouds. The talking and a megaphone became much louder.

"Nobody move. We're here to gather up what the leader of this great country has ordered. We will arrest anyone who violates this."

The first raid.

A sense of vertigo swept over my body, and for a moment, I forgot where I was.

The presence of two guards in the street to my right jerked me back into reality. One of them held a long gun, a rifle perhaps. Despite hailing from Texas, I knew virtually nothing about guns except they had a trigger and bullets. I could barely hold my phone up to record them as my hands shook uncontrollably. A tangle of pedestrians lined the curb, listening to the megaphone. Some held tight to their phones and smart-watches. Another crowd with signs reading "Go Back is Great!" and "Trash the Tech" gathered across the street. They carried long guns and wore mostly black.

I bumped into a crying, red-eyed teenager and stopped to say sorry. She tossed her phone into a passing car creating a crunch of glass and metal as the car ran over it and sped off. I worried she'd do the same with her body.

"Are you ok? Why did you do that?" I asked. Yet, I already knew. The Go Back rumors were true. Some of us could handle it better than others.

"It's over. It's all over," she sniffled.

I tried to meet her eyes, but she seemed to refuse. "What's over? Don't give up."

She sank to the ground like a melting popsicle.

I stuffed my phone in my pocket and turned to head back to my place, when someone called out. I kept walking, trying not to look in the voice's direction. I needed to get home.

"Hey. You." The voice got louder.

Despite all my better instincts to keep going, I turned around and saw a girl in her late teens standing in front of a corner bodega. She had long, brown hair with fiery purple tips.

"Where ya going?" she asked.

"Home."

"Can I come? Please. I'm so scared. Don't let them catch me. I need my phone. Please help me." she sobbed.

"Why don't you toss it?"

"I can't give it up. I can't. I need it to face-chat my boyfriend," she said. Her voice grew louder in the last few words.

I needed to move quickly. The sound of the megaphone grew closer.

"Um. Okay. But don't get any ideas," I said. "You'll leave when they do."

We walked quickly side by side, not talking. In the distance, I could hear the muffled sounds of megaphones and loud chatter of people and walkie talkies. Right before we got to my place, as I looked over to make sure she kept up, I noticed something shiny at her side.

"Gotta tie my shoe," she said, kneeling down.

As she did, her green jacket shifted. She had a holstered weapon. I had to think fast, so I told her I lived across the street. I pointed far away at a red and white faux-brick building. I told her to walk, so no one would suspect we were together. I told her I would meet her.

As soon as we parted, I sprinted towards my real place. I felt so bad, but "sometimes you have to be selfish," my mom always said. When I arrived at my apartment door, I glanced back to find the girl right behind me.

"You didn't genuinely believe I would be fooled by that, correct?" she said with a snicker.

"Sorry?" My throat felt constricted. I flinched at the sound of a megaphone down the street.

"That's understandable. I mean, the roundups and all." Suddenly, her face fully relaxed, and she didn't seem so anxious. "So, are we gonna go in or not?"

"I changed my mind. It's time to get my tech together to turn in." The space between me and the door seemed to grow tenfold in that moment. If I didn't get the door open right then, I never would.

"You don't believe they're just gonna let you turn it in and get on with things, do you?" She put her right hand on her hip right near the weapon.

"Well, yes, I do expect that to be the case."

"So, you're a journalist, huh?"

It was at that moment I truly understood. This is not going to end well. I dug my hand into my pocket. I could call 9-1-1. We were far enough away from the commotion that it barely filled the silence between us. "What the hell is this? Who are you?" I backed into my door. I wanted to run inside, but the iris recognition unlocking software wouldn't work. I fumbled for my actual keys. Thankfully, I always had them in case the iris recognition failed. That happened to a co-worker once and they had to wait three hours for a locksmith. No thanks.

She let out a loud chuckle.

"Give it up, Sarah. I hacked your Wi-Fi and your socials."

"Wait, when?" My door became blurry. I squinted, hoping it could see my irises.

"You really shouldn't have used the public Wi-Fi at the coffee shop." She pulled back her jacket to reveal the weapon.

My body shook. I felt weak.

"You're gonna let me in, okay? I know more than you think."

"Please." My voice shook, but I tried to stay calm through breathing. Surely someone would see us. A neighbor?

She said nothing as she punched a code into her phone. The lock clicked, and we entered the apartment. "Go get your tech."

"Okay. All right, now just calm down. I'll get it." I tried not to strain my voice. I'd been mugged before, but not with a weapon. Never even seen one close up. I raced through the living room past the couch, on which the girl made herself at home. Leather crunched beneath her.

"Nice place," she said and pushed the armrest button to bring down the TV screen. "Alright, let's do this." She stood and stretched her laced fingers to the ceiling. lifted both hands palms up to my side in a questioning gesture.

In my bedroom, a cardboard box that held the deepest memories of my childhood sat at the foot of my bed, its flaps open like a paraglider about to jump. Memories I meant to digitize, but never did. Ancient layers of tape revealed each of my moves. Scribbled in black permanent marker, the side that faced me read "Kitchen (breakable)"—a note from another time, another move.

Knowing I wouldn't have access to my digital pictures without my phone, I grabbed the top photograph from another box and shoved it into my bra. That's when the sound of a cough came from the bedroom door.

"That's not tech, Sarah." She flashed the gun again.

"Hold on." Another box sat next to my bed. In it I'd put some old phones that needed recycling anyway and an ancient laptop. "Who are you? Are you with the government? Where's your warrant, anyway? The draft hasn't even begun yet. My tech isn't due for another several weeks. I need to call my lawyer." The words came out in a babble. I looked at Mira, its square screen blank. I wanted to wake it up and tap the panic button feature.

"My name is Lily, and yes, I'm with the government. Figured we'd save you some time, since your number is first on the list."

No, it was not first. It had to be her because of the article.

Mira beeped and called out my vital signs. *Your heart rate is elevated. Please, take ten deep breaths. One ... two ... three.* My chance slipped away.

"Take that thing off," she yelled. "Give it."

I reluctantly complied. Breathing shallowly, I said, "Where are you taking me?"

"Who said anything about taking you anywhere?"

"Oh, it just crossed my mind that maybe people were being forced to turn in their tech." As I said that Lily turned Mira over and over in her hands. It had taken forever to save up for it. Now this Lily person with a gun had it. I pressed my fist to my mouth to suppress the expletives I wanted to yell.

"Naw, fake news," she said, rummaging through my box of photos and old love letters and sketches I made in middle school, mostly of my teen crush, Adam. "You think you have it all figured out, well you don't. And that source that called you? They're nobody."

My chest tightened, and I clenched my fists even tighter. She did know about the article.

"Okay Sarah, you're coming with us."

"Us? But you said you wouldn't—"

A man as wide as a linebacker appeared in my bedroom doorway. The TV still blared from the next room. I hadn't even noticed him enter the apartment.

"Yep, that's right." Lily pointed the gun, and the man crossed his arms, revealing bicep muscles bigger than both of my arms put together.

"Why? You have my stuff, so why?"

"Time's up," is all she said.

The man grabbed my arm and led me out of my apartment, not bothering to close the door.

6

SARAH

I BOUNCED AROUND THE BACK of the white van that Lily and her hefty accomplice threw me into. Every time we hit a bump my arms flailed around like half-cooked noodles. The padded walls meant no one heard me. Someone had also covered all the windows. I saw the back of the driver's head beyond the glass.

Two others sat across from me holding hands, not saying anything. The woman wore a black sweatshirt with the hood up. Black mascara ran down her cheeks. The guy had a nose ring, a flattened blond Mohawk with black roots.

"Why were you arrested?" I asked him.

He shook his head and looked at the floor.

"It's okay. I'm a journalist. I wrote—"

His head shot up. "The article? What the actual fuck—and now they have you?" He shook his head again. "They came to our place. I think they'd been scouting us for a while. We're part of the resistance."

"Which movement?" I asked. There were lots of resistance groups nowadays, hard to keep track.

"People United for Tech. One guy grabbed her, so I spit in their face. They took both of us and threw us back here." He kissed the woman on the top of the head. She said nothing, didn't even look my way.

"So, how'd you end up in here?" he asked.

"I heard the raid outside my window and went to see. A girl pleaded with me to let her hide out at my place. I told her yes, at first, but then realized ..."

"Realized?"

"Realized ... she wasn't some innocent kid. She was in on it. She forced her way in and before I collected any tech or anything, she and a huge guy threw me in here. I couldn't call a lawyer. I couldn't take anything."

My arms banged against the side of the van. No response. The woman suddenly sobbed, then fell silent.

"Damn, these Go Back fuckers are crazy," the man said as he shook his head.

He got quiet, and I saw a tattoo of the word "Fight" across the fingers of his left hand.

I reached into my shirt and pulled out the damp, crumpled picture I'd saved, one I printed off at home from my computer long ago. Opening it up revealed a picture of me about ten years ago, possibly 2028. I was about 18, just moving out to college. My sister Liz stood next to me. She held her little Labra-doodle puppy, Curly. I had attended school as far away as possible. That equaled Northwestern University in Chicago where I got my B.A. in Journalism. Memories in tow, I folded the picture and tucked it in my bra.

•   •   •

What seemed like hours later, but I didn't know because I had no Mira, the van slowed and jerked to a stop. The back door rattled open, and I squinted into the light. I desperately needed the restroom.

"Welcome home," the burly man who had thrown me inside said with a smile as he spat onto the gravel. I looked him in the eyes and let out a disgusted grunt. For a moment, I thought he might be apologetic. His frown disappeared and his eyes relaxed, but that didn't last long.

"What you lookin' at?" he growled. Then Lily came around the corner of the van and faced us. I gave her the finger. Burly Man let out a tsk and snorted.

"Watch it," Lily said. "You don't want to get on our bad side."

Behind them, I saw a four-story whitewashed brick building. It had a pitched roof with dormer windows on the top floor. The entrance looked grand, with two large, white pillars on either side of a wooden door. It had a huge grassy lawn with a majestic live oak in the center. I spied a wood around behind the building as the hot air from outside made its way into the van, and I wished I had on sunscreen.

"Well, come on now. Get out," the burly man said.

We all scooted to the edge and climbed out. I looked around, then at Lily and she shook her head as to say, *Don't even think about it.* Guess she knew I was thinking about running.

"What the hell is this place?" the male passenger asked. He held the woman he rode with tightly.

"The Center," Lily said, staring straight at it squinting her eyes. The purple in her hair shone brighter. She would have been so pretty if not for her terrible personality. "Hey, it's not all that bad. You should have turned yourself in sooner. It's like a spa."

I shuddered at hearing those words.

"We know it's not a spa," I mumbled. The dry, dusty air hit my tongue, making me even more thirsty. "This obviously isn't Austin. Where have you taken us? We aren't under arrest. You have no right to keep us here against our will."

As Lily laughed, heavy bags appeared under her eyes. Crease lines also told me she was probably older than I initially thought. "We have every right. Dec 466-92 suspends the writ of habeas corpus in cases of rebellion. We're here to keep the public safe." She smiled to reveal gleaming white teeth.

I ran the term habeas corpus through my mind several times. My fingers twitched, wanting to Google it. My breathing grew shallow, fully aware that I was incapable of doing this.

"No, fuck that. That's bullshit," the male passenger said, taking a big step forward, and that's when I saw the holster on the burly man's hip. He pulled out the gun in a flash. The dissenting passenger stepped backward and almost fell. The woman squealed and grabbed her stomach. I noticed a slight bulge, but it may have been her clothes.

Burly Man said, "Don't. Even. Fucking. Think about taking me down. We got eyes on you over there in the building."

We all stood at a frozen standstill, until the driver waved the gun at all three of us and said, "Go." He and Lily guided us up the bricked walkway to the door. I saw no address or any identifying features to tell me where I was. Lily pushed a button, and I saw movement behind the smoky glass next to the door. It opened and a woman in a lab coat stood before us.

"Hello and welcome to you all," she said in a soothing voice, with clipboards in hand. She appeared in her late 30s with smooth brown skin, and a pointy nose with a stud in the right nostril. She didn't appear to wear any makeup, and she smiled with her thin lips closed, revealing no teeth. Her lab coat reached her knees and underneath, she wore baby blue scrubs. She had a badge with writing too small to make out.

Oriental rugs and paintings of nondescript landscapes filled the spacious entryway. It seemed more like a mansion than an institution. We rounded the corner and came upon a waiting room area. My breath became raspy. Terror set in and I remained speechless despite my strong desire to protest. I wanted to go home.

"Hello new guests," the woman in the lab coat said again, holding out the clipboards. "Please fill out these questionnaires. After that, we'll then escort you to your rooms."

"I don't want a room." I crossed my arms. "I want to go home. I'm a U.S. Citizen, a journalist and I haven't even been read my rights. Neither have they." I motioned to the other passengers. It took everything inside me not to yell and run.

"Relax, Sarah. You'll be fine. We're just adhering to protocol initiated by the Presidential proclamation. Your article? Well, it's viewed as propaganda against the government."

"It was the truth, and I demand to see a lawyer."

"There's no need for all this. We'll provide a phone call after we admit you. Now, just fill out the paperwork and don't give us any reason to hold you further and you'll be right on your way." She smiled again. This time her thin lips parted, and I saw a bit of teeth. They were crooked and ugly, a total mismatch of her smooth, delicate features.

She stood there like a robot, arms outstretched, holding out the brown clipboard with a stack of papers attached. She shook it at me and finally I took it. Her black heels clicked on the marble floor as she walked away. I found it strange she wore heels with scrubs.

"This cannot be happening," I said to the two other passengers, who stood against a wall holding their own clipboards. The woman's black hair looked damp, and she hunched over next to the man. Then she put her hand to her mouth and threw up in a wastebasket. I looked at her sympathetically, though happy I didn't get sick as well.

A woman in orange scrubs came from around the corner and took the man and woman away, leaving me alone. I scanned the room for any sign of cameras. I spotted one in each upper corner. As I walked to the beige couch to fill out my paperwork, they moved to follow me.

The thick questionnaire asked me everything from my birth date to what technology I've ever used, to ratings scales on how I perceived and used certain technologies, to my mother's maiden's name, to my blood type, which I left blank. I thought they might try to make me a guinea pig in a medical experiment. Plus, what did that have to do with technology?

They had given me a ball-point pen, silver and heavy. It shone like a weapon, so I decided to unscrew it between my legs to hide from the cameras and put the sharp parts in my pocket. Just in case.

At some point, a man came to escort me to what I thought I'd be my room. It turned out to be like a doctor's office.

"Put this on," he said, handing me a gown that tied in back. After the door closed, changed into the gown, leaving on my undergarments. I didn't want to be so exposed if I had to run. After a few minutes, a woman's cries came to me through the door, then a man screamed.

I pressed my ear against the door, even though I would have been able to hear from a distance.

"No, don't take Rich. Please. He's all I have," the woman cried. "I don't have a phone to call him. Where are you taking him? Where are you ...?" Her voice dropped off and disappeared.

I sat in a metal chair next to the examination table. Unlike normal doctor's offices, I saw no medical instruments. Calls came over the intercom outside, muffled talking, and the sound of elevator dings outside the door. With nothing to do but wait, I looked at the ceiling and counted the tiles.

The door opened. A white-robed man with a thick red beard and bright smile stepped inside. He stood about 5'8".

"Good afternoon, Sarah. My name is Dr. Rose. I hope you've enjoyed your stay so far." He had a perky voice, like this was some sort of regular checkup.

"This isn't a hotel," I scoffed back as I squeezed the bundle of clothes I held in my lap. "I'd like for someone to tell me what the hell is going on. What are you going to do to me? Why can't I see a lawyer." I wanted to sound intimidating, but his flat expression told me I was not. Instead of folding to my questions, he went on as if I'd said nothing.

"I've reviewed your files, and everything seems up to par. We'll have you on your way soon, okay?" He took a step in my direction, and I could see his face clearly. Acne pocks dotted his cheeks. He licked his full red lips like a lion about to pounce its prey.

I recoiled and jumped off the table squeezing my ball of clothing to my chest. "Okay, but where am I? Do I need a lawyer? What am I charged with?"

"You're not charged with anything. This is the protocol under the President's executive order issued just 24 hours ago. Those who issue propaganda against government orders will end up here. I would have figured you, of all people, would have known."

My eyes focused on the silver push handle of the door. He stepped in front of me.

"What is this place? Is this a Center?" I said in my most serious voice. My heart pounded and my mouth turned dry.

"You're at a Center for Behavioral Re-Cognition," he said. "Now, I'm going to give you a drink of a solution. It will help you relax. Don't worry. It won't hurt. The drink will help with that. Oh, and don't run. There's a nurse and a guard right outside the door."

He made his way to the cabinet and pressed something on his watch. The cabinet door lifted, and I saw rows and rows of pre-sealed containers.

"Please, I don't understand. What did I do? Why am I here?" I demanded again. My voice cracked. "I mean, they got my phone and other tech. Can I please just go home now? I don't understand."

I said all this to his back. When I finished, he turned to me and said, "Sarah, you can make this easy on yourself or difficult. It's your choice. Drink. It will be okay. I promise."

I bit my lower lip and shook my head. I wiped my sweaty palms on my gown.

"Sarah. Come on. It's like a shot of whiskey. Surely, you've done one of those before. Drink up." He lifted the container and pulled the flap to open it. He held it against my pursed lips.

Without thinking, I screamed "No!" and slapped it out of his hand.

A buzzing alarm sounded and a red light on the ceiling illuminated. Three people wearing orange scrubs swarmed into the room and pushed me down on the table. My body thrashed side to side, but I was no match against them. They held my arms and legs tightly. I spat and it landed on one of them who had long brown hair. They looked about my age, and kind of reminded me of Liz, for some reason. I screamed "Stop!" and the person covered my mouth with a gloved hand.

The so-called doctor held my leg, and a needle pierced my thigh.

"You should have listened, Sarah. Don't say I didn't tell you so."

•   •   •

Artificial light. No windows. Both tricked me into believing it was daytime when I had no way of knowing. Still, some things did remind me of the outside world, like peeling gray paint, the closet with a lopsided wooden clothing bar, and the hospital-like bed. I tried to move, but the hard, narrow mattress made my back ache. Rubbing alcohol mixed with urine and sweat filled the air. A low hum of conversation seeped through the walls. The voices didn't sound alarmed, so maybe I shouldn't have been.

But I was. Because my wrists were handcuffed to the railings of the bed. Because of the IV drip. Because something firm jabbed into my backside.

How long had I been here? I looked down at my painted nails, which were an abysmal shade of bubble gum pink. They reached just past my fingertip. Hadn't been that long in forever. I had been a chronic nail biter—before.

The lock rattled, and I drew in long breaths through my nose that filled my diaphragm. A woman entered, opening the door halfway. She walked to stand next to me, her heels clicking loudly as she approached. She had straight dark brown hair slicked back in a bun, not one hair askew. "Relax, Sarah, everything is okay," she said.

My lips formed a circle to ask, "Wh…Where … ahhh … am I?" My head and lips had a heavy sensation.

The woman scribbled some notes on a clipboard. She paced the bed, stopped at the foot and stared. Her glassy blue eyes did not flinch in the light. Her taut cheekbones cast shadows on her face.

"You're at the Center for Behavioral Recognition. We're weaning you of the technology so many have grown addicted to."

I coughed. "I'm not addicted. I need a lawyer. I want to call my—" The words stumbled from my mouth. My thoughts had a mind of their own. I pushed up on the mattress, but my weight pulled me right back down. "This is against the constitution." The words came out in a whisper, even though I had been trying to scream.

The woman came closer and stopped by my right side. She shook her head and messed with my IV bag.

"Save your energy. Why do you think you're here, anyway? We can't have you interfering with our business." My fuzzy head felt like a bowling bowl. I jerked my right hand to try to pull the tubing out, but the handcuff banged against the bed rail. Pieces of felt swam in my mind. My brain fuzzed over from whatever they put in that IV.

"Get me out of here!" I wanted to yell loudly, but all that came out was a hoarse bark.

A rapid beeping filled the air, and my airway constricted. Then the room faded to black.

•　　•　　•

Days, hours, minutes later … after several times squeezing and lifting, my crusty eyes finally pried open. My pupils contracted against the harsh lighting. A woman in an old-fashioned nurse outfit had roused me. I saw a round face with crow's feet around her brown eyes. She had black eyebrows with dirty blond, slicked-back hair. Perhaps she had dyed it.

Faint beeping in the distance and shiny, silver, barren walls told me they'd taken me to a different room.

And this wasn't a hospital. I'd been in one of those before when I had my appendix out. There were windows and visitors. There were none of those here.

"We thought we lost you," the nurse whispered. As she leaned in, the sweet smell of donuts filled my nose. What I wouldn't have given for one of those right now.

"I. Where am—?" My words came out in an avalanche. I gathered my thoughts and rolled my tongue over my bumpy teeth. I must not have brushed in ages.

"Relax, Sarah. We're here for you," the nurse said. "You're in the best of hands. It's difficult but trust us." She chuckled and said, "Oh, and speaking of hands, I hope you don't mind, I painted your nails. You looked so sad, and I wanted to do something nice for you."

I wanted to say, "I never would have picked that color, crazy lady," and ask, "How long have I been here?"

She placed her cold fingers on my wrist to check my pulse. I shuddered to think where else they'd been. I studied her, trying not to stare. She wore a band on her left arm with a symbol on it. At first glance, I thought it was the Red Cross, which made me feel relieved, like she wanted to help. Like, maybe I had gotten out. As she leaned in, I got a closer look.

Stitched in red string were two uppercase letters. GB.

Go Back.

•   •   •

The movement had been infiltrating our lives for at least three years now.

It started with a shortage of raw materials used to make technology: tantalum, tungsten, tin, gold. So-called "conflict minerals." The headlines told it all.

BLOOD ON YOUR HANDSET

Is your cellphone made with conflict minerals mined in the
Congo? The industry doesn't want you to know.

and …

CELL PHONES ARE THE NEW BLOOD DIAMOND

7-year-old children mine the minerals used to make our cell phones and laptops.

The images in the articles were disturbing. Little Congolese boys, some as young as four, with dust covered hands squatting in a rock pile, pants rolled above their callused knees, pushing down sharp wooden instruments used to dissect the minerals. These children shed blood to gather these rare earths so us first-world citizens could have the world at our fingertips. But they couldn't keep up. Mines caved in, killing off the child labor force. Countries hoarded the minerals, and sold them on the black market at sky high prices. Inspectors deemed the one and only mine in the U.S. unsafe years ago. A trade war with China, the other rare earth provider, ended with that country issuing an embargo.

The government limited cell phone usage, hoping to extend the life of current phones. Problem was these conflict minerals were inside most tech, including DVD players, laptops and electric vehicles. The government went from suggesting limited technology use to requiring it, kind of like water rationing during a drought.

Then came a silent revolution on social media that lit up like wildfire. A radical nostalgia group called the Go Back Movement, or GB for short, latched on and infiltrated the general population, then the government. They claimed tech was a public health threat. They got to the President, even though he's more of a puppet now-a-days. Even he wants to "Go Back," back to the days when tech didn't "rule our life."

Social Media sites filled up with #GoBack.

No tech seemed like a good idea at first. People listened and did cell-free Friday. They did tech shabbats. They walked more. Spent more family time. Then, businesses banned cell phones. They posted signs saying, "Please silence your cell phone. We can't compete with your conversation," or "Please. No pictures. Security will confiscate your technology!"

So, people realized it wasn't worth it, but little did they know how bad it would get. It was so great at first, but it blindsided people. Politicians seized the opportunity, running on promises to Go Back, to Make America Real Again. Real conversations, real pictures, IRL or, *in real life* friends.

We all bought into it, even me.

7

OLIVIA

THE AROMA OF BURNING TUNGSTEN, aluminum and plastic would forever be etched in my nostrils; even though GB sealed the doors shut, minimal airflow causes the scent to linger. They restricted Sub Zero to mid-level staffers like me. It's an intricate, underground tunnel system.

Ed and I had chosen "vat duty" to further our plan. No one really wanted vat duty because it was time-consuming and hot, but thanks to my army background, we jimmied a two-way radio inside our helmets for communication. We smuggled them back and forth every day.

Daily, I entered a confined space to put on my GB-issued PPE. I tied back my long dreads and pressed the white button attached to the material on my left hip. The silver suit inflated, surrounding me with protection from heat and chemicals. The gold face mask shielded my eyes.

A black and white diamond-shaped sign with a skull and crossbones that read "Inhalation Hazard" greeted me at the door., and I walked in.

"Olivia, I need you back here," Ed piped into my PPE. His tone was urgent.

"Coming." Both of our voices sounded muffled. I took twice as long to walk between the large vats because of my bad leg. Dismantled tech swirled at 450-degrees Fahrenheit. It was only the outer shells, plastic, glass and copper. Once melted, we poured it into molds.

Many believed that GB either produced more technology or transformed everything into statues. Of course, Ed and I knew better.

"Come on, slowpoke," he wailed.

"I can't stand this room." Because of it, I'd been limping along for months. About a year ago, the system override had failed, and a vat overflowed. I slipped in the goo and broke my ankle, damaging the tendons for life. It took weeks to clean up the mess as we had to use big machines that looked like Zambonis to suck up all the goo before it dried, then the stuff that did dry, we had to chisel off the floor and re-melt.

"We got more shipments in. Where the hell you been all day?"

"Relax, man. I've been busy." Despite being a government organization, Go Back didn't have military hair rules. Ed, the hippie I always teased him of being, was now trying to get his dark brown ringlets to grow out to at least his ears. I finally had the dreads. As he moved behind the vats, I heard a rumble. He pulled out three large carts, the kind airports used to transport luggage on a plane, except the tech filled this one to the brim.

I glanced at a new vat. "Is it ready?"

"Sure 'nuff," Ed said and pushed a cart my way. "Is the load-bearer ready?"

I looked down and flipped the switch to activate the movable floor. Then, the iron gears squealed awake, and the conveyor belt moved upward. The cart filled with mostly iPhones and some other metal tech like Smart monitors, lifted toward the lip of the vat. Finally, as it reached the top, I flipped another lever, and the cart tilted at a 45-degree angle. With a lurch and a bang, the metal tech landed inside.

Our protective gear allowed us to avoid the thick smell of phosphorous.

We lifted and melted the tech three more times. Once it liquified, we flipped another switch to drain the vats into molds that looked like large ice cube trays. The machine stacked the trays in three-foot towers. When we finished, I moved to the door to show I was leaving the area. Ed replied with an ever-so-subtle head nod.

Inside the airlock, my suit decompressed, and I stepped out, then a voice from the intercom said: "Please report for lunch duty at 13:00 in the main cafeteria." My stomach growled as I had had nothing for breakfast.

"Can we just skip the required shower this time?" I asked Ed. "How would they really know if we took one?"

He stood next to me. Sweat ran down his face and onto his shirt collar. I could see curly chest hairs poking out.

"Ha. Well, regardless of the shower after vat duty rule, you still need one 'cause phew!"

I nudged him with my elbow. 'Who you callin' stinky? Speak for yourself."

Ed smiled. "I kid, I kid. But seriously, we eat together today, okay?"

•　　　•　　　•

The cafeteria was not large, and burglar bars covered what few windows it had, which meant minimal natural light streamed in. People sat alone for fear of being accused of collaborating, so Ed and I only sat across from each other at scheduled times. I grabbed a bowl of tomato soup from under the warmers and sat down. As I slurped, my mind wandered to the token in 609. Such a feisty one that Sarah, at least from what I've been told. Can't believe she's here, and it's all my fault.

"Hey," Ed said. As he walked by to sit across from me, he spilled some soup on my right leg.

"Dammit, Ed. Come on."

"Sorry. Let me clean that up."

"No, don't worry about it." He shouldn't be drawing any attention to us. I swallowed fast, and the broth went down the wrong pipe. I tried not to cough as I grabbed the napkin from his hand, plucked off a chunk of tomato, and ate it. We're penalized for wasting food around here.

"So, good job today. Sorry about the soup, and reminding you about your injury back there," Ed said.

I felt my face growing warm from annoyance. I dabbed a new napkin to my forehead. "It's fine. Can we just move on? My ankle is doing better now. Besides, we have bigger things to worry about. Like the future of our movement."

Ed rested his elbow on the table and shot me a side eye. "Keep it down. You never know who's listening," he whispered.

We sat and sipped our soup in silence for several minutes before Ed spoke again.

"Meet me in my room at 16:00, okay? We've got more to discuss."

"Why don't you just tell me now?"

"I've got papers to show you. I can't do that here."

"Sure, I understand. I get it." I spooned up the last bit of my soup and left.

8

OLIVIA

A LITTLE LESS THAN THREE HOURS LATER, after my mid-day workout, I made my way to Ed's room. He lived in the male sector of the Center, showed by the outline of a male figure on each automatic doorway. Go Back assigned everyone as male or female according to their sex at birth. They desired to return to a dual-gendered society and the use of only male/female pronouns. We were back to Don't Ask Don't Tell.

I reached the end of the well-lit hallway, exhaled, and rehearsed my reason for being here.

"I.D.," the man at the security desk at the front of the male wing greeted me.

"Oh, come on, Dean, you know me," I joked, fully aware I'd still have to pull it out.

"Sergeant Parker, you are familiar with the rules."

I pulled out the I.D.

"Reason for visit?"

"We need to discuss shipment status. The vat room may need to be expanded."

A wide grin filled Dean's face. What a moron.

"Okay, be sure to sign back out when you're done." He hit the buzzer, and the electronic doors swiped open to reveal the long residential hallway.

Ed opened his door almost at the same time. He had been expecting me, after all. He motioned me to his desk where I spotted a pencil and paper laid out.

"Howdy, Sergeant," he said.

I gave Ed the stink eye and sat down on his bed across from his desk while he closed the door. He sat at his desk chair. Our rooms were so small that if we both crossed our legs our feet might touch. At least we had small windows overlooking the courtyard. I came hoping he had more information about the Garden, our name for the headquarters of our resistance movement against Go Back. We'd been gathering recruits there from other stations for a year. The church building had been abandoned. The entrance sat far back from the main road and that kept it well hidden.

"Ok, so Gavin is MIA. At last report, the Garden had 221 recruits, but no telling who's stuck around."

"What's the plan going forward? Who's our intel?" I asked.

"Isobel is there. She's been able to hack through the firewall and send sporadic messages. But it's been weeks."

"I'll try to break through the firewall again after midnight. There isn't as much monitoring happening at that time. At least I hope not," he said.

"Okay, when you make it through, be sure to tell Isobel about the path through the town of Moffat. We need to update the maps. I gotta do that before I give one to anyone else."

He opened his mouth to speak, but then closed it. I felt guilty suddenly because I had been keeping a secret.

"There's something you should be aware of, and I apologize for not mentioning it earlier."

"What?" Ed's eyes squinted. "Come on. Tell me."

I ran my hands through my hair and exhaled.

"One of our recruits. I know her."

"You know her? How? Who is she? What?"

"Okay, hold on. I don't know her like that. I talked to her once. I told her. I told her—everything."

"What the hell you mean by everything?"

My throat tightened and I spat out, "I told her what's going down with GB. I called her at News Underground. She picked up the phone. I didn't choose her."

"Ok, shut the fuck up, Liv. What didn't you tell me this before?" He stood up and ran his hands through his hair and furled his brows.

"I wanted to, but there simply wasn't enough time. Please. Let's move forward with this. She's here because she wrote the article telling everyone what GB is up to, never planning to give tech back, using the mine collapse and tech shortage to re-form government, you name it."

"Ok, so what makes you think we can trust her?"

"Because she trusted me."

Ed sat back down and put his face in his hands. "Alright. Well, I trust you, so I guess that means I trust her, too."

I could always count on Ed to toe the line. This was one of our unspoken agreements. We had to trust each other's judgment to succeed. "I'd better go." I stood to leave. "Thanks for this. Thanks a lot."

"Yeah. See you soon." He opened the door and about three feet away stood a male janitor, mopping. A shiver of fear ran down my spine, and I sucked in a deep breath. My God, I hoped he hadn't heard anything. But as I looked closer, I noticed he had some headphones on. He didn't look at us. No one could be aware of our intentions. If they did, we'd be dead. Conspiring against GB is a capital offense. Automatic death penalty.

•   •   •

At the check-in desk to the women's unit, the guard greeted me with a nod.

Behind me, another woman approached. A recruit. Fresh blood, as we called them.

"Hi, um excuse me, Sergent Parker."

"Yeah, that's me." I squinted at her name badge. "Um, Private Burke."

"Please, call me Lily."

"Yeah." My mind spun, desperate to understand why she was treating me so nonchalantly. Was it a trick?

"I was interested in finding out if you've had the opportunity to meet Sarah Grimes, our most recent capture?"

My heart skipped a beat as I had just been talking about her with Ed. "Met her?"

Lily ran her fingers through her hair. "She's a journalist, as you may already know." An 'A'-ranking capture ... So exciting." She almost squealed.

"Indeed," I said. I blinked rapidly to remain poker faced. Who was this Lily character and why did she care so much about telling me about Sarah?

"Yeah, they assigned me her case," I said.

"Her case, huh?" GB often assigned recruits to cases like this. The idea is newbies would work their hardest to prove themselves. Plus, they were easily manipulated in believing they could do anything to a capture. Plausible deniability. I shuddered to think what might happen if this kid got her hands on Sarah.

"We're gonna get so much intel outta her," Lily said with a smile. I liked her purple hair but hated her sneaky personality. "Okay, well, thanks. Sergeant Parker. Apologies for the inconvenience." She turned, re-inserted her earbuds, and walked in the opposite direction of the unit.

"Olivia, your bravery always astounds me," Ed said into my ear. He'd been listening in the whole time because I'd forgotten to turn off my 2-way smart buds to his line.

"I'm not brave. That girl was ... well. Nothing. I'll see ya, okay?"

"Yeah, the vats are waiting."

9

OLIVIA

SURE ENOUGH, THE VATS WERE WAITING. The next day, Ed and I went back to our routine of melting tech and pouring it into containers to ship to GB allies. Those allies would make tech from our recycled rare earths, and we, meaning Go Back, would make a profit and continue our hold on the population.

"Over here." Ed's voice filled my helmet. He stood near one of our smaller, original containers.

"How is it going?" I asked.

"I contacted Gavin."

"What's the update?" We'd both been trying to reach him for some time. Ed and I both had the coordinates, but the connection was sketchy.

Ed faced me. "The Garden wants Sarah."

This didn't surprise me. We'd been sending the leaders of the Garden names of captives for months. "Don't worry, we'll get her out of here." I replied. But deep down, I felt terrible. I tipped her off, and she wrote the article.

He and I worked for more than an hour without speaking again. A sense of gratitude washed over me, knowing that my suit protected me from the noxious fumes released by the simmering and melting tech.

"How much more of this do you think we're gonna get?" I asked. "Central Texas has to be out of tech by now."

"It depends," Ed said. "GB has centers all over. In the past six months, they've added twelve more in the Southwest region. They want to expand in the Northeast, but that's on hold because of political stuff, but the GB says they're chipping away. At least that's what the latest update read."

"Well, I sure as fuck hope they're wrong."

I stepped away from the vat and walked towards the exit.

"Wait, we're not done here," Ed said. "You're conscious of the fact that leaving is not an option."

"I'll just tell them I inhaled fumes."

"You can't. Come on Liv. Let's power through."

His eyes got to me. They always did. Even through the smeared, thick plastic, I could still see them; gorgeous caramel-colored irises contrasting against those dark brown brows. His curls getting longer. His skin was such a contrast to my bronze. There was no attraction towards him from my side. I told him about being Ace when we first met. Still, I could appreciate his looks.

"Alright fine. I'll stay. You got me."

I walked to the smaller vat and pulled the lever.

We pushed on for another hour. I became a robot in a trance, pulling levers here, checking the temperature there. Soon enough, our shift ended.

We cleared out and walked to our respective shower units.

In the hallway, we walked in unison. My walkie-talkie piped out: "Parker, we need you and Cantrell in the conference room."

They've never requested us in the conference room. My mind went to the worst case scenario. They found the Garden.

"10-4," I replied. I turned to Ed. "I bet they want to talk about expanding the program."

"But how?"

"I have no idea, but we're going to figure it out."

We reached the conference room. I expected to see guards outside but saw no one. Then the white doors swished open in unison to reveal long, oval tables with at least two-dozen GB officers sitting, staring at holographic satellite images. One of them was Captain Allabaster; the one who made endless promises of a better, more peaceful world without all the tech. She had promised me a temporary detox. She promised lies.

Tech filled the conference room. I couldn't even recognize the purpose of some of the new-looking stuff. Behind one woman who sat across from me stood what looked like a robot, all white with its arms bend at the elbows. Its body looked like plastic and metal, but the face looked eerily human and malleable. Its eyes appeared to focus downward, not fully closed. I tried not to look at it. Allabaster held what looked like an old-fashioned remote control strapped to her wrist. She gave it commands by pushing buttons, and it responded. All this forbidden tech in one room. So, they were hoarding it.

Live news feeds from all over the world animated one portion of a wall. Another portion showed all the security cameras in The Center, another area showed all the GB vans; their dashcams and the ones parked in the garage.

A group huddled in one corner wore Virtual Reality glasses. Their heads pivoted and nodded.

"Please sit, Sergeants Parker and Cantrell," Allabaster said without even looking our way. "Thank you for your swift attention to my call,"

Ed and I sat next to two people I did not recognize. One was a man wearing all white, with a GB band around his right arm. His hair was short and slicked back like Allabaster's. The other was a woman with half pink, half black slicked-back hair. She wore SMART glasses, the kind with heat-sensing technology. She could pull up our chip information in seconds—our vitals, our background. Some said this was a new-fangled lie detector.

No one acknowledged us. It's like we weren't even there, except for Allabaster's greeting.

"Parker, we called you and Cantrell in because we have some new intel, and we think you may assist. You two have proven invaluable in the vat room. Your loyalty and dedication to our movement is extraordinary."

We really had her fooled.

I stared at her thin, slow-moving lips. She pointed her device to the wall and several charts replaced the news feeds. She pointed and clicked to zoom in on one at a time.

"I requested an update several weeks ago in order for everyone to be aware of where the tech stands." She looked at me for several seconds. I could not see her even blink. Her hair did not look real. Every strand of her hair was plastered down.

"Now, if I may." Allabaster zoomed into the area on the map again. It faded from map/street view to satellite, and that's when I recognized it. The 200-year-old church with peeling white paint, narrow steeple and unkempt grass—The Garden.

Fuck. I shifted in my seat to calm my nerves. My pulse quickened. It was impossible to suppress that. I felt the hairs on my neck rise. How did this happen? How did they find the Garden? This couldn't be happening.

"This is the target of our investigation. Activity has picked up here in recent months. A stockpiling of sorts," she said. "We've received a tip from the compound of an upcoming resistance strike. Details are sketchy, but it looks like a battle is imminent."

The others around the table looked up.

"Disconnect. Unite. Fight. Fight. Fight." We all said our battle cry in unison. To not say it would be treason.

"Yes, we will," Allabaster said.

She wrote on the table with a stylus.

Ed chimed in. "This tip? How was it received, Captain Allabaster, if I may?" I bit my lower lip. Hard.

"Under GB ordinance 7065B, that information will come at a price, Sergeant Cantrell."

Ed and I exchanged glances. We were both aware of this, as we were on the committee that helped pass it years ago.

Ordinance 7065B: *Those privy to intelligence that could be destructive to the movement upon release are sworn to secrecy. Violators will be permanently banished and re-chipped with a new identity.*

"Yes, ma'am, we understand the repercussions."

And it didn't matter because we're getting out of here, anyway.

"Well, okay then. We have men on the ground in almost every

city, some as law enforcement. Our spotter near Moffat sent us pictures of the activity. Hard to say what's going on. When we get closer to the area, all we see is an old church. Baffling."

My breath grew raspy. I gripped plastic armrest of my chair in terror.

"An old church shouldn't be too hard to infiltrate," I said, trying to push my breath out. "And why would people even want to hide out there?"

"Parker, I appreciate your input, but we must continue to monitor the situation," Allabaster said. She pursed her lips and made them disappear into the creases of her face. "However, as soon as we get clearer details, we want you two to be our intel on the ground."

"Yes, of course," I said.

An alarm blared near the two-toned hair lady.

"Ma'am, the detector senses an irregular heartbeat in Sergeant Parker."

"Really?" Allabaster stared me down. I relaxed my expression and focused on my breathing. I remembered the military relaxation method:

1. *Find a quiet, comfortable place (not happening).*

2. *Close your eyes (also not happening).*

3. *Take a few slow, deep breaths. (Done)*

4. *As you inhale, tense and hold each muscle before you move on to the next part of your body (don't have time for all of that)*

5. *Tense the muscles in your feet by pointing your toes and tightening your feet as you inhale. Hold the tension briefly, then relax. (No time for that, either)*

6. *Press the balls of your feet into the floor and raise your heels. Contract your calf muscles. (Done)*

7. *Squeeze your buttocks muscles. Inhale and exhale, allowing your muscles to relax. (They would notice this)*

8. *Continue through your body, your stomach, hands, arms, shoulders, neck. (Can't do all that)*

9.   *Finish by tensing all the muscles in your face. (can't do that)*

10. *Let yourself be still for a few moments and experience relaxed muscles. (I think this happened).*

We sat for what seemed like minutes, but it was likely only twenty seconds. My exercise must have worked because the alarm stopped and Pink-Haired Lady said, "Normal heart rate detected. Must have been a glitch."

Allabaster typed something into her device. "Well, Parker and Cantrell, I thank you again for your service in the vat room. I understand it is a demanding task, but you are required to complete it. The minerals we receive from the melted tech are a landmine for us. Keep up the good work" She stood. "You may be excused and remember the consequences for sharing information."

We all stood and saluted her. The doors swished open, and we stepped out.

I let out a long sigh. "That was fucking unbelievable."

Ed was silent.

"Aren't you gonna say anything? I mean, how crazy was that? I can't believe her."

"Liv," Ed said.

"Yeah?"

"It's time."

"Yeah, I know," I said, looking straight ahead. "I know."

10

OLIVIA

THE TIME HAD COME to initiate the plan and leave this place. The next day, I walked to Sarah's room to switch out the drugs for saline in her IV bag. She needed to be alert to escape. She looked so peaceful hooked up to the IV. Arms crossed, shoulder-length, auburn hair swept off her face—no sign of fear, except for constant rapid eye movement beneath her lids. Her chart labeled her a "flight risk" and "sedation underway." Anyone who tried to escape moved down the hall to secure rooms—which were more like prison cells.

Sarah captivated me. She reminded me of my sister Kiwani, who I hadn't seen in over three years, pretty much ever since I joined GB. She's the one who helped me realize this was all bullshit. Like for real. She sent me encrypted pictures with people being rounded up against their will, empty shelves of tech, shuttered businesses. Mass homelessness. GB was supposed to be recycling tech so the economy could grow, but it crumbled and fell. President Gibson, so embarrassed, or better yet incompetent, denied everything. Even more reason to get out of here, blow it up and start all over. I pushed my dreads aside again. I'd let them grow far longer than I ever wanted these three years, but they seemed to suit me.

Sarah's chart looked standard:

✓ *Tech confiscated*
✓ *Personal Dwelling Secured*
✓ *Tracking Device Implanted*

Her intake chart included her hometown of Austin, her employer, and her reason for capture: Sabotage.

They would never let her walk free. The door creaked as I pushed a wheelchair inside. My limp felt more pronounced, so I relied on the handles for support.

GB had released people from here, but only after they signed an agreement not to gain any tech and to adhere to the three principals of Go Back stated in the pocket-sized pamphlet we all received. It's a lifelong contract that also included prohibiting active resistance against GB and the government.

The alert of Sarah's arrival came via the inter-web labeled "urgent." Because of my ranking, I was pre-screened and pre-approved, so could provide backup if people fled. I watched Sarah behind a one-way glass as she filled out her forms. She took so long, I figured she must have been in shock over the transport. It was then I'd learned of her identity.

They took her and the other passengers with her to intake first. That's where GB physicians took vitals and gave sedatives if needed. They separated everyone, even children and babies, from their mothers and each other. Release was contingent on compliance; and, as my superiors told me, they gained compliance easier when people are alone. When they released mothers contingent upon being reunited with their families, they complied better, they told me.

Just before her intake, Sarah sat there nibbling her nails as she looked around. At one point, it seemed as if our eyes met, but I knew that was impossible through the one-way glass. After they took her to the back, I snaked through the halls until I could eavesdrop on her conversation with Dr. Rose. All of it alarmed me. The threats exchanged, the desperation in Sarah's voice.

I bit my lower lip and shook my head. My palms became damp with sweat, then I heard screams and an alarm. Rapid footsteps approached. As other guards entered the room, so did I and saw Sarah passed out on the metal examination table.

I stood there as my chest moved with my breathing.

"Sergeant Parker, assist or leave," Doctor Rose ordered, so I assisted by lifting Sarah's feet.

Five of us carried her that evening. Once inside her room, Dr. Rose took over, checking her pupils for dilation, blood pressure, and heart rate.

"Thank you for your swift action, Dr. Rose," I said. I secretly wanted to kick him where it hurt.

He smiled back. The good doctor seemed to like me for whatever reason. We'd often worked together photographing new intakes. He said he chose me because of my combat photography experience.

"Anytime, Parker," Dr. Rose said. He paced the room, then added, "Grimes is a great addition to the movement."

I chose my words with caution. "You think? And how so?"

"She's young, malleable. I can see that she'll be a real ally." He put his hand on the doorknob to leave.

"Yes, she will be," I replied.

•   •   •

After I filled the I.V. with saline, I sat at Sarah's beside. I skipped lunch and exercise duty. Told my superior I had a stomach bug. When the saline kicked in, her eyes peeled open.

"You're getting out," I told her.

She looked at me through squinted eyes. "What?"

"I'm Olivia. I called you. Told you—"

"You're the caller? You told me everything." She coughed. "It's true, isn't it?" Her voice sounded haggard, dry.

I put my hand under her head and lifted a glass. "Here, sip some water. I'm gonna get you out of here, but it won't be easy. We've assembled the resistance at a place called the Garden."

Sarah pushed her hands down to sit up. She slurped the water and some rolled down her chin. "I'm so weak."

Months of little to no activity did that.

"No. You don't understand. This is how it is now. Go Back has its tendrils in everything. The rules have changed." I unlocked her cuffs.

"Here, take this." I handed her one of GB's thick rectangular pamphlets. "There's a map inside. Study it. Don't lose it. Hide it in your pillowcase."

The glossy front cover of the pamphlet displayed a family picnicking under a gigantic oak. Sarah held it open and appeared to read.

A WORKING GUIDE TO THE GO BACK MOVEMENT

Who we are:
We are politicians, parents and citizens concerned about the negative impact of technology (including cell phones, artificial intelligence, digital assistants). We are just like you.

Our history:
The Go Back Movement, or GB for short, is based on the Luddite uprising in early 19th Century England. The Luddites rejected the machines that vied for their jobs. We believe technology is vying for our need for human connection.

[DEPICTION OF LUDDITES DESTROYING MACHINERY.]

FAQs

Are you against ALL technology?
We are not technophobes. We believe in the power of certain technologies.* We also know that, even in it's best form, and with the best of intentions, technology can become addictive.

What are you doing?
With the full support of the President of this Great Nation, Ronald Gibson, GB is providing accelerated treatment programs. We have more than 52 Centers across the U.S. And plans for more are in the works!

Why can't we keep our tech?
We believe society is on a death march and that technology must be resisted. Go Back is working in your interest on this matter. No longer will we be slaves to the screen. Resist with us and you will see. Freedom is yours for the taking.

* Acceptable technologies: Cars (non-autonomous), phones (land-line only, or cell phones with no internet access)

* Unacceptable technologies: Autonomous (self-driving) vehicles, internet-connected/Wi-Fi cell phones, tablets, smartwatches (I.e. any device with internet connection as this has proven addictive and destructive to personal and familial life or has the valuable rare earth elements—see the handbook for further information)

"This is all such propaganda! How can they get away with this?" Her voice raised and her eyes widened as if she couldn't believe she could speak. She pressed her hands to the mattress and tried to scoot back to sit up in the bed.

"Here, let me help," I said. I placed my hands under her arms and lifted as she pushed again. "There. Better?"

She nodded. "How long have I been in here?" she asked. She raised her hands and stared at her nails in confusion. Her forehead wrinkled. Despair and confusion. She knew nothing.

"Six months. Almost seven," I replied.

"How can they hold me this long? And drugged like this?" She pointed to at the needle in her arm.

I leaned down to whisper. "We have given you food through an NG tube, so you will notice weight loss. I know it's crazy, but we are charging you with sabotage. If you want to get out of here, we have to do this the right way, please."

"I'm so weak," she said. "I'm afraid I won't get far out of here."

I placed my hand on hers. My earbud announced dinner in five minutes, so I stood to leave. "I'll arrange for PT for you to build back your strength. You were pretty strong before. It should only take a few weeks. Oh, and don't mess with the chip, either. We'll take care of that right before."

Her eyes glazed over, foggy with tears. "Chip? What chip?"

"We're getting you out of here, Sarah. Trust me, like I trusted you," I said. "Oh, and whatever you do, don't go home."

•　　　•　　　•

PRESS BRIEFING
by Press Secretary John Dickerson
James S. Brady Press Briefing Room
1:11 P.M. EST

MR. DICKERSON: Hello, everyone. Good afternoon. Yesterday, the United States witnessed a tremendous historical event: the opening of a dozen more Go Back Centers. President Gibson promised to help this country recover from tech addiction in record time, and President Gibson delivered.

The president has also worked tirelessly since the closure of the Mountain Pass Mine to ensure every American will continue to have access to necessary technologies. However, he recognizes the need to wean Americans from their tech, especially cell phones. Cancer deaths are up twenty percent from ten years ago. Research suggests cell phones are to blame. Texting and driving accidents are at an all-time high, even with the growing popularity of ride shares and autonomous vehicles. And, in other terrible news, the marriage failure rate is at 65 percent. An all-time high linked to excessive social media and Internet usage.

Earlier this year, we heard from several news outlets and so-called fact checks that President Gibson would quote, "take away all tech forever." That was an NBC News article. USA Today warned us that, quote, "despite well-meaning intentions, the seizure of tech quote, 'was a permanent solution'" end quote. These reports are false.

President Gibson directed the Go Back movement to build and fill these centers to rehabilitate the tech-addicted public. It was a novel approach, indeed, and led by President Gibson. President Gibson also directed Go Back to recycle old tech to preserve the rare earth elements that have now become exceptionally rare due to trade embargos.

Together, these steps play a significant role in changing the course of tech addiction and boosting our economy. Thank you to President Gibson.

And now, I will take questions.

Cynthia.

Q: John, you mention the cancer rates at an all-time high. What studies prove that cell phones are to blame?

DICKERSON: There are several studies out there, all available to the public. You can find them at whitehouse dot gov.

Q: There are rumors of a tech roundup. Is there any validity to these claims?

DICKERSON: These claims are false. I'm not even going to entertain such nonsense.

Q: Are people being forced into centers? Why can't the press go on a tour of one?

DICKERSON: There are HIPPA laws. Remember those? It would be against the law to expose patients like that. As for the first part of the question, that's ridiculous.

No further questions. Thank you.

11

SARAH

YOU'RE GETTING OUT. Olivia's words filled my head like music. The ceiling tiles looked even clearer, if that was possible. Just as my mind began to relax, the door creaked open, and a nurse stepped inside holding what I assumed was my chart. I hadn't seen her before. She wore a white, cotton pantsuit, her mousy brown hair sagged. She appeared very young, her porcelain cheeks rosy, her almond shaped green eyes alert. I slumped back down in bed to pretend someone hadn't switched out the IV fluid.

"You're new?" I asked.

"Been here a few months," she replied. "I'm going to take you to another room. Please use caution as the effects of your Phenobarbital will be wearing off."

So that's what they've been giving me! I relaxed my face and moved my fingers slowly as to appear calm and drugged. My tongue felt like a cotton ball.

"Can I have some water, please?" I asked taking my voice down an octave to sound more subdued.

The nurse smoothed down her white cotton pantsuit and filled a glass for me. I chugged it down. She grabbed a pen inside her pocket. She scribbled something on my chart.

"We're going to the Information Room in the Commons."

I pressed my bottom into the bed and moved to the edge as slow as a snail while the nurse pulled up my rough, wool socks and put some white slippers on my feet.

"Put your hands on my shoulders, and don't do anything stupid."

I complied, slid off the bed, and my feet hit the floor. She helped me into a wheelchair and buckled me in like a baby.

"You eager to meet the others?"

I squeezed my eyes together. Did I just hear correctly? Others? "Yeah. I am. Thank you," I said.

"You know Ms. Grimes; you will enjoy it here. I know I do." She said it in a robotic tone.

Why would someone so young buy into all this? I kept the conversation going. "Do you miss it? Your tech?"

"Don't ask such questions. You'll see. It's all worth it." She changed her voice, as if speaking to a child. As if something that banal would convince me.

She wheeled me out of the room. I could only assume the buckle locked, preventing me from escaping. I heard nothing, only the thud of her feet on the floor and the occasional wheelchair squeak. After about 200 feet, we paused next to a door with a glass window. She tapped a code, and the door buzzed open.

"Here we go. You'll see, Sarah."

The room smelled musty. A brown and yellow plaid couch from the 70s sat against the back wall. People sat in metal chairs facing a whiteboard.

"I think I can walk from here," I said to her, but when I tried to lift myself out of the chair, I remembered she had secured my legs.

"Here, let me get that for you." She put her hands on mine, then reached over and swiped a key card over the buckle and it opened.

"Hmph. So that's how it works. Clever technology, eh?" I snickered. She gave me no response.

"Take the seat up front, next to the window."

I shuffled to the opposite wall. The nurse had rolled up my starchy, medium-blue scrubs because they were too long. They were too tight on the thighs, but as I walked, they didn't rub together like they had in the past. The effects of a liquid diet, I guess.

I reached the seat and lowered myself into it. A heavy-set woman with short, frizzy brown hair sat two seats over on my row. She had the same medium blue scrubs on. My heart danced with happiness as I realized how close I was to another person, causing my words to stumble out in excitement.

"Hi there. You okay?" I asked.

She looked at me with kind eyes. "No, not really. You?"

"No." My stomach rumbled from hunger.

I caught the faint sound of little feet and whispered conversations behind me.

"They're coming. Be silent," the girl said.

People wearing GB uniforms and others who looked like patients (or rather prisoners) entered through the door, a swarm of bees to the hive. They filled every other chair in the room. I dared to look at them. One had crimson hair. She walked like me, slow and staggering. She did not look my way but sat facing forward. I could only guess they had heavily sedated her. Another sat behind me. A man, in what looked to be his late 30s. Short hair with gray around the edges. The others filled in, too quick for me to notice and before I knew it, a woman stood behind the desk in front of the whiteboard. I recognized her from my intake. She had the pulled back hair, not one askew.

"Greetings, all."

"Greetings," we all echoed back, even me.

"Welcome to the GBC, or the Go Back Center. We are so thrilled to have you all here. We know it may seem daunting." She cleared her throat and reached for the half-filled glass of water in front of her. She held it, pinky out, pressed it to her lips, and took such a small sip the water level looked the same. "But rest assured, we have secured your technology, and after your rehabilitation, we will release you back into society, ready to conquer all." She raised her right hand to the ceiling, her thumb and index finger pressed together in some sort of symbolic gesture that looked like the Okay sign.

"Here at GB, we believe technology like cell phones, self-driving vehicles are responsible for the downfall of society, but I think it would be better to read the pamphlet," she said. Then several other GB workers came around, giving us each a white trifold.

Before I had it fully open, I sensed a presence over me.

"What do you think, Sarah?" the woman from the front of the room said. I looked up to see her hovering over me. She came around to face me, and I read her badge: Cpt. Allabaster, GB.

"Sarah?"

"Yes Ma'am." I had no idea how to address her.

"What do you think? Sounds good, yes?"

I froze. Some of it sounded appealing, but how were we supposed to just go back to before the internet? How could we?

"Uh. Sounds interesting, but how is it even possible?" It was the only thing I could utter in that moment.

"Sarah, surely you can understand why technology is bad. We've been monitoring the population's use and perhaps we should just show you. Perhaps we should show all of you," she said even louder.

Then she pulled out a remote control and turned on the TV screen.

A woman sat alone in a room at a long table. She said nothing but she cupped her hands, left hand holding the right as if holding a device like a phone. Her thumbs flew back and forth. Texting. Then up and down. Scrolling

"You see. This. This is what it has become. Those we've rescued have all the symptoms."

Then the woman at the table looked up straight into the camera. She appeared to fix her tear-filled eyes on me.

"Go back. I want to go back. I'll do it, okay. Please, please … just help me. Help me." Tears ran down her face. Before she could go on, a man entered the frame. I instantly recognized him as Dr. Rose, the man who injected me. A shiver ran up my back.

"Thank you, Penelope. It's okay. Come, come with me," he said as he helped her up. The TV turned black.

I looked around. Many sat with their mouths open. A few women cried. then a man's voice cried out.

"This is bullshit. You brainwashed her. No one wants your Go Back crap. I never signed up for this!"

That voice sounded familiar. When I turned to look, I saw Chris from the Elephant Ear.

I couldn't believe this. He stopped yelling as our eyes met and, then some orderlies grabbed his arms and dragged him away. My voice forgot how to work. I wanted to stand, but as I placed my hand on the armrest of the chair, an alarm blared.

"That's all for today, folks," Allabaster said. "You will all be escorted back to your rooms." My nurse stood at my side.

"Don't try anything stupid," she said in my ear.

"I won't."

"Good, now get in the chair," she said not offering to help me this time.

Some walked, some rolled, but we all meandered back to our rooms. Doors closed. My chest tightened at the thought of where they took Chris, the thought of him in this place, too. I had to find him again. We had to get the hell out of here.

12

SARAH

MY MEMORIES FLOWED like a swollen river after a heavy rain. In and out of sedation, I remembered the room, the chairs, the people. I struggled to remember the events. Then I saw a woman's face, bronze cheeks, thin dreads framing it. She gave me a pamphlet. Inside was a map.

Olivia. Yes. Her. She promised I'd get out of this hell hole, yet I'm still here. At least I'd been doing PT every other day in the yard. I felt my legs getting stronger along with my will.

Ever since seeing Chris, the pang in my heart sharpened. We had only just met, but seeing someone from the "real world" gave me hope. I didn't believe in love at first sight or fairy tale stuff, but we had something, and I had to get back to him.

After Olivia had left, I'd used my teeth to cut the string on the side of my pillow to create a small hole and slid the map inside.

Now, I pulled it out and unrolled it. The paper looked like brown craft paper, and it fit in the palm of my left hand. One side had what appeared to outline the Center. An X showed my room location in the northeast corner according to the compass. A red "E" marked three exits. I traced my finger along the routes to the female and male residential wings. I stopped at the cafeteria. A down arrow indicated a basement level, labeled Sub Zero/Do not go. An up arrow indicated a second floor labeled GB offices/Do not go.

On the other side I found a map leading to the Garden. Its legend had a series of hand-drawn symbols which indicated different places and instructions:

> Temporary location
> The Garden
> Pack up and Go
> Follow the trail for water and food.

I thought of the pamphlet and its propaganda. Go Back had some ulterior motive for all this. I wanted out. I had to. No, Olivia was the key. She always had been. I resisted the urge to rush and instead embraced the need for patience. I put the map back inside the pillow.

Soon after, the same nurse from earlier came inside.

"We're going to the—"

"Information Center. Yeah, where else," I snapped.

We went almost every day. She explained that we needed to undergo reprogramming to successfully reintegrate into a society without modern technology. "Are there still planes? Cars?" I asked one day.

"Of course. Haven't you read the pamphlet?" She snickered. She smoothed down her white nurse hat. The only hair I saw was a thin line of brown and a tiny bun behind the hat.

"Yes. I read it all right. Makes sense. I guess. I just don't see why I'm here. Why can't I get—"

"Better not to ask, Sarah. You know about declaration 466-92. We all do." Her lips formed a small smile.

I gave up. No sense in wondering when Olivia was going to get me out. Or was she? Where was she anyway? All kinds of paranoid thoughts ran through my head.

"Come on now. We can't be late," the nurse said and hoisted me to stand.

•　　•　　•

I didn't see Chris again.

I spent most of my time in the Information Center watching propaganda about the perils of high tech and the need for minerals, how our society failed us and how we needed to sacrifice for the good of the nation.

The rest of the time was spent between PT, the dining hall or in my room. I could sense myself becoming institutionalized. I wondered when I would get out. No one would ever tell me.

One day I saw the man from my van ride and sat across from him.

"How've you been?" I asked. His eyes darted around, and he didn't touch his food. He looked forward then back over his shoulder.

"You shouldn't be talking to me. We were wrong. We were all wrong."

"Wrong about what?"

"Wrong about trying to fight back. We just need to go along. To go back."

An unease swept through my body. This guy had been on the front lines of the resistance. What had they done to him? My stomach and chest tightened. I wasn't hungry anymore and wondered if the implanted chips could manipulate our emotions. Then I questioned my own.

I wanted it out. When was Olivia coming back?

●　　　　●　　　　●

Back in my room, the IV tethered me, though I'd felt more lucid. Still, they deemed me a flight risk and decided to sedate me. I scanned my body the best I could with my hand and searched for any evidence of a chip. Nothing. They had stopped handcuffing me for certain stretches. They'd said I'd been a "good girl" at the information sessions.

I turned my head and spotted a wheelchair next to my bed. I felt lightheaded, but not faint, so I sat up. The plastic casing of the IV had tape over it. I ripped it off to reveal the needle below. I might have done this a long time ago if it hadn't been for the handcuffs and drugs. No, probably not. Needles scared me. I stared at it almost willing it to fall out, but knew that wouldn't happen, so I pressed down on the port with my right hand, closed my eyes and ripped it out with my teeth. A liquid that tasted like rotten grapefruit splashed inside my lips. My tongue found the cloth of my scrubs to wipe it off.

A strong pressure formed between my legs and as I reached down, I touched something hard down there. I lifted my left leg to scoot over, and a stench filled the air, like an overflowing toilet. My knees on the edge of the bed to stand, something warm flowed down my leg, and I spotted a bed pan. The stench told me I'd been drugged for a long time.

Gasping, I took the top sheet of the bed and wiped off my leg. I shuffled and propped my hands on the edge of the bed and moved towards the wheelchair. I didn't know where I was going, but I had to get out of here.

My bottom slid into the seat and my hands grasped the wheels, but I couldn't get them to move. Once I did, I almost crashed into the wall when I figured out a way to steer it back towards the door. Clutching the door handle with my sweaty hand, I turned it to enter through the doorway.

I found myself in a narrow, dark hallway with hazy, flickering overhead lighting. Doors with small windows near the top were on both sides of me. Chattering came from behind some of them, but I rolled on. Tapping came from behind others, but I rolled on. Then something made me pause. Inside one room, came faint singing.

Outside the door, I tried to push myself into a standing position, but my legs gave out, plopping me back down. Up again I pushed. This this time my feet touched the floor. I reached with my left hand up to grab the window's edge and reached up with my right to stabilize myself. As I pulled myself to a full standing position, I peeked inside. I looked down towards the sound and saw a mess of dark curls.

It was Chris.

He crouched in a corner, with his knees pulled to his chest. His blue scrubs sagged around his legs. His shaggy hair fell over his eyes.

My legs strained under me. As I reached my hand toward the glass, my left leg gave out and I slipped halfway down, twisting my ankle. I winced in pain. It didn't hurt as badly as I thought it should, leading me to believe they had, in fact, drugged me.

As I reached up to grab the wheelchair armrest to hoist my body back up, footsteps and the telltale clicking of heels echoed far away.

I pulled as hard as I could and pressed my feet into the ground to stand. I pushed my bottom back into the seat and attempted to roll, but I moved in the opposite direction and collided with the wall.

The clicking sound got closer.

I maneuvered the wheels as fast as I could towards my room, then the clicks subsided.

"Sarah. Stop," she called out to me.

I stopped without applying the brake and crashed into the wall again. This time my toe jammed, and I yelped out in pain.

"Why have you left your room, Sarah? It's not safe out here for you. These rooms are for those who, ahem, have not acclimated to the GB movement. Let's just say they need a little more convincing."

I almost believed her, but never turned to look at her. Instead, I sat and whimpered. My toe and ankle hurt, but the fear hurt more.

"Let's go back to your room. You're not ready for the real world yet. I don't want you to end up here, Sarah. So, let's be more cooperative from now on, 'eh? No more leaving the room," she said in too sweet a tone. I knew she was faking. My skin crawled.

She turned me around to face her and said nothing. I sensed her intense stare even though I concentrated on my thighs. I looked up and saw her subtle grin. Her pen was in her pocket, clipboard tucked under her right armpit. I couldn't read her expression at all. She handed me the clipboard and came behind me to push me back to room 609.

The door was already open. Two orderlies in green scrubs waited for me. I said nothing as they hoisted me into the bed and started up the IV.

13

SARAH

I N MY DRUGGED STATE, I had ample time to reminisce about the past.

Before guards. Before raids. Before being arrested.

Going Down
The Possessed (2012)
You're blown up and then some
You don't belong (don't belong)
So, stand up and fight this
Or you're going down
You're going down

My mom played that song over and over during my childhood. The lead singer's epic voice, the drawn-out electric guitar solo, stuck with me somehow. I even tried to learn how to play it as a teen but failed.

"What's it about, Mama?" I'd ask.

"Well, it's about being able to hide away from the real world. It's about not having to worry about it getting to you. Like protecting yourself."

My 6-year-old self-accepted this explanation without another thought. Today, those lyrics seemed so much more poignant. The tech world had blown up. The Go Back movement was in full control.

•   •   •

No calendar on the wall, no ticking clock, just me and my thoughts, lying on this damn bed with a molded pan between my legs that caught my waste. I stared at the ceiling and counted the tiles. One, two, three, four … Such a useless pastime. There were forty-four. Despite being aware that one tile was broken in half, I still counted it.

I lay there for what seemed like hours when the door creaked open, and someone entered. Instead of the familiar clicking of heels on tile, there was a muffled sound resembling loafers. Dr. Rose strode into the room. While I lay paralyzed in my own feces, he leaned over me, oblivious.

"How are you today, Sarah?"

I wondered how I was supposed to respond to this. They caught me fleeing my room and since then I'd laid there, too scared to move. I had seen Chris singing to himself, going crazy in this new reality.

I paused, took a breath in and out, and planned my words. "I'm okay, however, I'm not sure," I said. It came out sounding more like a question than a statement.

"Hmm, well, I think I have something for that," he said and held up a large vial filled with clear liquid in one hand and a needle in another to put in my IV needle.

I crossed my arms across my chest in protest. My body became rigid. He looked at me, hesitating, with the needle in his hand.

"I don't want that in me."

"Alright," he said in a gentle voice, and he placed the needle on the shiny silver pan next to me.

I breathed in a sigh of relief, hoping he wouldn't hear, but he did.

"Sorry to scare you like that." He leaned closer. Was he trying to take advantage of me? His breath had a sweet fragrance, reminiscent of chocolate.

"It's okay," I stammered. What an idiotic thing to say. Someone comes at you with a needle, doctor or not, and you say it's okay? I was crazy.

He looked at me like a puppy who'd been waiting to be adopted for months. Like a hungry puppy whose spine and ribs showed. He lifted my right eyelid and shined a light. He did the same for the left. I lay motionless and didn't say a word for fear he'd drug me unconscious again. I thought about finding a phone, but even if I did, I couldn't remember anyone's number thanks to speed dial. I could call 911, but what if GB had bribed the operators?

"All clear. We must keep you here for a few more days. Remember, the punishment for leaving a room is severe, but we'll cut you some slack. You didn't get far," he said.

He turned as if to leave, but then looked back.

"I like you, Sarah. I wouldn't want anything bad to happen to you out there. Stay put, okay?" Then he walked out the door.

I didn't hear it lock behind him.

14

OLIVIA

T HE CLOUDS RACED ACROSS THE SKY like a marathon with no finish line. The thunder cracked, and I felt the coming rain in my joints.

I sat alone on the bench outside the Center as I did on a rest day. It's our one-day-a-month to roam the grounds. We're free to write home, but we're never free to leave except for raids or pre-approved business.

As I relished the Zen of solitude, I felt a thud next to me.

"Hey Liv." Ed plopped down beside me on the garden bench. "What're you doing?"

He always appeared so fucking chipper. I hated that about him and loved it, too.

"Nothing, just thinking," I answered. An earthy scent and Nimbostratus clouds promised approaching rain. A crow cawed in the distance.

"Naw, I can tell it's more than that." He nudged my arm.

I stood up, and the pain in my ankle shot up my thigh.

"You know what I'm thinkin'. Why do you always have to play around, Ed? Oh my God, it is so irritatin'." I felt like I could explode. I struggled to push back tears, but they came full force.

Ed jumped up to face me. "Liv, wait. No, I didn't mean to."

"You didn't wanna what? Piss me off? Push my buttons?"

"Sit down, Liv. They're watching."

As much as I wanted to yell and run away, I dd it. He was right.

We sat in silence as I wiped my eyes, and then I spoke up. "I'm worried, Ed. Our plan is falling through. They're on to us, the Garden, everything. And Sarah is still here."

"It will happen." He placed his hand on my knee. "What would you be doing right now if this whole thing hadn't gone down?"

What kind of question was that? Nothing like that mattered anymore. Still, I caved and answered. "I planned to be a live music photographer with a blog and/or photography school, but here I am at this Center, melting down tech and drugging people. Not at all what I expected."

Other voices filled the air. Ed raised his index finger to his lips, and we tiptoed closer. A line of bushes prevented us from getting near the open basement window. We laid down and propped our chins up against the sandy soil.

"It's time," a muffled male voice said.

"Yeah, it is. So, what then?" a female voice asked.

Ed and I exchanged glances. The gravel underneath me ground into my elbows. I shifted around and my arm bumped into Ed's. I could smell his musty cologne and see his short stubble on his face from lack of shaving.

"We can't let this happen again. We need Sarah for—" The voice went silent.

"Shit," I mouthed to Ed.

He pursed his lips and shook his head.

"We need her," a male voice, which sounded a bit like Dr. Rose, added.

"Yes. It's okay. We got it," the female said.

Ed and I slithered backwards on the ground and

"What the hell was that?" I asked, panting.

"No clue, but it's obvious they're gonna make a move."

Thunder boomed in the distance. Ed reached an arm around me. "We're going to the Garden, start a new life, ya know? We've done all we can here."

Sitting there, motionless, the sky and my stomach churning in time to the thunder. The low bushes around the Center swayed in the wind. It gusted every few minutes, creating a peaceful rustle. I imagined what it might be like to be away from here. Ed and I bowed our heads to contemplate the thought.

"I'm getting her out, then we're making our move, okay?"

"Ok, I'm in," Ed said gave me a side hug. "Good. This is good."

Rain hit my forehead. "Yeah, it's good. We're getting out of here."

15

SARAH

T HROUGH THE BLINDING HAZE, I remembered.
I peeled open my eyelids and looked around the room: white walls, silver chair, chart hanging on the door, teal, fuzzy bedspread. My head also experienced a fuzzy sensation, but to a lesser degree.

Chris remained in my mind. We'd barely talked, barely touched, but I wanted to see him again. He was so close, yet so far away. And he sent me a friend request the day of my capture. What crazy timing. I wondered when they got him. God, what did they do to him? I've got to get out of this room, but Dr. Rose's words scared the shit out of me.

He didn't change the bedpan. I pushed my legs to the side and look around for a call button. There was none. I yelled out, "Help!"

Nothing. Where was Olivia?

I swung my lead legs over the side of the bed and steadied myself to walk. My feet hit the ground. My hands still on the bed, I walked around it, the molded pan still wrapped between my legs. I'd kill for a shower.

As I looked around, I didn't find anything capable of cleaning me. I walked to the door. Wished I had that wheelchair back because my legs were weak.

I stumbled to the door and reached for the knob. It clicked and opened. I put my head out without care. The empty hallway revealed no bathrooms. I knew they'd cleaned me at some point. Why couldn't I remember when?

This ain't right … It ain't right … the lyrics from "Drowning in Circles" by The Oh Yeahs kept running through my mind. I stumbled outside my room. I knew Chris had been to my left, so I turned in that direction and steadied myself on the wall. A shadow approached. My breath left my body. But I didn't hear heels, only the steady rolling of what sounded like a cart. The hair in the shadow looked thick, like dreads. Olivia.

"Sarah, back to your room," she said.

As I walked back, I was aware of her behind me at every single moment. Thankfully, it only took about twenty steps. Once inside, Olivia stood inside the room, half a foot taller than me. I rested my hands on the cart. It had a bucket full of water and a bottle of soap.

"Sit down. I'm gonna take care of you now."

"But what about the orderly?"

"Don't worry about her. She's on desk duty." Olivia's round, green eyes blinked more often than I thought they should. She rubbed her hands together like lathering imaginary soap. "I just want you to know I'm sorry for what happened to you. I feel like it's my fault. And I'm gonna get you out of here. Now, lay on the bed."

I laid like a baby on a changing table. She curled her fingers underneath the hard plastic of my molded bedpan. Then I heard a large snap, and we tried with all my might to pry it off. We gave about three huge pushes and the right side ripped off and with that, I smelled the most horrendous thing I've even smelled in my lifetime. Pure stench, worse than a sewer, and it had come from my body.

We did the same trick with the left side and the more stench came pouring out. A huge, crusty lump came off my body. I swore we removed skin. I dry heaved. Guess I hadn't had enough solid food to throw up. Olivia wiped the water on my skin over and over and over again. I winced through the pain, but did not cry. We couldn't let them hear me.

I'm not sure how long this lasted, but the water cleared up. I was clean enough. I dried myself with a huge roll of brown paper towels, then Olivia helped put on a pink t-shirt and pants that looked less like scrubs and more like lounge pants, dark blue with a draw string belt.

"You still have the map?" she asked.

"Yeah. I've looked at it. And wondered what the symbols mean."

"They are lookout symbols. For on the road. There are helpers and there are sweepers. Avoid the sweepers."

"Yeah, sounds good. Listen. I have a friend, Chris. Down the hall. I hate to ask this—"

"Consider it done."

"Consider what done?"

"We'll get him out, too. Whatever you want. It's my fault you're here, Sarah. I never should have called you."

I found it hard to accept what I heard. Was there really a way to trust her? She seemed to trust me. It's all we had to go on at this point.

"Listen. I have to go. I'm going to help you and Chris. Don't worry. Study the map. But don't go anywhere before we get your chips out, okay?"

"Yeah. Thank you so much. Oh, and Olivia," I asked. "How much has the world changed since I've been in here?"

"A lot." She turned and went out the door. And yet again, I'm left alone with only my thoughts and ceiling tiles to count.

Right about tile number forty-two, I heard it; the telltale clicking sounds. Oh, God. She was coming.

Talking came from outside the room and a loud response that sounded like a two-way radio.

"Yes, I'm on my way. I alerted everyone," she said. Sounded like she's right outside the room. The heels stopped.

I muffled my breathing inside my shirt.

I thought of Chris inside his room, or cell, as I should call it. I thought of him thinking of me and wondering where I'd gone. Or maybe he didn't think about me?

"What? No, that's not what I said to do. Hold on, I'm coming. Stay there. Stay right fucking there. We'll lock it down," the voice outside yelled, contradicting her usual calm nature. The clicks faded away.

•   •   •

Later, the sound of the door latch made me hope it was Olivia, but instead I saw Dr. Rose. He stepped inside the room wearing green scrubs. His perfect red hair stood askew like he had bed head.

"You've been bad, Sarah. I warned you."

I had been scared here before, but at that moment I was more scared than ever. "I'm sorry," is all I spat out. Tears flowed. I didn't have to make them up. They were real.

He sat next to me and smirked, then slid off the bed to stand, and I breathed a sigh of relief.

"Why are you here?" I questioned as I wiped my tears. Instead of fear, I now felt determined to get some information out of him.

He hesitated. Ran his fingers along my thigh. I shuddered and pulled back, but that only made it worse. His hand moved to my inner thigh.

I want to kill you, I thought. I put my hand in front of his to push it away, or at least away from my inner thigh.

"I'm here to move you to a new wing; one with a little less freedom because of your recent escapade." I assumed he was talking about my leaving the room.

"I didn't mean to break the rules. I just needed to clean up, but no one came when I called." I pulled away and scooted towards the wall.

With that, he grabbed my wrist, which gave me time to spot a syringe in his shirt pocket. I sat upright and called out again for help. That's when I saw his other hand reaching for his pocket.

I covered my mouth to hide the intense scream that fought to come out, jumped up and got more leverage to yank the light off the wall. It was rectangular, with a base made of some sort of thick plastic resin. As I grabbed it, my bottom slid off the bed and I fell to the floor, ripping the fixture from the wall. It fell to the floor and partially shattered.

He lunged, and I smashed the broken, jagged end of the light into his face. He rolled to the floor with a grunt. Blindly, I thrust it into his face again and again as hard as possible.

He laid motionless, blood pouring from his eyeballs.

Oh my God, I'm a killer. My body shook, bile rose to my throat, but I swallowed it down.

I tossed the sheet over his body. I saw it rise and fall, so maybe I wasn't a killer. The door cracked open. There stood Olivia, with her mouth ajar.

"Oh shit," she said. She put the tray of food she brought me on the ground and closed the door behind her. I found it strange she seemed more concerned about me than the covered body on the floor. On the tray, I saw a small potato, and a torn piece of bread. I picked them up and shoved them in my mouth. I couldn't remember the last time I'd chewed food.

"I had to," I cried with my mouth still half full. "He had a needle. He was going to take me to another room. I thought I'd never see you again."

Olivia's face tensed and I saw lines form on her forehead. "Change of plans, okay? Grab his arms."

We dragged him and pushed him under the bed. Olivia pulled out the syringe and injected him.

"To buy us more time," she said. Her eyes locked onto mine doggedly.

I felt like I couldn't get enough oxygen in my lungs. "More time for what?"

"You can leave in five minutes, okay?" Olivia blurted out. She pushed back her long dreads. "Don't forget the map."

I pulled it out of my pillowcase, along with the picture of my family I had stashed in there too, and placed both in my sock. My only two possessions now.

"As for the chips," Olivia said. "Here. You'll have to cut them out under your right arms. And soon. Unfortunately, with this new situation, we have to get moving."

She handed me a box cutter attached to a carabineer. She also handed me a rolled-up ball of gauze.

The thought of having to cut this tracker out of me made my bile boil.

"Don't tell them I helped you or I'll be dead." She started for the door, but before she left, she handed me a key.

"It's a skeleton. It opens all the doors on the wing."

Her eyes glowed. Were those tears I saw?

I thanked her, but then asked about Chris.

"He'll meet you at the exit. But if you don't see him, go anyway. Don't stop. And whatever you do, *don't go home.*"

I nodded, then exhaled through my nose like the whole of my lungs had to come out.

Without a word, she turned and hurried out the door, leaving it open.

My body thrust into action. I took the map out of my sock and opened it with shaking hands. Just like men, I never had a talent for deciphering maps, so relief washed over me because a series of arrows told me where to go. They led away me from Chris's room. I wanted to turn back. The thought of being out there alone; I didn't even want to think about that. But Olivia had told me Chris would meet me at the exit, so I trudged on. As I turned the final corner to the exit, a voice emerged.

"Sarah."

There he was, a shadow of the man I'd met at the Elephant Ear. He still wore loose fitting scrubs but had a small backpack on.

"Olivia said to meet you here," he said with a smile.

In that moment, anything was possible, but knew we had no time for chit chat.

"Yeah, I know!" I said and blindly grabbed his hand and tugged. "Come on."

We looked left and right. Seeing no one, we proceeded. Our slippers made the faintest pitter patter on the tiled floor. The walls were shiny and gray and lined with doors. A clock perched above one of them. It read 16:05, military time for 4:05 p.m. Rectangular fluorescent lights lined the ceiling, but only emitted the faintest light.

Voices echoed from around the corner, and then we observed a door labeled storage. I used the key to open and we entered. We used what little light coming in from under the door to look at the map. From what we saw in the ten seconds we studied it, and from what I remembered, we had to go through Exit 3 that lead to the courtyard.

We pressed our ears to the door to listen for any sounds of people and stepped back outside.

"Stop you two. Right now." In front of us stood Captain Allabaster and, to my surprise, Olivia.

Nausea overcame me. Allabaster looked at us with cold, hard eyes, and repeated, "Stop. Do not leave."

"We're not trying to leave," I responded.

"Then, where are you going?" Allabaster said in a sarcastic tone. Just then, an alarm sounded, and a voice blared on the intercom. "Code Red. I repeat, Code Red. Everyone must report now to their assigned duties. Medical staff. Get in position."

"Captain, if you don't mind, I can escort these two back to the rooms," Olivia said. After speaking her expression fell flat and emotionless, however I could see beads of sweat forming along her hairline.

Allabaster spoke into her walkie. "Code Red, repeat your status."

"Ma'am, we have Dr. Rose, down in Patient Wing One. Facial lacerations and possible concussion. He's unconscious now. Over."

"Got it. Be right there." Allabaster's mouth opened and closed without her speaking. Her lips furled back revealing her perfect veneers. "Yes, Sergeant Parker. Take these two and meet me in medical. Lock their doors and we'll deal with them later."

"10-4, Captain," Olivia said.

Allabaster's departure created a lengthy pause.

Olivia pulled something from her waist, and before I knew it she held a knife to her collarbone and sliced it. She held out the knife to us. "Here, take it," she said with a pang in her voice.

I stood motionless in shock. Chris squeezed my hand then reached with his other and grabbed the knife.

With a strained voice Olivia said, "When they notice you're gone I can say I tried to stop you, but you put up a fight. Go!"

I shook my head in disbelief. I couldn't believe Olivia would intentionally hurt herself to help us, plus the sight of blood made me queasy. Chris looked back at me with glossy eyes. He seemed frozen. I took a deep breath in, clutched his hand again and our sweat came together in our palms. I pulled, then we raced to the exit.

The door had a long, silver push handle. We both crashed into it, exposing the air outside. Sunlight blinded me. Not sure how long it had been since I'd seen that. We ran down a long sidewalk, following it as it curved through bushes. My thighs throbbed and my breath raced. Chris huffed and puffed as well. As we ran, I realized I didn't even read the instructions for what to do after I got out.

We reached the end of the sidewalk and saw a tall brick wall. Chris bent over and motioned for me to step on his back. Without hesitation, I did it and climbed to the top.

I sat on top and looked down. His eyes studied mine, pleading. I wanted to help him, but how?

He jumped to grab the top but missed. I heard voices yelling.

"Oh My God, Chris, come on."

He jumped again. I sensed his weakness.

His fingers clasped the top of the wall, and I grabbed his wrists. I had little strength, too. His feet pressed up against the wall. Then I saw the dogs and people coming straight for us. They were ready to take us back or worse.

With all my might I hoisted Chris to the top of the fence. As dogs barked, we jumped to the ground on the other side. I fell into my knee, my ankle twisted, and I screamed in pain. Gunshots fired in the distance.

"Run like hell," Chris said.

As I ran, the pain worsened with each pounding step.

Then, the sound of dogs and shots faded. Chris had to help me. We found a wooded area beyond the field and ran into that. It looked like there'd been a recent fire. Half of the treetops had no leaves and were black with soot. Running further, the forest grew thicker with trees, bushes and fallen branches.

We ran and ran and ran, forever. Our breaths pounded against the wind. The dogs and voices grew fainter. We hit a pile of leaves and slid down a hill. I grasped Chris's shirt, and he grunted and tried to grasp my waist. We stopped at the bottom. Chris landed on a tree root and cried out in pain. I reached for him and motioned towards an overhang in the hill. We rolled over to it and lay there, trying to silence our breathing and groans of pain.

16

SARAH

W E DIDN'T REST FOR LONG. The echoes of dogs in the far distance were more than enough to keep us up and moving.

My knee hurt and ankle, but that didn't stop me. Plus, Chris pulled my hand at every turn.

Right before my knee seemed on the verge of breaking, we noticed a small cave and quickly entered. Chris's presence provided me with a sense of security even in this chaotic situation. In the light, I studied his attire, dark blue hospital scrubs, and some gray slippers.

He turned to look at me. "Your knee. How is it?"

I looked down and pulled up my pants leg. It appeared larger than usual. For good measure, I checked my other one for comparison. Yep, I was right.

Chris reached out his right hand and squeezed my shoulder. "Are you okay," he whispered.

"Yeah. It hurts bad, though." That was an understatement.

I pulled the box cutter and the roll of gauze out of my pocket.

"You have to cut the tracker out of me." My chest rose and fell as I sucked in the breath. They put them in our right armpit."

"Oh my God, what?" He reached his hand inside his shirt and felt around. His eyes squinted against a sunray. "Hm, I don't feel anything. No, wait. Oh wow, I do feel a little lump."

I widened my eyes. Was this really happening? I passed him the box cutter.

"Just do it. Come on. The chips track us," I pleaded. Could I have ever imagined I'd be in a situation like this? Never.

"My hands. They're so shaky."

"Chris. You're the only one. I trust you." Between him and Olivia, I was trusting more people than ever nowadays.

"Lay down," he said.

Crunchy leaves and a rock poked into my shirt against my back. I wiggled away from it.

"Should I take off my shirt?" I didn't have time to experience self-consciousness.

"Yeah." Chris looked down at the ground. I saw his full lips, and a pang of desire filled my chest.

"Shit. Okay, um. Is this thing even sterile? I don't want to cut you, Sarah," he said.

"It can't be that deep." I raised my arm over my head. I looked over and saw how thick my hair had grown there. "Shit. How are we going to find in all that?" I smiled and Chris smiled back. His smile gave me some comfort.

Chris said nothing but took his index and middle finger and pressed from the outside in, like a self-breast exam in my underarm.

"Think I found it."

My chest tingled. "Really?"

"Well, there's something irregular in there, and I can only hope that's it."

"Do it."

I wasn't sure how much time had passed since we started all this, or how far we'd gotten from the Center, but we had no time to waste. I grabbed the corner of my shirt that lay across my chest and bit it. Chris handed me the rock I'd laid on before and I squeezed it in one hand. Our eyes met, then I closed mine.

The blade entered my flesh. I'd never had a high pain tolerance, and this hurt worse than most things I'd experienced. Thankfully, he didn't have to make a large gash. A warm burning, like fire shot down my arm, then he squeezed.

"Holy crap. It came out." He unrolled the gauze and wrapped it under my arm and around my shoulder. He handed me the small brown tracker. Its oblong shape reminded me of a pinto bean, but smaller.

"My turn," he said.

"Lay down," I said with a grimace. Would I be able to do this? Chris took off his shirt. I noticed he had very little hair and no tattoos. He raised his arm. I pushed my fingers around like he did and felt nothing. He tried, too.

"Found it!" he said.

I experienced extreme emotional distress as I pressed the blade into his skin. The chip slid out, and I wrapped him up.

"We need to get out of here," he whispered.

I knew he was right. "Let's look at the map. Olivia gave it to me."

"Can we trust her?"

"What else do we have to go on? She said we had to head to a place called the Garden which is labeled here on the map. about a two-day walk or three-hour drive from here." Chris traced the jagged path northeast with his finger.

"There. We gotta take, looks like highway 16 to 290. East. North. Then Northeast. Maybe we'll find a car. Or a bike."

My knee swelled like a sausage.

"I can't do this. Not with this knee."

"You have to. I'll find a walking stick for you." And before I could protest, he took off.

While I waited for him, I wondered if I'd die alone. I resisted the thought, but I longed for the ceiling tiles to count. The sound of crunching leaves startled me awake from a daydream.

"Hey. I'm back. Look what I found."

I rolled over and saw him standing there with a long tree branch. It had three arms with leaves still attached. I smiled at the thought of what we were going to do with this thing.

"I figure we'll break off these two sections and make this into a crutch for you," he said. "What do you think?"

"That is great. I think it'll work. Let's do it."

We worked, trying to break the arms of the branch while creating a crutch. With Chris's help, I stood to place my arm inside it. The sharp edges ground into my left underarm, but it had to do.

"Practice," he said.

I placed my weight on the crutch and tried walking around. The scratchy parts pressed into me.

We sat down again and reviewed the map. It showed the Center surrounded by an enormous field, a wooded area, and then some roads.

"Looks like we should head through this wooded area to the main road. Do you recognize Tynewood Highway?"

I shook my head. "I'm lost without GPS. Truth be told, I got lost even with GPS."

Chris flashed his pearly whites. His eyes twinkled. Why did we have to be in these circumstances right now? I'd kill to just go out to eat or catch a movie for a first date.

"Let's get going. It's gonna take you awhile."

He leaned against me, and I took the crutch in my left armpit. We walked in unison on the soft ground. Every sound, no matter how faint, worried me. Was it them? Had they found us? It seemed every step we took forward, we took two back.

I looked up to see a divided highway. We stopped before crossing.

"Where are they?" I asked.

"I don't know. I don't know," Chris looked both ways. I could tell he was worried.

From out of nowhere we heard barking in the distance. They found us.

We looked at the road. Cars raced by here and there. One slowed down. It had a symbol on the lower left front windshield. Was it a temporary location symbol? The old Cadillac parked on the shoulder, and the driver waved for us to get inside.

Before I verified the symbol, Chris grabbed the metal handle of the rear passenger side door, but it fell off. He then opened the front door.

"Do you have tech?" The male driver screeched at us.

Chris and I looked at each other, and before I said a word, he said, "Yes! We have some," and he gave me a gentle nudge into the passenger seat. He climbed over me to get to the back. I reached over to close the door. It was so heavy I feared I wouldn't have the strength, but somehow, I gathered it up from every inch of my ailing body and pulled it closed. The car tires squealed.

We were on the road.

PART TWO

APART BUT TOGETHER

17

OLIVIA

NOT EVEN THIRTY MINUTES after the alarms, Captain Allabaster called me into her office. She sat behind her large wooden desk holding a pad of lined paper in one hand, a pen in the other. The sun rays coming from the small rectangular window behind her created a halo of light around her head.

"Sergeant Parker, what do you recollect?" She pressed the pen to the paper.

"I was escortin' Ms. Grimes and Mr. Cameron back to their rooms when they fled."

"Did you attempt to capture them?" Allabaster grilled me.

Her annoyance radiated out of her body as she pressed her pen against her lips, then tapped it up and down against the pad of paper.

"Captain, I called for backup because I wasn't sure if they were armed. I also knew they couldn't get far in the courtyard." I knew she wanted to know why I didn't run after them.

She glanced at my blood-stained shirt where Sarah had slashed me. Thankfully, the wound was superficial.

"I notice that you have been injured."

"Yes, Ms. Grimes had a box cutter and slashed me with it."

"I see. We will review the video footage." She wrapped her fingers on the table so I could hear each of her nails hit. The sound waves seemed to bounce against the walls and onto my head.

"Of course." I wiped my palms on my pants to remove the sweat. "How is Dr. Rose?" I wanted to divert her attention from Sarah.

"We found him unconscious, with multiple stab wounds to his face, likely inflicted by a broken lamp."

"So, Grimes hit him with a lamp?"

"It appears so. We're still investigating."

Allabaster got up and paced the room. Her heels clicked on the tile floor. Her face revealed the fine lines etched deep from years of scowling and worrying. She glanced at her notepad but wrote nothing else. She continued to look down for several moments, then said, "Sergeant Parker, I need you to go secure the vats. The meltdown is suspended during the investigation."

$\bullet \qquad \bullet \qquad \bullet$

We headed to secure the vats after my interrogation. Ed and I removed any melted tech and inventoried what remained.

I spoke into the suit's microphone. "Hey. How's it going?" I tried to keep things light before divulging how much shit we were in.

"It's okay. You don't have to play it cool. I already know about the escape. Got the alert five minutes ago."

We finished up our work and made our way to his room. As we sat next to each other, I saw the glossy glow of sweat on his forehead. I rested my head in my left palm in sheer exhaustion after my interrogation.

"Okay, so. Things are ramping up. I didn't expect Sarah's escape to be so dramatic. I thought we had more time, but Dr. Rose fucked things up," I said.

"We've gotta push up our departure," he said.

He walked over, arms outstretched like he was ready to embrace. I stepped back hoping to discourage him. His brows furrowed, lines forming like deep crevices of pain, aftershock of all we'd been through.

"Look, Liv, I know. I know. Alright." He stopped his forward movement but continued his fixed gaze.

"You know what, exactly?"

And that's when he stepped forward. His arms wrapped around me and we were like one person. Together. Unified.

I breathed in his sweet scent before I attempted to pull away.

"Ed. Stop. This. Now." I tried to wrangle free. "Ed."

His grip loosened.

"Sorry. Olivia. I'm so fucking sorry, but I care about you. I want to make it out of here with you."

Ed's eyes glazed over, red with more intensity than I'd ever seen. He was like a machine when he got going. The first time I met him three years ago, he taught me how to use the vats, how to suit up, and proper temperature control. He taught me to care about this shit. Now, he would help me unravel it all.

18

OLIVIA

THE NEXT DAY, after securing the vats, Ed and I went to my room to iron out our plan. Inside, my nylon curtains fought to keep out any remaining daylight. A stray sunbeam hit the green wool blanket on my bed and exposed a flare of dust motes. Ed sat down next to me.

"Now, it begins," I said. I stood up and paced in front of him, my mind racing. Sarah had escaped, and they were onto us.

"The plan?"

"Yeah. The plan," I said.

We had planned to leave after we secured things at the Garden, but GB now knew about it, and Sarah escaped. That moved our timeline up.

Our plan was to make maps to Moffat and the Garden and give them to select patients escaping the Center. We ended up contacting Isobel there, after trying frequency 76501 on two-way radios—the town's zip code. She told us she'd escaped from another Center and found the Garden.

"Hop off," I motioned to Ed.

He stood, and I pushed the bed away from the wall and pulled up the fitted sheet to reveal a long slit. I pushed my hand inside. I felt scratchy polyester and foam that sent shivers along my shoulders. I'd always had a heightened sense of touch. I pulled out a leather portfolio which held the maps I'd made and lists of what to bring. I laid one map out on the bed and traced my finger along the route leading from the Center to Moffat. I'd copied the map from satellite maps. I knew we wouldn't be able to take any traceable tech once we left.

"When are we gonna take our chips out?" he asked.

"Tomorrow," I said and folded the map and placed it along with the bed. "You're in charge of rations. Get as much dehydrated food packs as you can along with water filtration tablets. Stash it outside behind the water tank. Meet outside the infirmary at oh-five hundred. We'll remove our tracking chips there. I'll swipe the meds and dressings from the infirmary."

"Okay," Ed said. "You sure we can't take any tech?" he asked right before he left.

"I'm going to secure a satellite phone. The chips are easier to remove from them. The only problem is getting one without them noticing, you know," I said. He nodded and gave a concerned look, then stepped outside.

He left me left alone with my thoughts. Prayers never got me anywhere.

I loaded up my backpack. Three pairs of socks, two tank tops, one pair of pants and shorts, one long-sleeved shirt and one light jacket. Spring meant the temperature could go up and down. A handful of underwear. Deodorant. Toothbrush and fluoride powder. Empty water cauldron. 2-way radios.

Pacing back and forth, I worried about this flawed plan. Sarah got out. She had the map, but would she be able to get to the Garden? Would Ed and I be able to get to the Garden?

I sat back on my bed. I knew the maps and I would be gone by this time tomorrow, and this left me with a deep uncertainty. Joining the Army was a motivation for me. I wanted rules, I wanted direction. Now, I had none of that. It started out that way, but it morphed into some unfocused photograph with blurred edges.

I stared at my packed bag on the edge of the bed and placed it inside my closet. This had been one of the longest, stressful days of my life. I got dressed in usual nighttime attire, scrub-like nightclothes, and slipped under my sheets.

19

OLIVIA

I MET ED AT THE DESIGNATED TIME at the infirmary. I spied no one beyond the glass doors.

He pulled out something that looked like an allen wrench from his pack, gripped one tool and jimmied the lock. I watched him with admiration because of his utter determination. I heard a louder click, and the door opened.

"Ah ha," Ed exclaimed, like a winner of a very precarious game. "Let's go in."

We stepped inside. Several rows of silver tables with containers of gauze, Q-tips and cotton balls on top stood in front of us. A box labeled "Hazardous Waste Only" sat on a counter.

"We need a scalpel and tweezers, but we need to sanitize our skin first," Ed said. "And put on some anesthetic."

We rummaged through the cabinets and drawers. I found what we needed.

"Lay them on the table. Rub the scalpel down with this." He handed me a bottle of rubbing alcohol and a piece of gauze.

I slid the wet gauze over the instruments. "That should do it," I said.

"Ok, sit down. This is gonna hurt. Bite down on something, okay? Oh, and sorry in advance."

I sat on the cold metal table. Ed held my right hand in his. Blindly, I pulled him to me. "I just want to say. Thanks." I leaned close, kissed his cheek, and pulled away.

He stood dumbfounded but cracked a smile. "Liv, you never cease to amaze me."

"Just cause I'm Ace doesn't mean I have no feelings. I am glad we're friends," I said.

He smiled, looked at my hand, and injected the anesthetic in the area between my thumb and index finger, where the implant was. GB put the trackers in its worker's hands for easier access. It put them in the captive's underarms for better concealment.

"It still might hurt despite the anesthetic. I'm so sorry."

I bit down on my right sleeve and nodded for him to begin.

"There's scar tissue. Making it hard to get it all out."

I felt a big tug. Thankfully, the anesthetic seemed to be working.

"There. Man, I thought this thing would never come out." I heard a "plink" as the chip dropped into the metal pan.

Ed dressed my wound. He was up next. His chip was embedded and took twice as long to dig it out. When we finished, we disposed of everything in the hazardous waste bin.

At the door, he stopped me. "Are you packed?"

"Yep. Ready to go. Have to say, I won't really miss this place."

"Me either."

"Okay, so this is where we split up. Meet at van number three in one hour, okay?" I told him.

"Yep. Got it. See you soon, Liv. We'll be on the outside." Ed said and left.

•   •   •

Inside my room, I looked around. So sterile. The gray walls were bare. My green wool blanket sat on the bed pressed against the wall. The one small window that looked out into the field behind the Center has been my view for the past three years.

I looked for anything I may have missed. We planned to leave right after the dinner call. Everyone would be in the cafeteria, so they would be distracted. Inside the closet, I found several GB-issued shirts hanging. I ran my hand along one of them, the first one I received when I had been so proud to be a part of this movement. To make the world better. Free of tech addiction and dependence. I wanted to save the planet by recycling all the old tech. I thought I'd be doing the environment and the economy some good. Well, no more.

Oh, what the hell. I tossed the shirt into my bag.

The hours passed like days. When the time came, I pulled my backpack over my shoulders and left the room, not looking back.

Nearing the cafeteria, I heard chatter and the clanking of dinner plates.

"Hey, you two! What are you up to?" a familiar voice interrupted. "Oh no! What happened to your hand?"

I turned around and saw Lily.

My heart beat at double-time. I stopped just before entering the cafeteria.

"Had a little incident in the vat room," I said.

"Oh, wow. Hope it isn't too bad? You reported it, right?" Lily said and looked closer at my hand. Other recruits brushed past us. Inside, others carried food trays. The smell of meatloaf wafted to my nose. My stomach growled.

"Not yet. Ed and I wanted to get it wrapped up first, but it's on my to do list." I said.

"You know the punishment for not reporting workplace hazards, right?" Lily said, inching even closer.

I scratched my head and ran my fingers through my hair. Our plan had to work.

Lily's face lit up. "Oh my God, you heard about the escape, right? Allabaster says she's sending out top recruits to find those two."

This was the true test. I gave my best poker face. "Oh yes. I was involved! That Grimes girl slashed me right here!" I pointed to my chest, hoping my shaky finger didn't call my bluff.

Lily started to say something else, but I interrupted. "We will, Lily. Now if you don't mind, I'd better get to it. Thanks for reminding me to fill out that incident report."

"Anytime. Take care. And remember, disconnect and unite."

"Fight, fight, fight," we said in unison. To not do so would be like kneeling during the pledge, or God forbid, burning the flag.

Lily went into the cafeteria, and I kept going to the monitoring station three hallways down where I had to disable the security cameras that faced the loading dock. I went inside and found camera three and set it to black.

Outside at the loading dock, all the vans looked the same white with no windows.

I rounded the corner to the number three slot and saw Ed sitting on the rear bumper of the vehicle.

"You made it," he said with quiet excitement. "I have everything. Didn't even forget the water purification tablets."

"Great, now, let's get the hell outta here before they catch on."

20

SARAH

N O ONE SPOKE.

The mystery driver looked to be in his mid-40s, with a graying mid-length red beard and a worn, blue backwards-facing baseball cap covering his red hair. The vehicle reeked of cigarette smoke but wasn't smoking. The man had on a faded black T-shirt that hung over thin, hairy pale-skinned arms. The seventies rock he played on a cassette deck sounded like something my grandparents may have listened to.

The road wound through a wooded area flanked by abandoned homes in desperate need of a power wash and a lawn mower. Where was everyone? The weeds overpowered the flowers. We blew through four-way stops. All the shop windows read *Closed*.

I wanted to ask questions or to look back at Chris, or better yet, jump over the front seat to hold him, but I decided against it for fear of injuring my knee further and angering the driver. We passed empty grocery stores littered with abandoned carts. Cars sat in spaces, but no one came in or out.

The bleak landscape made me want to cry, made me want to scream. But I had no cell phone to call for help, only a crumpled, hidden map.

"Where are we?" I asked the driver.

"We're near Girvin, baby," he snorted.

Don't call me baby.

"Hmph. Never heard of it. We're trying to get to Moffat."

"Ain't about what you want now, lady. I mean, you two got into my car, so you can shut your pie hole now. Look," he said, flooring it. "This is just how it is, folks. You either come with me, or get caught by them Go Back people. I assume that's who you were running from."

"Maybe," Chris said. "Where are you taking us?"

"Don't worry Mr. Long hair. We'll be there soon, and you'd better have some tech."

I shuddered and stared out the window, wondering what we'd tell him once we got to our destination. We'd have to cross that bridge once we got there. Along the road, only small shrubs and unmarked buildings filled the empty fields. No sign of a town. We passed a few small oil rigs. I saw hills in the far distance. Leaning my head against the padded door frame, I closed my eyes.

•　　　•　　　•

I must have fallen asleep because the car had stopped. My head lifted off the window, and I rubbed my eyes.

"Home sweet home," the driver said. Several dogs barked in the distance.

We were at what appeared to be a two-story abandoned farmhouse. The second-floor windows had shutters with peeling green paint, one of which hung by a thread. It had a wraparound wooden porch piled his with junk including a rusty refrigerator from the 1950s.

I turned around to look at Chris and he leaned forward and touched my hand. I looked back at the driver.

"Thank you so much for the ride, but we really must be going."

He let out a loud, disarming laugh.

"Get your tech ready. I was supposed to bring some back, and if Damon finds out I got none, we're in trouble. Plus, if those sweepers come by, we're all in for it."

I hesitated and tried to figure out a way to gain his sympathy.

I had to come up with something fast. "Yes! The sweepers. We're running from them too."

He scrunched his elongated, red, bumpy nose.

"I know we told you we had some tech, but we were scared," I explained, saying that we had to get away from the sweepers because we had just escaped their prison.

He looked at me without saying a thing. I thought maybe he was on our side, at least for the moment.

"We just need a place to crash, and we'll be out of your hair. We will try to find you some tech and bring it back." It was all I could think of at that moment. Chris remained silent in the backseat. I heard his body shift on top of the vinyl seats.

Please don't be thinking of running. Not without me.

"Alright, pretty lady. Don't. Fuck. This. Up. For. Me," the driver said after what felt like two hours. As he spoke, the lines on his forehead spread across his face in waves. I felt scared.

"Yeah. No. We won't. We will do anything you want," I replied.

I glanced back at Chris, who gave me a half smile. I could tell he was desperate for something—a bathroom, water, or food or sleep. It had been so long since we'd had any of those things.

The man opened the driver's side door and a gust of cool air rushed past my face. I sucked it in like it was my last breath. He gestured for us to get out. I pulled the metal door handle and pushed my foot against the door to open it, wincing in pain from my injured knee.

Before I knew it, Chris stood next to me. We walked in unison to the steps, then up each one until we reached the front door.

Inside, I saw an open room devoid of furniture except a saggy salmon colored couch along the left wall. A guy wearing loose khaki pants, a faded t-shirt, and a bandanna on his head laid on it facing away from us. He remained that way upon our entrance, so I figured he was asleep. The room had scratched up wooden floors and a fireplace on the opposite wall. I couldn't tell if it was wood-burning or gas. Faded green wallpaper with vertical white stripes lined the walls. It smelled like a thousand unchanged cat litter boxes mixed with stale air freshener. I breathed out of my mouth to avoid the stench.

Chris stood to my right. His arm brushed against mine as he shifted his weight. He smelled musky. We hadn't bathed in so long.

Our driver stepped over to the man on the couch and poked at him in the shoulder. Chris and I stayed by the door.

The man on the couch stirred and sat up to face us. "Hunter, bruh, why you take so long?" He looked over at us. "Who the hell are these fuckers?"

I feared he would soon demand the tech we didn't have. Hunter shot a look at us too, then quickly looked back at Damon. "Sorry I took so long, man, but I couldn't find anything." His voice seemed to go up an octave. "I tried, Damon. I tried. I really did. I thought the store on F-M 980 would still be okay, but when I got there, it was cleared out." Hunter stopped.

Damon stood up eye to eye with Hunter. I looked over at Chris. He stood motionless, and I did the same. Hunter stepped back.

"Don't you fucking say that," Damon said at almost a whisper. "Don't."

I felt the crumpled map Olivia gave me back at the center in my pocket and heard her words.

Don't go home.

"But hey, D-man, I found these guys, and they have tech," Hunter spit out, and before I could even blink, Damon slashed his face with a knife. Warm blood splattered everywhere. I screamed, then covered my mouth just as fast.

Hunter grabbed his face and fell to the ground, cowering. I wanted to flee. I'd only seen this in violent movies, but that was make believe. This was not.

Damon wiped the blood from the knife onto his pant leg and turned to me and Chris, who stepped in front of me. If my heart beat any faster, it would have popped out.

"So, whatcha got?" Damon said, moving closer to us. "Phones, smartwatches, heck I'd even take a broken tablet."

Chris put his arm behind him to motion me to stay put. "Wait, Damon please. We never told him we had tech. We just needed a ride. We'll go," Chris said.

"Yeah. I bet," Damon said.

Hunter lay in a fetal position in the same spot, moaning.

"Hmph, yeah, well, Hunter ain't the brightest bulb in the box. I'm feeding this one to the wolves. Sweepers will be back soon, and if we don't ante up, we'll be in for it." Damon looked over at Hunter.

"Sweepers?" asked Chris.

"Yeah, boy, you know sweepers? They rule this area now that GB runs shit. Ever since the collapse."

"Collapse?"

"Where you two been, anyway? Who you running from?" Damon seemed to have caught on to something.

"We're not running, just passing through. Looking for work."

"Yeah," chimed Damon. "It ain't easy being holed up all by yourself. We've been doin' our best, but ya know. Hunter was gonna get tech for us for when the sweepers came. Then he was supposed to reach out to our people out west, but well, he's always disappointing. So, let me say this. You two can stay the night, but you gotta help us get some tech after that. Follow me. You two can sleep in the spare room."

"Yeah, okay," Chris said, looked over his shoulder at me and nodded.

"Thank you," I added. I got a closer look at Damon. He was thin, even thinner than Chris, but taller, at least 6'3 or so. Chris seemed to be about my dad's height, or about 5'10.

We walked past Hunter into an adjoining room filled with not much, except for a lopsided wooden dresser and a bare mattress on the floor.

"You can sleep here."

"Yeah, okay." I wondered if those were the only words in Chris's vocabulary now.

Damon turned around to leave. His back to us, Chris and I looked at each other. Chris's eyes were as hollow as I'd ever seen. He seemed like a shell of what he once was. I probably looked the same to him.

Damon left the room without closing the door. I pulled it closed and sat down at the edge of the mattress, and put my hands on my face. My knee still hurt, but not as much. Still, I worried about what would happen if I needed to run again. I wanted to cry or scream, but nothing happened. I only heard my muffled breathing as I wondered when Chris would come sit next to me.

Seconds later I felt a thud to my left as Chris sat down, and he let out a muted "umph."

I felt his warmth beside me. I leaned towards him and rested my head on his shoulder. He didn't pull away. Then I felt his arm around my back. His fingers coiled around my right arm, like a glove.

I lost it and started shaking. I didn't think I'd cried since this whole thing began, but seeing this violence combined with escaping the Center had me at my breaking point.

Chris clutched me tighter.

"It's ok, Sarah. We're gonna get out of this," he tried to reassure me, but his voice had a tremor to it. The uncertainty made me want to cry.

"Can you believe? Can you? I can't." My mouth couldn't form sentences.

"Yeah. I know. We gotta get out of here," Chris whispered. He held me tighter and stroked my arm.

Then he did something unexpected. He hummed. I couldn't recognize the tune, but I loved it. His voice soothed my eyes shut. We rocked back and forth on the edge of the mattress. He then lowered me down as he continued to hum and stroke my arm.

21

SARAH

I WAS STARTLED AWAKE and saw Chris sitting up beside me. His back rested on the wall behind our heads; his shoulder length hair wet with sweat. The dark blue light outside the window indicated nighttime.

"How long have I been sleeping? You shouldn't have let me," I said.

"Just a bit, but you needed it," he said. He patted my left thigh. "Besides, I've been keeping watch the whole time and trying to figure out how we can get out of here. We can't help these guys get tech. This Damon guy's crazy." He laced his fingers together and pressed his palms together.

"Maybe we should just tell them the truth, that we escaped the detox center?"

"No way!" Chris shot back. "Those guys are desperate for money. They would turn us in for sure. No, we need to get out of here."

We heard what sounded like tap dancing coming from the other room, mixed with the low growl of what we assumed was Hunter and Damon's voices.

"Okay, you win. We need to get out of here, but how?" I said, trying not to sound too scared. I also worried if anyone else besides Hunter and Damon were in this house. Both Chris and I still wore what we left the Center with, hospital-like scrub tops with denim-mesh bottoms and hard-soled slippers. We needed other clothes and real shoes.

"Let's try the window. Front door doesn't seem like much of an option right now," Chris said. He stood up next to the window and pressed his hands to the glass. It had a sheen to it and looked thicker than modern-day windows. The sash looked like someone had painted over it two dozen times, with the current coat a thick, flaking eggshell color. Chris tried to slide the latch open, but it wouldn't budge.

The noise in the next room got louder and we heard what sounded like muffled cursing.

We tore up the room in silence, looking for something to scrape the paint to open the window. We looked everywhere. Then the horror of our surroundings unfolded with a closer look at the brown carpet that looked like unvacuumed acrylic yarn. Heaps of stuffed white garbage bags lined the walls. A big brown stain in the corner to the left of the door looked thick and crusty.

I went to the tilted dresser, hoping to find something, maybe a nail file, to scrape the paint to loosen the latch. I pulled the one and only drawer but had to rock it back and forth to open it. It only held dust and some ancient looking black and white pictures. One showed a man in overalls holding a pipe and a woman in a plaid dress standing by a huge tractor. I squinted my eyes and noticed the house in the background was the one we were in.

Chris stood on the other side of the room, digging through piles of papers. He must have found nothing because he headed into the closet. I followed. We closed the door and pulled a string to turn on an overhead light. A few long sleeve plaid shirts hung inside. They seemed innocent enough until we spotted the sewn-on arm bands.

GB. Go Back.

"Chris. He's one of them." I pointed to the band on one shirt.

"Shit," he blurted, then grabbed one of the wire hangers, tossed the shirt to the floor, and reached to open the closet door. He pointed to the metal hanger with wide eyes, then to the closet door. I realized we were going to use it to open the window.

I pulled the cord to turn off the light. We stepped out of the closet, and our plan went to shit.

Damon stood in the room with his hands on his hips and what looked like an automatic rifle slung across his chest by a black strap.

"Well, well, well. What do we have here? You two been doing seven minutes in heaven or what?" He let out the loudest and downright scariest laugh I'd ever heard.

I honestly didn't know what to do, so I grabbed Chris's hand and looked up at him.

"Yep, you caught us," I said with wide eyes and a smile. "Best seven minutes of my life. And now, we'll just get out of your hair. Thanks for the place to rest."

Damon said nothing for what felt like ten minutes, then let out another, not-so-sinister chuckle.

"No worries," he said, then spat right into the brown carpet.

I couldn't muster the courage to contemplate what else hid in there.

"We don't need your help with tech, anyway. Oh and, uh, don't worry, we'll be dropping you off in a safe spot. One thing, though. We're gonna have to make sure you can't find us again, see?"

Hunter and another man entered the room, walked right past Damon and straight to us.

I squeezed Chris's hand, and he squeezed back. As he looked down, his hair covered his face, and he mumbled something. I couldn't quite make it out, but I thought he said, "I'm so sorry, Sarah."

Then Hunter struck him in the head with the butt of the rifle, and before I had time to react, I felt a thud on my head and the room went dark.

22

OLIVIA

SWEEPERS PATROLLED EVERY MILE of road between here and Moffat. Since leaving the Center only 45 minutes ago, Ed and I had been dodging them left and right. They drove in unmarked tall, white cargo vans with no back windows. We spotted one parked with some people we recognized standing outside. We needed to up change our looks.

"Let's stop in there," Ed said, pointing to a small, red bricked building with a rectangular overhead sign that said Value Drug pharmacy. As we approached the door, a dirty sign inside a sheet protector read, "no public bathrooms." The door let out a two-toned ring as we went inside. It smelled of lilac, faint music played overhead, but half of the fluorescent lights were on and many of the metal shelves were empty.

A thin, older white man with curly hair down to his earlobes and a yellow, wooden pencil his ear sat behind the counter to our left, looking down at a book of crosswords, could have been Sudoku. "Howdy y'all," he said then looked back down.

We returned the greeting and walked to the aisle labeled cosmetics. I picked up scissors and some hair bleach. Ed picked up some blue dye. We also got sunglasses. We'd punch out the frames later to make them look like glasses.

"Looks like that's it. Let's go." Ed said. We walked to the counter and the man sat up straight.

"Find everything? We're still waiting on a shipment."

"Yeah, we're good," I said and placed the items on the counter. I could see little bottles of five-hour energy drinks and little lighters that looked like pistols.

"That'll be $32.79," the clerk spat out.

Then he tilted his head to our right, and his mouth hung open. He raised his left index finger and shook it at us. "Hey, aren't you from that Center? Saw your picture on the TV just a couple a minutes ago." Every evening at 17:00 GB authorities would send pictures and details of fugitives to local news. The stations continued to run on an analog signal.

Run, Ed mouthed to me. He grabbed the items, and we bolted to the van. I yanked open the passenger side door and got in. Ed already sat in the driver's seat and punched it into reverse. The tires screeched as we pulled out into the road.

"Holy. Shit. Ed."

"Holy shit is right. They're on to us. Not surprised, but crazy hearing it," Ed said. "We need to find a place, and I think it's also time to ditch this van."

"Yeah, you're right. I know we removed the tracking devices in our bodies, but maybe there's one on the truck."

"Shit, why didn't we think about that?"

We drove into a neighborhood and spotted a one-story red brick home at the end of a *cul de sac* with overgrown grass and bushes that covered the windows. It had a long driveway with a garage to stash the van. We grabbed our packs and walked to the front door. The air felt fresh. Ed's curls blew every which way in the breeze.

"Stand back," Ed said. He kicked the wooden front door hard a few times, but it wouldn't budge.

"So, this is where you show me how manly you are?" I said with a chuckle.

"Oh, be quiet. Let's try a window around back. The bushes here are too thick out here to get by."

"I could've told you that."

Out back, puffy dandelions grew in patchy grass. A wooden privacy fence darkened by years of mildew and tannins kept us out of view from any neighbors. I spotted an already broken window next to the sliding glass kitchen doors. Ed grabbed a nearby branch to punch out the remaining shards, and we climbed inside a tiny bathroom. An overpowering smell of dust and something rotten penetrated our noses.

"I don't know if this'll work," Ed choked.

We walked through the house filled with lots of worn carpet but no furniture.

"This is so gross. It's stuck like a hundred years in the past," I said, trying to waft away the foul air with my hand.

"Yeah, and no one's cleaned in that long, either," Ed replied.

Only one bedroom had a mattress in it. It lay on the floor with a sheet thrown on top.

"Welp, it's better than nothing," I said with a shrug. I opened the window and went into the en suite bathroom. It smelled better than the one we had climbed into. I took the dye and scissors out of my pockets and put them on the closed toilet seat.

"Come here, I need you to cut my hair."

Ed came into the room. I saw him behind me in the mirror. His eyes looked darker, circles forming underneath. He was tired. Worried. We both were.

He took the scissors and pulled one lock away from my head. "How short?"

"Halfway."

Ed took the lock and snipped it in half. It fell to the floor. He continued, lock by lock, round my head until I had a bowl cut.

"Oh, this looks ridiculous. Cut it closer!"

Ed cut and cut and cut until I had two-inch nubs protruding from my scalp. I applied the bleach cream and tried not to wince from the smell and burn on my scalp.

I cut Ed's hair shorter, applied some bleach, and applied the blue coloring. Some of it stained my hands.

"I feel like a blueberry! I waved my hands mischievously in his face.

"Yeah, what do you think I feel like?"

"Yeah, okay. I get it. I think you look good," I said, and I wasn't lying. Ed had never looked this good. The blue brought out the green specks in his eyes.

My own eyes burned from the chemicals. I turned the water back on and washed the bleach from my hair, then scrubbed my hands, but the blue remained. Shrugging, I knew nothing lasted forever, especially hair dye.

I stared at my much shorter dreads in the bathroom mirror. It felt surreal. My hair hadn't been that short since grade school. Ed kicked them into the corner of the bathroom next to the pink-tiled tub and under the pedestal sink. I almost didn't recognize myself. No longer did I have the heavy locks to hide behind. My exposed face made me feel so vulnerable.

I went into the bedroom where Ed had unfurled his red sleeping bag onto the mattress. I heard a thump as he laid down.

"What I wouldn't give for the Internet right now," he said. "I'd make a post on MyTime, telling the world we're gonna defeat the GB and get all our tech back! HA!"

I came in and sat down beside him.

"Yeah, well, I'd give anything for a pillow right about now and some clean satin sheets!"

We looked at each other and laughed at the ridiculousness of it all. A gentle breeze came in through the open window and we sucked it in.

"Wonder what Allabaster's doing right now?" Ed asked.

"Probably shitting her pants. I mean, who's gonna melt the tech?" I snorted.

"Not us, Liv. Never again."

I pulled the crumpled map from my pocket and traced my finger along our route. "This setback is costing us, man. I wanted to get to the Garden tonight. If we don't find another vehicle, we'll have to walk longer than a day."

Ed sighed and blew a raspberry. "We'll find something."

We sat there in silence for a while. Later, we scoured the rest of the house for anything useful and found a flashlight in a closet, a disposable razor in a bathroom, and a couple of cans of generic brand chicken.

•　　•　　•

"Want me to sleep in my sleeping bag?" I asked right before we called it a night.

"No, let's use yours as a blanket. Plus, if anything happens, we'll be close enough to let each other know!"

"Okay." I unrolled my sleeping bag and threw it on top of Ed, hiding his face.

He moved around under it and said in a muffled voice, "Help, I'm trapped!"

I'd never shared a bed in my adult life. Anyone I'd ever hooked up with, I'd always slipped out. Never get too close. That's my motto, and this world has made it easy to stick to.

23

SARAH

IN MY RECURRING DREAM, I am a seven-year-old sitting in a magnolia tree, whistling to the birds and they replied in our own special language. I could have stayed up there forever, but I knew my mom would worry if I didn't get back inside the house. The branch bent beneath me, like a vine. The trunk was stable, but the surrounding branches stretched out like swings. I stood on them and grabbed the upper branches to balance as I bounced.

I climbed down to the next level, grabbing onto the upper branch. My feet found the bottom rung of vines. A song I heard in a movie pumped through my head, then came out of my mouth. I bounced to the beat.

My backyard was like a forest, an anomaly in our city neighborhood.

Vines covered the ground interspersed with poison ivy. The trees are small and in need of pruning. An uneven brick path wound through the yard.

I jumped off the vine and walked the path back to my back door. I heard classical music reverberating through the walls, a telltale sign of my father practicing the piano. The sound produced a calming sense of normalcy. I walked along the path parallel to the practice room window, the sounds of Chopin getting louder with each step. Then the music changed from beautiful to banging. I stopped to listen in when it sounded out of tune.

Can't be. Dad's a professional, been doing this his whole life.

I walked toward the window of the practice room; I felt the leaves and twigs crunching under my feet, but I couldn't hear them because of the awful sounds coming from inside. As I pressed my nose against the cold glass and peered in through a crack in the curtains, I saw my dad facing the piano. He swayed back and forth. I felt scared. What should I do? Why was Dad playing like this? Was he sick?

I tapped on the glass, and Dad turned his head towards me. He doesn't stop playing. I looked at him with tears in my eyes and raised my hands in a questioning gesture—like "what is wrong?"

He stopped playing and hurried to the window, mouthing something.

I cried, "WHAT?" and pointed to my ears.

As he came closer, his mouth formed an "O," and his muffled speech became clearer. As he reached the window, he pounded on it. He yelled, and I heard him loud and clear.

"GO BACK. GO BACK. GOOOO BAAAAACK."

He said it over and over. Tears flowed down my cheeks.

I stepped backwards. I turned and ran. Where? I didn't know. I ran to the driveway and toward the street and stopped. I'd never been around the block by myself.

I saw a parked car with its lights on and a man inside. It was the same man I saw in my front yard one year before.

No. No. NO! I screamed and cried. Go away. GO AWAY. GO AWAAAAAY.

•　　　•　　　•

My body jerked awake as my eyes peeled open. My breath felt heavy. Just a dream. Or was it?

I was on my right side on a cold concrete floor, gagged. I tried to speak, but my tongue felt glued to the cloth, and I could only hum in agony.

My ankles were bound, too. I saved my energy and tried not to fight too much. Instead, I turned my head, looking around for Chris. Breathing was challenging. My nostrils felt tight, and my head and knee hurt badly.

There were stacks of cardboard boxes of various sizes all around me. Some were open, some knocked over.

Where the hell am I? How did I end up here? Ending up in an unwanted change of scenery was becoming way too commonplace.

I slowed my breathing to listen. Then I heard a low grunting sound. Must be Chris, but I couldn't tell where it came from. I hummed as loud as I could, then waited.

The grunting grew louder. Sounded like it came from behind me. I got on all fours despite being tied up. My palms and knees on the ground, I inched along to where the noise came from.

Behind the boxes, I spotted Chris, tied like I was with his back to me. I slinked around to the front of his body. When our eyes met, I noticed his were wet and hollow.

After several tugs here and there, we freed our hands and mouths. We propped ourselves up and gasped. I crashed into his chest and exhaled.

"I thought I'd lost you," I breathed out, my head still resting on him.

"Me too," he said.

I looked up, and he put his hand under my chin and mumbled, "How miserable would that have been?"

He leaned in and our dry lips touched. We didn't know if we'd live or die, but that didn't matter because we had each other. I pressed into him. Our mouths opened, and I tasted him. I'd longed for this moment since I met him, but now it took on something much more than pure passion. Our sheer will to survive and hold on to whatever we could drove us.

I broke away and held him. Our tied feet hindered us, but we were together. I couldn't hold back the tears. I felt Chris stroking my tangled mess of hair.

We had to get out of here.

24

SARAH

W E UNRAVELED THE TIES on our feet and pulled ourselves back upright. We figured we must be inside a storage facility because row upon row of boxes and metal shelves filled the room.

Navigating the rows felt like a never-ending maze. I spied a box on its side with a bunch of pamphlets inside spilled on the floor. I looked closer, and saw the GB logo. In my pocket I felt the paper map but waited to take it out until we figured out where we were.

Chris and I stumbled along in the semi-darkness for some time, walking through each row. Finally, we found a metal door with a push handle. Before we pushed it open, we looked at each other. Chris put his index finger over his lips to signal my silence.

He put his right hand on the handle and pushed. He leaned against it, and, to our surprise, it opened!

Blinding sunlight pierced our retinas. We shielded our eyes with our forearms. Squinting, we stepped outside onto a sidewalk. The door slammed shut behind us. As our eyes adjusted, we found ourselves on a street corner with cars parked to our left and right, but we saw no one.

Chris grabbed my hand, and we stumbled down the sidewalk to our left.

Abandoned storefronts that looked like they belonged in a quaint old town lined the sidewalks with a red brick road in between. Chris and I were the only window shoppers. I almost wished we saw someone, anyone. I peered into a shop called "Mama's Treasures." It had a huge a bay window and lace curtains, but the smeared glass made it difficult to see inside. Straining my eyes, I saw mannequins inside and tiered displays with crystal vases jewelry cases along the walls.

Our feet shuffled on, hands holding on to one another for dear life. Still, we saw no one on either side of the street or inside and of the shops.

After about five minutes, we heard the roar of a car engine behind us. I spotted an alley to our left and pulled Chris in that direction. We ran past dumpsters and fire escapes, but at the end of the alley we spotted a chain-link fence that looked to be about six feet tall.

"We have to go up," Chris said and pulled me towards one of the fire escapes. Unfortunately, the fixed ladder hung too high for me to reach.

Chris crouched on all fours, and I stepped on his back. I had to stretch a bit to grab the bottom rungs of the fire escape. I pulled up as hard as I could and swung my legs like I would dangle on monkey bars. The car roared, but it sounded like it went past the alley. Chris jumped a few times and pulled himself up as well. We both climbed the steps up as quickly as we could.

About eight floors up, I heard tires screech. Chris tried to open the closest window with no luck. He kicked it and it cracked. I looked down and saw the car stopped at the fence. The driver must not have seen us.

Chris kicked again, and the window gave. The glass shattered at our feet and half inside. We went in without stopping.

Inside the dark, dusty apartment we tiptoed away from the broken glass that littered the linoleum floor.

"Now what?" I asked.

Chris shushed me and motioned for me to go to the wall. He looked back and closed the curtains on the window.

I blew out the breath I'd been holding for what felt like hours. We stood in an open kitchen/living room area. I ran to the cabinets to forage. I found a box of plain wheat crisps, opened it up, and shoved a handful in my mouth.

"Slow down. Help me find a bag, okay?" Chris requested.

I set the box down and looked under the sink. Nothing but several dead roaches and an empty bottle of cleaning solution.

"Look at this," Chris exclaimed. He held several cans of tuna. Guess that would go well with the crackers.

I surveyed the nearly empty pantry. On the ground were several empty re-usable grocery bags. We tossed the tuna and the box of crackers in one. To our surprise, we also found about eight water bottles on one of the upper shelves.

When the GB movement started, they banned water bottles and plastic bags. If government workers spotted you with any, you'd get a ticket.

We headed to the front door.

"Wait." I stopped to look at Chris. "Where are we going? I mean, no one is here, obviously. We could stay here. Lock up. We could put something in front of the window."

"Okay. Yeah," he said. He set the bags down and went to another room. I tiptoed to the window and pulled the curtain back about a quarter of an inch. I looked all around, but didn't see the car anywhere. Hopefully, they had given up and went back from where they came from. I turned back to look at the side of a flat-screen TV that sat on a black stand with glass cabinets. Chris came around the corner pushing a wooden dresser. We shoved it against the window in front of the curtains.

"Let's push the couch against the door," he said.

When that was done, we sat down on the floor against the back wall of the room. Chris opened a water bottle and handed it to me. I took a swig and Chris did the same. We sat for a while, not talking.

I got up to find a bathroom. I found it around the corner, right next to the bedroom.

"I'm going to take a shower," I told Chris.

"Sounds so good, but I don't think the water is on. Use one of the water bottles we found, but just a little."

"Shit, you're right."

I compromised with a "sponge" bath using my shirt as a makeshift washrag and a crusty, used bar of dial.

As I dabbed water on it and scrubbed only my smelliest areas, I could tell I had lost at least twenty pounds, something I always wanted to do "back in the day," but never like this. I heard a soft knock at the door.

"Hey, I found some clothes in the closet. They smell musty, but do you want some?"

I grinned. "Yes, please!"

He handed me an oversized "I Love NY" t-shirt. I didn't try on the pants he gave me. They looked way too small.

I poked my head out of the bathroom and went into the bedroom. I looked inside a mostly empty dresser and found some boy-short underwear. They were snug and caused my belly to spill over the elastic. I also found some baggy gray sweatpants and put them on.

Back in the living room, Chris sat on the couch wearing a faded, black Nirvana shirt, the kind the cool kids that never even heard of the band used to wear, and cut-off jean shorts.

We sat on the couch and stared at the TV. I wondered if it even still worked. We couldn't find out without power.

"What was your favorite show, you know, back then?" Chris asked.

"I don't know. I rarely watched stuff. I usually caught up on streaming six months afterwards. I liked that one zombie show, though."

Chris chuckled. "I never could get into that." Chris groaned and stretched both arms to the ceiling. "God, I'm tired," he said. He looked at me, his eyes hollow, yet so deep blue. I remembered looking into them what seemed like ten years ago after that show at the Elephant Ear.

"Yeah, me too."

Chris stood and reached out his hand. I latched on and he guided me to the bedroom. Suddenly, I felt exhausted at the look of the bed with the plain, baby blue fitted sheet; like it could have belonged in a 5-star hotel.

"Hold on," Chris said. He went to the closet and came back holding a huge, colorful quilt.

"Where did you find that?"

"It was up on the top shelf," he said, pointing to the closet.

I chuckled, knowing only someone his height could see something like that.

He spread it out on the mattress and we both lay down on our backs to stare at the ceiling.

"I'm so glad you're here," I whispered.

He grabbed my hand.

"Me too."

My body felt so heavy, I fought to keep my eyes open. Before I knew it, the morning light shone on my eyelids to wake me.

25

OLIVIA

E D AND I TRAVELED FOR HOURS on foot through mostly empty towns. Any people we spotted looked dazed; businesses shuttered. The tech shortage, then the GB seizure, crashed the stock market. With limited-to-no Internet and cell phones, most companies faltered. The economy lay in ruins and Go Back pulled the puppet strings.

We stumbled onto some bikes.

"Weeee!" Ed cheered, going down a hill at breakneck speed.

"Slow down!" I yelled, trailing behind him. I'd never been steady on a bike.

Ed's brakes squealed as his bike rounded a corner.

"Shit. Shit. Shit!!!" Ed called out, then turned out of sight. I saw him crash.

I pedaled quicker, but not before checking my own brakes, and they seemed fine. I found him around the corner laying on a lawn on his right side, his pack about ten feet away from him. As I slowed, I spotted a maroon sedan in the distance heading towards us. We hadn't seen any cars for quite a while. Maybe two towns back.

"Ed, come on. Come on. Get up and out of the street," I said. I put my hands under his arms and tried to lift him up. He put his hands on the grass, and I noticed a large, bloodied scrape on his left one. He grabbed his head with his right hand.

"I'm sorry. I'm sorry. Ouch. I'm so sorry," he said.

"Okay, just get up. We'll talk about it later," I said. The sedan got closer and slowed.

As Ed and I got onto the sidewalk, the car paused in front of us. An older, bald black man rolled down the window.

"You two all right?"

"Yeah, just took a tumble," Ed said. He grabbed his head.

"Do you need a doctor, son?" the man asked.

"Oh, no, sir," He put his bloodied hand behind his back. "Really, I'll be fine."

"Where you two from, anyway? You don't look like you're from around here. Where you live, gal?" He stared at me viciously. Like he'd never seen a black girl and a white guy traveling together.

"Um … we're just passing through, really," I said. "Thanks for asking. We'll be on our way now."

"I reckon you should come with me," the man said. He placed his left arm out of the window and curled his index finger towards the vehicle.

"No, really, I'm fine. I'll just—"

"You'll just get in this here car, boy," the man said. His right hand yanked a gun out the window and aimed it at Ed. I gasped and stood in front of Ed.

"No, wait. We mean no harm. Really! Please, sir. We're going. You'll never see us again," I begged.

"Do as I say, and nobody gets hurt. Ya see, I know the authorities are on the lookout for the two of ya'll. Seen your picture in the feeds."

Shit. Shit. Shit. How do we get out of this?

I felt Ed's hand on the small of my back.

"It's okay. Okay. We'll come with you. Just let me pick up our stuff." Ed and I turned and leaned over to pick up his pack.

"Run," he whispered under his breath.

"Hurry up, you two. Now!" the man demanded.

We both turned away from him, and I darted behind a house. I turned around, thinking Ed was right behind me only to see the car speeding off and Ed gone; his pack still on the grass.

I was alone.
Ed was gone.
Now what the hell am I going to do?
I collapsed to my knees and cried like a wounded animal.

PART THREE

THE GARDEN

26

SARAH

"**M**ORNING SUNSHINE," CHRIS SAID in a near whisper. I rolled over and saw him looking at me.

"Hi."

For a moment, everything felt so normal, like we were a normal couple, waking up, about to plan breakfast. But that fantasy only lasted about thirty seconds. As I glanced up at the stained ceiling and empty dresser, I remembered our situation, and my body shuddered.

"Are you cold?" Chris asked, then stroked my shoulder. His touch gave me a tingling sensation up and down my body, starting where his hand met my skin.

"Um, no ... but," I looked into his eyes and couldn't figure out what to say. I sensed my face scrunching up. His eyes did not wander for even a moment. His gentle hand gave my shoulder a squeeze and pulled me closer into his chest. Chris was a tall man, his shoulders broad, but his body was lean. I sank deeper into his chest and sighed.

"I wish we didn't have to go back out. I know we have to, but I don't know where to go or what to do or ... or ..." I stammered.

"Yeah, I know," Chris said as he stroked my hair. "We've got to find others. We need to team up somehow. I don't know how, but we do. I don't know who to trust anymore. All I know is that I trust you, Sarah."

Just as quickly as my name came out of his mouth, our chests pressed together and before I knew it, he pulled my shirt up and off. Our mouths pressed together like before, but this time our breath was heavy, and I could not control my longing.

Afterwards, we laid tangled together, stroking each other's hair. At one point, my fingers got caught, and we chuckled.

Like a normal couple. I took in a deep breath. No ceiling tiles to count. For the first time in I don't know how long I felt liberated physically and mentally. I wanted to be in this moment forever, but I knew it was impossible. I closed my eyes and then I heard banging.

We both shot up in the bed.

"Oh my God," I whispered.

"Put on your clothes." I could tell by his tone it was not up for discussion. We put our clothes on quickly. I had my shirt on inside out and he didn't even button his.

We stopped at the bedroom door.

He looked at me, put his left hand up in a stop motion, then put his right index finger to his mouth to silence me. He handed me the bag full of food.

No! What are you doing? I mouthed. I shook my head in disapproval, but he waved me off and went out the bedroom door into the living room. I stepped into the hall between the bathroom and bedroom and saw him making his way to the front door. He went out and closed the door behind him.

I went to the door and set the bag down. I listened. Nothing.

My heart thumped. My breath felt heavy with fear. What if I lost Chris? I'd be alone. I had no way of finding anyone else, like my sister Liz or Mom. Or anyone. I had memorized no one's phone number and had no internet to look them up. No GPS, no Google Maps. How dependent we'd all become on these things. Maybe GB had a point. I shook off the thought.

I stood there for a moment, listening to my breath. Chris was somewhere out there. What, or who, was beyond the door? The not-knowing made me crazy.

I looked at our pathetic bags of rations. I was hungry. I grabbed the remains of the water bottle and took a swig, chased it down with two crackers. I knew I needed to eat more, so I peeled back the tuna can's lid. It smelled revolting. I stuck my fingers inside the can. I wished I had mayo or something, anything to make it tasty. But, of course, I didn't. We found no condiments in the refrigerator or pantry.

I finished the can and licked my fingers clean. Eating took my mind off the thought of possibly losing Chris.

My mind wandered to last night. Chris and I hardly knew each other. I'd lost all sense of time and space since being locked up in that place. I knew I needed to help Olivia out, but I couldn't even think about that right now. All I could think of was finding Chris.

My personality found doom and gloom wherever I went, a depressive state I'd learned to live with or against. Pick your poison. I was so attracted to Chris. He took care of me and didn't yell, unlike my absentee father. Chris paid attention to me. I didn't know what else I could want.

Before I had time to think any more, I heard a sound, and the doorknob rattled. I stepped back and Chris slipped inside. I instinctively grasped onto him for dear life. He hugged me back, then pushed me away.

"I found nothing. I couldn't hear anything anymore. Did you hear anything else?" he asked.

"No, I didn't. So, no one was out there? Where did that banging come from?"

"I don't know. Maybe we should camp here and come up with a plan."

He locked the door and sat by the bag of supplies. He pulled out the water and another tuna can. I chuckled.

"What?"

"Nothing. It's just, I ate the same thing for breakfast," I said with a smile.

Chris gave me a side smile and dug in. I sat near him, saying nothing.

"I think we should try to search the other apartments. You know, get more rations, or even find others," Chris said with a mouth full of tuna.

I looked at him with wide eyes. "What if the people we find are dangerous?"

"There must be more people around here. We can't be the only ones that got away or let go. There must be others like us," he replied, wiping his mouth with the back of his hand.

He said those words like we were a part of a special society or something. I saw us as two normal people trying to escape this bizarre situation.

"Yeah, probably. But it sounds too risky to go inside apartments like that. I mean, do we knock or just go in unannounced?" I asked.

"I don't know, but need to get out of here and find others."

"Okay, Chris. I want ..." my voice faded. I felt like I was going to lose it.

"You want what?" He looked at me with those eyes and I almost forgot what to say.

"I just want to be with you. As long as that happens, it's fine." There, I said it. Now he'd push me away or agree.

Chris took a few steps towards me and placed his hands on my shoulders. "Yes. We stick together, Sarah. No matter what."

He leaned in to kiss me. His lips felt softer than I remembered. His breath reeked of tuna, but I didn't care. I sucked in his sweetness and never wanted to stop. I aspired to be back in that bed intertwined, feeling like a normal couple, not one that lived in a parallel universe.

"Wait," I said in a hushed voice. "What if we're separated? We've never talked about how we'd find each other. We don't have phones." I felt the map inside my pocket. "Let's check the map."

I pulled it out and Chris studied the paper further. "Look, Sarah! Look! I think this is where we are," Chris says as he pointed to an intersection. "I remember passing Swift Street. It was right next to that store with the mannequins."

He was right. I remembered that, too.

"So, we're here?" I pointed to the intersection and to a building that looked like the one we climbed into.

"I think so," Chris said.

"How the hell did we end up right where she said we should be? How ...?"

"I have to think about this," Chris said. "We gotta go. It looks like the map is telling us to go east from here, to a place called The Garden in a town called Moffat."

"Okay, well, we'll just head that way. There's something going on here. We gotta figure it out. Let's go". We copied the map twice onto scrap paper, studied it and took one each and put the original in our pack. We marked meet up points, then put them away.

I leaned down to grab our ration bag, but he took it from me. "I got it," he said.

"Okay ... let's go."

Chris unlocked and opened the door. I wondered what time it was. We stepped into the carpeted, stale-smelling hall.

Door after door stood in front of us. Which one would we try first?

27

SARAH

WE TIPTOED ALONG THE DIM, CARPETED HALL. Chris walked in front of me. Right before we reached the end of the hall and the stairway down, I heard a thumping. At first it sounded like someone pounding the wall, but as we got closer, it sounded more like a television and some heavy bass, either music or a loud movie. Chris put his hand up.

I froze, but he kept walking right up to the door where the sound came from and put his ear up to it. I wanted to run, grab him, and pull him to the stairwell, but I was also curious myself. What was behind that door?

I took a few steps forward and heard voices from what sounded like a television. Sounded violent. I heard a lot of screaming and banging.

Chris ushered me next to him. I stood next to him and pressed my ear to the wooden door. I heard people laughing and talking. Sounded like at least ten of them.

"What do we do?" Chris asked.

I turned the knob and gave a slight push. The door cracked ajar and through the opening, I saw them; at least eight. Four on a couch and four standing. They all smiled and talked and laughed. Tons of papers sat all over the rectangular glass coffee table.

I gave Chris a definitive head tilt toward the room.

The laughing stopped, and everyone stood up to face us. One man stepped forward and yelled at us to close the door. We stepped inside, closing the door, while I stood behind Chris.

"Hi, it's been so long since we've seen people. I can't believe it," Chris muttered.

"Yeah. The last person we saw ended up sliced in the face. I mean, can you believe that?" I said and chuckled.

The man in front glared at us. He had broad shoulders and looked of Hispanic descent. He had straight shaggy hair in the shape of a bowl cut long enough to cover his ears. He wore jeans and a black and red striped t-shirt. "Anyone else in your crew?" he asked.

"No, it's just us," Chris said. "Look, we're passing through here and heard some noise. We're lookin' to meet up with some people. We need help,"

The man paused, then smiled and let out a loud whistle.

A door opened to a bedroom opened and a woman stepped out. She was short and stocky, older, maybe 70 or 75, and hunched over. Her wavy short gray hair looked like it hadn't been brushed in some time. She wore a white, flowing shirt with lace on the sleeves, and blue nylon trousers.

"Hello, you two," she said. "What brings you here?

Gee, old lady I don't know. We managed to escape an institution that is detoxing the population of all technology, we were chased down, slept in a cave, hitchhiked to the farm from hell, were knocked unconscious and left in a storage facility and managed to stumble into this apartment complex, but not before nearly being run over. Does that about sum it up?

That's what I wanted to say, but instead something much more civilized came out.

"Ma'am, uh you see, we're kind of on the run. We don't know where we are, and we're looking for this place and we're not even sure why, except for someone at the Center told me to."

Her dark eyes widened. "The Center? How you get out?" the old woman asked in choppy English.

Chris jumped in. "It's because of this map. Some doctor gave it to Sarah and told her to find the place on it." He motioned to me, and I pulled it out.

"Bring to me," the woman said.

I'm not sure why, but we both decided to trust this stranger. I just hoped it worked out better than the last time.

The man who questioned us when we came in took some glasses off an end table and handed them to her. The woman put them on, then took the map from my hand and studied it, turning it around and over.

"El Jardin!" she exclaimed. A hush fell over the room, then muffled talking.

"The Garden? Yeah, that's what the map says." Chris said to her.

"You know this place?" The old woman took a step back, with the map still in hand. The others took a step forward in what seemed a protective move.

"No. Not really!" Chris tried to assure her.

"Oh, I hoped maybe ..." the woman looked down and the map fell to the floor. I ran over and grabbed it.

The woman sobbed. The man put his arms around her. The others stood with their heads down, sullen.

"We tried to get in there three months ago. They wouldn't let us in. Said we were *them*. That we were 'backers,' but we ain't. Now we're stuck in here, trying to make the best of it. There are about 40 of us in this building. We only go out during nighttime. We don't wanna get caught, by *them*."

"We can help you," I blurted out.

"Yeah. We can," Chris said, following my lead. "We can get you into the Garden. I mean, we have this map. They will let us in."

The old woman looked up revealing her wet cheeks. Her almond-shaped eyes sagged with the weight of her wrinkled skin. Something about her gave me comfort. She was like the grandma I never had.

"Come child." And I did. She held me. "Thank you, child. Thank you."

"For what?" I asked into her shoulder.

"For giving us hope. It's all we have." She released her grip and walked to the bedroom doorway. "Devon, give them soup. Go now."

She then walked back into the room she came from.

Shortly after that everyone in the room started excusing themselves for home, saying they need to get ready to gather supplies for the next day.

After the last person left, Devon headed to the kitchen.

"Make yourselves at home guys."

We sat on the couch and heard clanking. We placed our bags of rations between us.

"Be cool," Chris whispered. "He doesn't have to know everything."

Devon stepped back in the room with two bowls in hand. "Don't get too excited. It's cream of mushroom. Only thing we have left right now."

"No worries. Thank you so much," I said and immediately started chowing down.

Devon sat across from us in a beige recliner.

"So, you two were in a Center, right? Haven't met anyone who's come out of there. We've heard rumors about what's going on, though. The Backers have been hiring people to work there, not really by choice. It's more like a draft. You know, like, with the Army?"

"Yeah, I got the sense that was the case," I said.

"How'd you end up there?"

He doesn't have to know everything ...

"I got caught up in it all. I got caught in a raid, that's all. I didn't have any tech to give them, so they arrested me," I said.

"Well, we'd better be heading back," Chris said. "Thank you so much for the soup."

"Back where," Devon asked with a puzzled look.

"Back to our place. We were thinking of leaving, but now we've met you, we should team up, figure things out, ya know?" Chris said casually.

I couldn't believe he said this. My nerves told me to get out of here.

"So, it sounded like a TV or something when we came in. How did you manage that?" I asked.

"You can get Satellite TV's and generators on the Dark Net."

"You mean there's still Internet?"

"Spotty, but yeah. It's tricky though, man. You encrypt it and stuff. My Tio knows how to do it."

I nodded slowly and scratched the back of my neck. I felt Chris give me a nudge, but I kept going. "So, on our way here we saw some cars driving very slowly. We thought they might be following us, so that's how we ended up here," I said.

"Yeah. We didn't know that. Thanks for that info," Chris added. "So, thanks for the food and the talk. We'll be heading back now. See you tomorrow, bro?"

"Yeah, um, sure," Devon said and stood extending his hand.

We turned to leave. I felt so paranoid, like Devon would literally stab us in the back. But he didn't and we walked out the door like we just met our new best friend.

Back in the hall, I asked, "Now what?"

"Follow me." We walked towards the place we slept before, but then passed it. Chris went to a stairwell and we walked up.

I was too tired to ask any questions.

We walked up about five flights before Chris went back into a hallway that led to more residential doors. Chris cupped his hand behind his ear and pressed it to the door.

"Listen."

I didn't hear anything except our feet making the floor creek. We opened it and walked down the hall of the apartment. Then Chris stopped and turned to one of the doors. He put his ear to it, stepped back and turned the handle. He shushed me and it opened it slowly. Chris motioned for me to wait and went further inside. The uncertainty of it all was way too familiar.

I stood in the hall and waited.

28

SARAH

I STOOD ALONE, our pathetic rations at my feet. Then Chris appeared with a big smile in the doorway and said, "Come inside."

I walked in. A window gave off minimal light; enough for me to find my way around. I set the rations down on an overstuffed black leather couch and sat down. The unit had wood floors, as if someone had remodeled it. The kitchen looked newer too, with stainless steel appliances in the u-shaped kitchen. A couple of framed art pieces hung on the living room walls. One looked like an imitation Picasso; a mingling of black and gray-angled objects that somewhat resembled a house.

Chris stuck a wooden chair underneath the front door's handle to further secure it. He sat down on the floor cross-legged and exhaled.

"This should give us time to plan our next move. Devon and the rest could still find us here easy. We need to keep up like we're on their side. We need to pretend."

"Why?"

"Because it's all we have right now. I don't know what else to do, but until we can really trust them, we can't, okay?"

"Yeah, ok? I'm thirsty," I said.

Chris and I headed to the kitchen, and we peered into the refrigerator. It smelled stale because of no power, but it sat mostly empty. We found a gallon of water inside, an opened box of baking soda, and little else except for a stick of butter and some condiments, maraschino cherries, soy sauce, and capers.

"Give me that." I motioned to the water bottle. I opened it and took a swig. I handed it to Chris, and he took a little. He put it back inside and we headed to the living room again. Chris entered the hallway with three closed doors.

What if someone's home? What if ... someone's dead inside? Wait—wouldn't we smell it?

Chris opened the first door on the right. He flicked the switch, and nothing happened. He walked in and I followed.

"Stay back," he said, but I ignored him. I wouldn't be out of his sight again.

We tripped over what felt like pillows or stuffed animals. Chris opened the blinds to reveal a bit of outside light, and we saw a young boy's room filled with toy boxes, overflowing with things like stuffed animals, books and Legos. An unmade single bed had a train comforter draped halfway across it. Inside the closet, hangers dangled, some on the floor, like someone ripped the clothes off in a hurry.

I hugged Chris from behind, and he held my hands in his. What happened here?

"Wait," He whispered.

I wanted to get out of here. This room made me think of my sister, Liz. She was obsessed with trains as a kid and even aspired to be an engineer later in life. I wanted to know where she was, if she was okay. I left the room and opened the other closed door.

Chris stood right behind me, but I was getting sick of him always making the first move. I needed to toughen up.

I saw a queen-sized bed. Light from outside filtered in through open curtains, and I noticed a floral duvet on the bed and opened drawers on the wooden dresser.

"Let's sleep here tonight," I said in a breathy, seductive way.

Chris hesitated and looked around. "I need to check out the rest of the place first, okay? Wait here."

"No, I don't want to wait. I want to come with you."

"Wait here. You're tired. I need to make sure we're secure, okay? Plus, I can look in the kitchen for more food. I'm still hungry."

Why can't I say no to this man?

"Okay, I'll just be here," I said, too tired to argue, but knew I would have to take the lead at some point. Chris left.

I stared up at the ceiling, the outside light making shadow creatures. The bed was much more comfortable than our original one. Our first apartment was so minimal and gross. This one seemed like the people had a maid, or barely lived here at all.

Chris came back into the bedroom. "All clear. The other room is another bedroom, but looks like an office or something. We'll check it out more in the morning. Here, hold out your hand."

He handed me a chocolate chip cookie. My mouth fell open with amazement, then I inhaled its sweet scent.

"Where did you get this? It can't be good!"

"It was still in a sealed wrapper. Try it out. Mine was tasty!"

I took a small bite to savor every morsel. The chocolate melted in my mouth and the rest crumbled away into sweet nothingness.

"Um ... Yum. Thank you, Chris."

"Well, thank me later, okay. We still need to find toothbrushes. Our teeth are gonna be black soon!" Several minutes later, he went to the bathroom and came back with two toothbrushes, one an adult size, the other a child size with Snoopy on it.

"You take the big one."

"Or we can share."

"We may need to at some point."

We went to the bathroom and used baking soda from the fridge to scrub our teeth.

Back in the bedroom, I laid down next to him. We both looked up at the ceiling for a while. Then Chris jumped up and locked the bedroom door.

"Just in case, you know?" He climbed back in bed.

"Do you trust Devon?" I asked.

"Not yet. I've never been able to trust anyone, really. Not even my own family at times."

"Sorry about that."

"No. It's okay. I'm used to it. I used music to get out of my head, you know. Started a band. We got pretty good, but things fell apart. Things have a way of doing that."

"I'm sorry," was all I could think to say. "I would have liked to hear you play. What about your job? Trust anyone there?"

He chuckled. "Music was my way out of the trenches, too. I'd give anything for a phone or iPod or something. Hell, even a CD player!"

"They still make those?" I jabbed at him with my index finger.

Chris started humming, then singing a song I had not heard before.

We laid there awhile, and I took it all in. Where did this voice come from? It flowed like honey, with the right pitch and pinch of angst.

"What is that? It was amazing."

"Just an old Dylan song I gave a little twist to," he said modestly.

"Thank you so much. You should sing more often."

"Well, we should find a guitar. Once we get more settled, I'll get one and sing to you every day."

My heart grew three sizes in my chest and a warmth flowed over my body.

29

OLIVIA

I TRIED THE SATELLITE PHONE AGAIN and again and peddled as hard as I could in the direction the car sped off but couldn't contact or find Ed. Anywhere.

In the next town over, I found an empty house and unfurled the map on the bed. It highlighted several routes to Moffat. Green showed highways and quick routes by vehicle. Orange showed quick travels by foot. By all estimations, I could reach the Garden in nine hours or sooner if I got a car.

But I couldn't leave Ed.

I put my head in my hands. Think, Olivia. Think!

Out the window, I saw fuchsia clouds. Darkness would be here soon. My eyes felt heavy, but I needed food. I looked through my pack and took out a dehydrated apple package.

I stood up and wandered around the house to gather up anything I had left behind. In the bedroom, I spotted some costume jewelry scattered on top of a three-drawer wooden dresser. I opened the drawers and found some mismatched socks, a T-shirt and, ironically, some negligee. I chuckled and tossed it back into the drawer. Guess whoever left it here deemed it unnecessary for their trip. And where did everyone go, anyway? Back at the Center, we had heard stories that most people in the nearby towns came to work for us, but that was hard to confirm because we had limited personal conversations. Ed and I broke that mold. Somehow, we found a way to each other during a simple dinner conversation years ago.

Ed had sat across from me. He seemed pissed off; heavy breathing, furled brows.

"What are you lookin' at?" he'd asked me.

"Nothing. Cool your jets," I said and continued slurping my tomato soup.

"Food here's awful," Ed said.

"Yeah, sure is. Are you new here? Nice to meet you, I'm—"

"Aren't we not supposed to talk to each other? Also, I can see your name on your badge. You're one of them, eh, Sergeant Parker?"

"Well, yeah," I said, confused. "Of course, aren't you?"

Ed tilted his head and shook it back and forth. "No. Not by choice at least."

Silence."You know you shouldn't be telling me this. You could get in big trouble," I said.

Silence.

Ed slurped down his soup and stood up. "See you around. Sorry for talking so much. I'll stick to the rules, okay? Please, just don't report me, okay?"

I watched him walk away and wondered how the hell he got to the Center. Until then, GB had signed up everyone I'd met, or recruited them. That would soon change.

Ed and I continued to sit next to each other. Most times we wouldn't talk, but occasionally we would, and that led us to know we could trust each other. I learned Ed was part of some first tech roundups and someone gave him an ultimatum. He could work for GB and get paid, or they would release him into a society with a crumbling economy. With his IT experience, he'd likely be out of a job. Ed took the job, but not without hesitation.

Once I found out GB rounded him up and pushed him into work, my suspicions about the movement's intentions grew and grew. Soon, Ed and I were partners, working in the vat room and making plans. Plans to get out.

With Ed's tech expertise, we hacked into the GB inter web and learned about outside resistance movements. We communicated with the people at the Garden with encrypted emails.

We got closer and closer until we got together.

It happened right after my accident.

"Ed, please. Just go back to your room. You'll get caught here. We can't be hanging out like this. I'll be fine!" I said, my leg propped up on a chair.

"No, you won't, Liv," he said.

He took me aback because no one had ever called me that. No one except for my younger sister, Kiwani. Last I saw her was before I left for boot camp. We emailed and chatted on the phone often. Once I got to the Center, communication lagged. I'd been so busy planning the Garden, I hadn't had time to message her. I kept thinking I would and then the plan went to hell.

"I don't trust Doctor Rose. I mean, why do we only have one doctor here, anyway? Like 500 people living here and one doctor? How good could he be?"

"He's okay. But yeah, I agree. We need more doctors." I shifted my weight and my foot rolled. I winced in pain.

Ed came over and put his hand on my shoulders. And that was that. That was everything. He stood there for some time, rubbing them. Then I thanked him with a kiss. He ended up carrying me to bed and lying next to me all night. Early the next morning, he slipped out, but not before telling me he was falling in love with me.

I told him no. Don't say that. We can't do this. I told him again and again and again. I cared about Ed, but had only felt love for family, not really romantic love.

He never brought up the love thing again.

•   •   •

Yeah, I had to find Ed.

At first light, I gathered my pack, along with some added supplies from the house, and peddled. I pointed the sat phone to the sky, turned it on and dialed.

"Ed, can you hear me? Answer, please!" Nothing.

I realized I might never find Ed. Hopefully, he had escaped

and would find his way to me. I peddled northeast and hoped to find a car sooner rather than later.

But mainly, hoped to find Ed.

30

SARAH

I ROLLED OVER TO FIND an empty spot next to me, jumped out of bed, and found my shoes. Is it morning or overnight? I felt exhausted, so I assumed the latter.

Where did Chris go?

I stepped out of the bedroom and into the living room. I heard nothing except some birds chirping. Then I noticed the couch pushed away from the front door. I turned the knob and slipped into the main hallway. "Chris!" I whispered as loud as I could. I pulled the door closed behind me. The only place I could think of was that he would be back at Devon's place, but why?

I went downstairs and pushed open the exit door. Then, I saw Chris's back. I called out, then heard a mumble of someone else's voice. I closed the door and left it open a crack to hear the conversation.

"Devon. I told you, man, we can't really help you out," I heard Chris say.

"I don't really think you have an option here, buddy. I mean, what else are you gonna do? You told me you need people," Devon said.

"I know, but—"

"So. Come on, dude."

"I'll think about it. Look, I gotta get back before she wakes up," Chris said. I sensed the irritation in his voice.

"Okay, but I need an answer by daybreak. We're gonna work together or you gotta get packin'. No hard feelings, bro."

I closed the door gently and made my way back up the steps. I stumbled a few times hitting my shin and put my hand over my mouth to suppress a yelp.

I reached our floor completely out of breath and headed to the door at a brisk walk. Inside the apartment, I went to the bathroom. I heard the door shut and rustling feet.

"Sarah, is that you in there" he called out from behind the door.

"Yes," I said. I hated to lie. I opened the door and there he stood with messy tendrils spilling onto his face.

I took a step back and gasped, trying to act like I hadn't noticed he was gone. I rubbed my eyes. "Hey. Where'd you come from?"

"I had to go out," he said matter-of-factly.

Chris stared down at the floor.

I slid past him out of the bathroom. His face had a look of concern.

"Okay. Where did you go?" I played along at this point.

"Devon's apartment. Before we left the other day …" Chris paused. "Can we go back to bed?" he stretched out a hand. I took it and he led me back to the bedroom like a lost child. Before climbing in, he turned toward me. I pressed my face into his chest and breathed. "What's going on?" I asked.

He pulled away and sat up. "Devon wants us to join his team. He says he knows where the Garden is. He says it's the place everyone is trying to get to. He knows about our map. He thinks we can get him and his group in, but I don't know. What if they blow it for us? What if, there is no Garden? What if? Oh, what the fuck am I talking about, anyway? I don't know anything anymore." He spat this all out like word vomit.

Chris looked down with utter defeat crossing his face. His lips pursed and he exhaled. He put his hands on his knees and cupped his head in his hands.

"Chris, we can't give up. I mean, if we have to join Devon, or at least pretend to, we'll do it. I wish I had the answer. Can't we sleep on it?"

"He wants to know by sunrise," Chris said, not even looking at me.

I threw my arms around him.

We laid back on the bed, both staring at the ceiling. Shadows bent and fluttered. I wondered what the shapes represented. I wondered who else Devon asked to join his group.

"He gave us food, you know? Maybe we can trust him," I said.

"Yeah. I don't think we should trust him, but I think we need to figure out what he's up to. Maybe we can get him to lead us to the Garden then throw him off somehow."

"Yeah, maybe.,Chris. I don't know what I'd do without you,"

"Me either. I mean, who knew? We met at a concert, and now this. Crazy," he said and leaned in for a kiss. Our lips locked. He kissed me hard and held me like it would be our last goodbye. Despite wanting to give in, I pulled away.

"It'll be okay. We have each other, and we'll find others we can trust. If it's not Devon, then it'll be someone."

"Yeah, you're right."

"Let's get some sleep. We'll see Devon in the morning and tell him we're on his side," I said. "Oh, and hey."

"Yeah."

"Sing again, soon, ok?"

"Ok, baby."

Hearing that term of endearment threw me off. It's the first time he'd called me anything other than my given name. I went to sleep with that, and the day ahead of us on my mind.

31

SARAH

THE NEXT MORNING, we got up without saying much. Chris gathered our few belongings. He found a backpack in the closet and more nonperishables in the pantry, like some fig bars, two cans of minestrone soup, and a can of sardines. For breakfast, we split a can of tuna on crackers then stuffed the remaining food inside the backpack, along with a half-used roll of toilet paper, a toothbrush we found underneath the sink in the bathroom, and the baking soda. We also found three bars of Irish Clean soap and a towel. Chris gave me the backpack, and he carried a sack filled with water bottles and canned goods. We kept the maps inside plastic bags.

"Ready?" Chris asked, like we were going off to battle or something.

"Yeah."

Then we heard a bang on the door, along with Devon's voice. All of the breath left my body. Chris's body startled and bumped into me. I clenched the backpack straps and stood frozen.

"How did they find us?" I whispered.

"I had to tell him when we met up," Chris said with a hint of regret.

"What? So, why did we leave the last place?"

"I wanted to find more supplies. Plus, I knew if I told you I teamed up with Devon, you might not agree."

I felt hot and my chest tightened.

"You there, dude? Let's talk!" It sounded like Devon, all right. The southern drawl, mixed with a slight Spanish accent, gave him away.

"Yeah, okay! Hold on," Chris said. He opened the door and Devon stood on the other side, with his "posse" behind him.

"Oh wow. Didn't realize you were bringing everyone. Come on in. Make yourself at home. We don't have much, but ..."

Devon cut him off. "Enough with the bullshit, dude. This ain't no social call." This is not the way he had talked in front of Grandma. He shoved his way inside and the rest followed. It looked to be the same people we met before. I counted five men and three women. Several sat on the couch. The largest man closed the door, then stood in front to guard it. Chris and I stood next to our belongings.

"So, you thought much about what we talked about last night?" Devon asked.

Chris looked at me sideways, then faced Devon. "Yes, and we accept your offer. Thank you."

"Good choice, dude," Devon said, then smiled, flashing a few silver caps. He ran his hand through his hair and put it in the pocket of his jeans. Devon was taller than Chris, standing at least 6'5" and very intimidating. He wore his pants loose, like they were the only pair he could find, or maybe he'd lost weight since all this went down.

"So, what's next?" Chris asked.

"I'll be the one to decide that," Devon retorted.

So far, I had remained silent, but after that, I jumped in. "Yes, we're with you. So, whatever you decide."

"No one asked you, woman," Devon said with a snarl. Several in his posse chuckled. I recoiled at the comment. I wanted to rip his face off.

"Okay, we're with you, so now what? Chris said. "Leave her out of it, okay? She's with me, so that means she's on your side, too, okay?"

"Yeah, okay, bro." Devon looked around. "So, what you got for us? We're ready to go. You got that map? We wait till dark to avoid them sweepers, a'ight?"

"Yeah, um. About that map. We're not sure where it went. We had it, but it must have fallen out of our stuff or something. But don't worry, we memorized it. We know where to go."

Devon sucked his teeth and grumbled. I could tell his patience was wearing thin. I had to think of something. My mind churned.

"Really, we know where the Garden is. It's about eight miles northwest of here. We can get you there!" I chimed in.

"But we need that map to get in, woman!"

I looked over at Chris with concern, trying not to tick these people off. Chris patted my shoulder. He tried to divert the conversation. "Take it or leave it. Look, we'll get you in there. Tell me, what have you heard about this place? I know you tried to go there once."

Devon looked confused, like he didn't know what to say.

"Sandy, you tell 'em," Devon sighed, then sat on the edge of the couch. A woman stood up and paced.

I shifted my weight and studied her. She looked about my age. What was she doing with this group of hoodlums?

"We heard about the Garden shortly after the guards came to this area. They wanted our tech, but we wouldn't give it to them." She looked over at Devon as if seeking his approval to continue. He nodded. "So, we had to do something we didn't want to." She looked at her feet.

"Go on, woman! Tell 'em,'" Devon chimed in.

"We had to kill the first couple of guards. After that, the rest got the hint. They left us alone, you see. They got scared. I mean, someone forced them into that job, they didn't want it. We felt bad about killing them," her voice broke.

I felt bile rise in my throat and covered my mouth in horror. A group of killers stood in our midst.

"Wow," I said in almost a whisper. "That must have been very hard. What did you do with the bodies?"

"We, um ... well. We buried them out back; dug a big hole, then dropped them in." Her voice changed pitch, going higher like a child's. "So, anyway. There was this one guard. We were about to have to kill him, but right before we did, he came right out with it and told us about the place. He told us the Garden has everyone's tech. It's all being re-booted or re-furbished or something. Also, there are people there who are trying to overthrow the Backers. So, we got him to take us there. We tried to get in, but it didn't work!"

"But what?" Chris asked.

"But we couldn't. We just couldn't." Sandy turned away.

"Oh, damn woman, it ain't that bad. Finish the damn story."

"Let me take her to the bathroom to freshen up," I said.

"Ok but hurry you two and don't get any ideas."

I walked towards Sandy and put my hand on her back. "It's okay, come with me." I hoped to gain her trust, like a reluctant source.

We stepped inside and she went to the sink and turned on the water.

She leaned over, her thin frame much taller than mine, and she pushed her long, straight hair over her shoulder and splashed her face with water. She scooped off the excess water with her hand since we didn't have any towels.

"Sorry 'bout that," she said. "Devon makes me so friggin' nervous sometimes." She chuckled softly, as if to dull the awkward moment between us.

"It's okay. But tell me, are you okay? Devon seems pretty aggressive. Are you two together?"

"Well, yeah," she said with a smile. "Course we are. I mean, without Devon, I'd be locked up somewhere in one of those Centers. Couldn't have that. I mean Mama and Daddy and Sis already went. Don't know if they're out yet, but I hope so. I hope we can find them in this Garden palce. It's what I've been waiting for all this time."

Sandy stopped. Devon stood in the doorway.

"So, you done in here, ladies? Let's finish up our conversation, 'eh?" He smiled, I cringed, then we all walked back out to the living room. Chris looked relieved to see me. Devon went back to his spot on the edge of the couch.

"So, now that Sandy's powdered her nose, we can get on with this. Go on now, girl."

Girl. Woman. Decide, you jerk.

Sandy continued. "So, uh. Anyway, we got to that gated place with the guard. He tried to tell us he gave us what we wanted and begged us to let him go. But we needed him, ya know? So, we didn't let him go.

"We waited until we saw someone walking on the other side of the gate. It was a young girl. We asked her what they called the place, and she told us about the Garden. But then she ran away, like she got spooked or something'."

Devon cut her off.

"Sandy, that's about the stupidest story I have ever heard. Sit your dumbass down, woman."

She did what he said. I couldn't believe this. Chris and I looked at each other. I wanted them to leave. I didn't want to even pretend to be a part of this group. This was wrong. So wrong.

"Look man," Chris jumped in. "No matter what happened at the Garden before, doesn't matter. We'll get you there again and we'll tell them what's up. That someone at the Center gave us the map and so they have to let us in."

"What makes you think they'll believe us?" Devon said.

"Because I memorized the map's details. I can tell them. I can prove it," Chris said.

"I'm listening." Devon said as he crossed his arms and leaned back onto the couch. Most of his posse now stood spread out around the living room. One man with a sleeveless Megadeath shirt and black jeans with rips in each knee lit up a cigarette and blew the smoke right towards us. He looked at us through his long scraggly bleach blond hair with about two inches of black roots.

Chris held my hand and squeezed. I assumed he hoped they bought it.

Devon stood up and approached us.

I looked up at him and said, "There were symbols on the map. Special symbols. When we draw them for the people at the Garden, they'll believe us."

"You better be right, woman."

"I am. Look, we need some time to pack. Can you give us a moment?"

Devon let out a loud breath. "Hurry up. We ain't got all day. We'll be out here, so don't try nuthin'."

Chris and I went to the bedroom.

32

SARAH

CHRIS AND I TOOK OUR PACKS to the bedroom and closed the door.

"Not all the way!" we heard from the living room. I pushed it open about two inches.

I sat on the bed and rubbed my temples, hoping to release some tension.

"We have to get away from them, but how?" I asked.

"Let me think." Chris paced. "Hide the maps. They might rifle through our stuff, and if they find them, we're dead! You heard what they did to the guards." He went to the closet and came out with a metal hanger, pushed the two long sides together and then bent it in half. He untwisted the hook and formed a peak. "We'll use this if we have to."

I opened my mouth to speak, then closed it. My eyes blinked with concern.

"Right, so, okay. We'll fold up the maps and put them in our shoes. Then, shortly before we reach the Garden, I'll distract them by saying I need to go to the bathroom. When I do, I'll sneak away, then you'll come and find me." I pulled out the map and pointed to a street about five blocks away from the entrance.

"They won't let me do that alone. Or you!"

"I don't know what else to do, Chris. There are so many of them! Why did you have to go to them? Why?" I pinched my lips together to avoid screaming, crying, or both.

"I'm sorry. I am so sorry, baby. I thought I was doing the right thing. I had no idea. Devon seemed so … normal in his apartment." Chris had bloodshot eyes.

"You two okay in there?" Devon yelled from the living room.

"Yeah, we're coming!" I yelled back.

"This will work," I said, putting my head on his chest.

"It has to," Chris said as he stroked my hair.

"What happens if we get separated? What then?"

"The meet-up point. We meet halfway between here and there at the library, ok?"

I'd studied the location of the library over and over. Still, the plan worried me. What if one of us got injured or, worse yet, held prisoner?

"It's okay, baby. We got this. Don't worry," Chris said.

Oh, how I wished I could believe that. Just then I wondered if Olivia had made it out of the Center. Was she already at the Garden? I heard a bang on the door frame.

"Time to go, lovebirds. We're ready," Devon's voice said.

Chris grabbed everything and went to the living room, where we found everyone standing up and the front door open. Devon stood in the kitchen doorway.

"I simply cannot believe nobody came back here, ya know? They'd rather be out there detoxin'," he said. For a moment, I almost believed his concern, but then he spat at the refrigerator.

"Pussies," he said and headed to the door.

I didn't like this guy or trust him, but we had no other options at this point. We never should have gone into that apartment. Chris and I followed Devon out, not looking back at what we left behind.

We stepped into the hallway, our future unknown, but at least we were in it together. I squeezed Chris's hand as a sign of reassurance.

I felt the hallway carpet press under my feet with each step. With each step closer to Devon's apartment, my heart pounded harder. I saw the open door, and I heard the low mumble of voices inside.

Devon pushed the door open and stepped in. The rest of his posse gathered in the small dining area next to the kitchen, some sitting around the table, others standing.

"Come on here, Chris, and figure things out with the men," Devon said, and Chris walked over.

Sandy walked over to Grandma, who sat on the couch just inside the door. I gave Grandma a smile and sat down in a recliner.

"Hello again," I said. She gave me a puzzled look. I figured she couldn't hear well, so I repeated myself louder.

"I can hear you, child, but I don't know who you are," she replied.

"I'm Sarah. We met the other day. Me and my friend Chris came by and had some soup. Remember?" I asked.

"Oh child, my memory is rusty as a '67 Chevy." She let out a raspy chuckle. I wanted to laugh with her but felt scared. I wished I could forget everything. Her loss of memory was a blessing, at least in this new world we found ourselves in. I guessed she was in some stage of Alzheimer's. Who knew? Maybe not even her.

We said nothing for a while. Chris and Devon stood huddled with several of the other men. I should go over there. Instead, I stood back, next to Grandma.

After a long while, Chris broke away from the group and headed towards me.

"Okay, We'll leave when it gets dark. Devon wants to lead, so I told him the general way to get there and drew a rough map," he said in a hushed voice. I knew that Chris drew the main entrance and left off the part about the secret entrance.

Devon stood by the door and cleared his throat loudly. "Okay, folks. This is it. We're headed back to the Garden. We found it kinda by accident at first, but now we're lucky enough to have these kind folks to get us there again. Give Sarah and Chris a big round of applause."

Everyone clapped, but not for long.

"Now, now," Grandma said in a raised voice. "You people need to mind your manners! Keep it down. There could be people sleeping."

"I know, Mee Maw. I know," Devon said. There he was with that fake sweet voice again. "We'll be good, Mee Maw. Don't worry."

"You'd better be, Grandson. I'm counting on you. I need ... I need." She sat with a grimace which enhanced her wrinkled. "Damn. I forgot."

"It's ok, Mee Maw. We'll get you more tuna out there. We'll get your medicine, too," Devon said. His tone sounded like a young boy, almost like being around her brought him back to his childhood. I wish I could relate. I had always wanted a Grandma, someone close who could keep me safe and tell me stories.

Devin looked around the apartment. One of his posse, a large woman wearing overalls and a yellow long sleeve shirt sat slumped against the furthest wall from me. Her wavy brown hair hung in her face like a curtain, still I could tell she was about my age, no more than 30. She had an elbow propped on her knee. I looked down to break the spell. I wondered what she was like, before. Had she been just like me? A woman working for a living and trying to earn respect. How did she end up here? Did she come on her own free will?

Chris gave me a nudge. "You okay?" The look on his face showed concern.

"Yeah," I replied.

"Okay, it's about two hours until sundown. We get some rest, then move on out? Got it?"

We all grumbled in affirmation. Chris and I sat next to the door, and I laid my head on his shoulder.

•　　　•　　　•

A thump on my right side awakened me. Devon stood over us.

"Enough beauty sleep, you two. Time to bounce," he said.

I rubbed my eyes and looked at Chris. He stood and took my hands to help me up. His felt cold and clammy.

Devon headed out the door and his posse followed. Sandy remained on the couch next to Grandma.

"Aren't you coming," I asked them.

"No. Staying behind. Gotta mind the shop. Devon says he'll be back for us. He's gonna find a vehicle," Sandy said.

"Oh, well, I hope you two will be okay," I said.

"We'll be fine. Devon knows what's best, so ..." Sandy whispered and looked down.

"Go on now, child," Grandma said to me. "My grandson needs you. Go. Go now ... go!"

"Okay. We're going. Thank you!" I let out, then Chris and I turned and walked out the door. Chris closed it behind us. We grasped our hands together. Find the familiar. Hold on to it.

We walked down the hall, step by step to the exit sign in front of us. Devon turned around and yelled, "Come on now. Don't slack behind, losers. We got places to go!"

What had we gotten ourselves into?

33

SARAH

O N THE FIRST FLOOR of the apartment building, before stepping out into the world, Chris and I went over our silent signals in case we ran into trouble. A hand over the heart meant "wait," two fingers meant "run" and pulling on an ear meant "stop/or they are lying." Devon kicked open the exit door with a bang and we went outside onto the complex parking lot. Several cars sat parked; one Toyota Prius had written in dust "Go Back" circled with a line over it.

We crossed the street and walked past empty storefronts and alleyways. No one seemed to be around. We stayed together, not speaking. Then, out of the corner of my eye, I spotted movement on the other side of the street. I looked over and saw two people going through a trash can. A crow cawed in the distance.

"We see you!" Devon yelled over. The two people looked our way and put their hands up. They said nothing and ran away. Devon chuckled.

"Damn, them rats are so stupid," he said.

We kept walking.

Moments later, I heard the squeal of tires.

"Get down!" Devon yelled.

We all rushed to find somewhere to hide. Chris and I tried opening doors to the shops. The second one opened, and we rushed inside along with several others. We got down on the floor on our stomachs. Devon was nowhere in sight.

"Must be the Sweepers," Chris whispered.

We waited, our breath slowed by the pressure on our chests against the ground.

Outside, the squeals got closer, then stopped. I looked over at Chris. He shook his head to tell me to stay put.

A car door slammed shut. I heard two voices and some footsteps outside.

"Where are they? I know they're here. Where?"

I could only make out some of it, but it seemed these people were searching for us. I remembered the coat hanger in my backpack.

"Ok, let's go." I heard footsteps. "This way."

Chris looked over at me. I could tell he wanted to make a move, but I really didn't want him to.

"It's Sweepers," I whispered.

"I know, but we need to ..."

Just then, the door to our hideout opened. Devon stood with two men I could only assume were the men that we just heard outside.

"Listen up, people," Devon said. "Sit up."

We did. Chris and I sat right next to each other, our knees touching. We did not hold hands.

"So, these two guys are looking for volunteers to help with their mission. Their mission is to track anyone down who still has tech. It's important, so come on now, we need two people to speak up and go with these people. That way, no one will get hurt." I saw beads of sweat on Devon's forehead. I couldn't tell if it was from sweat or nerves. Either way, I did not like it.

I looked over at Chris and shook my head in disapproval. No way were we going with these strange guys.

Moments passed, but it felt like hours. No one volunteered.

Devon looked desperate. "Ok then, people. I'll choose." Devon pointed and did the eeny meeny miny moe game. He almost picked me twice, but finally, he chose two women who joined us today for the mission.

"Get up, you two, and hurry up," Devon snapped at the women.

They stood up and went to the men, who put their arms around them. The man on the right looked very interested. He leaned in and licked the woman's face. She looked repulsed, but did not pull away. Anything to survive.

The four of them stepped outside. We heard an engine roar and speed off. This left seven men, including Chris and Devon, and one woman: me. Two men wiped tears from their eyes.

"So, you bunch of pussies really gonna cry about this? What good's that gonna do, huh?"

"Naw, Devon," a man with a red plaid shirt chimed in. He looked like he'd been down on his luck for a while. Several of his teeth were missing, and he was thin and dirty. "It's just Jennie and Marissa don't know what end is up, ya know? They're never gonna survive out there!"

"Oh, hush up, Vern. They'll be okay. 'Sides they ain't our concern anymore. We got these two." Devon pointed to me and Chris. "Come on, we got work to do. Move on out," Devon said loudly.

Chris poked his head out the door and called the coast clear. We all headed back outside.

We had about ten miles to go to get to The Garden. Chris told me he'd signal me when I was to take my leave. Until then I'd keep my head down.

Boarded up businesses lined the abandoned downtown. Still, some looked like they could open at any time. Through one picture window I saw a shelf of old-fashioned porcelain dolls. They wore frilly, colorful dresses with puffed sleeves. Some had bonnets, a few wore stiff shoes with real laces. I'd loved dolls as a kid, but these creeped me out. They stood motionless with no one to play with, no one to brush their hair and change their clothes. Other shelves held books and nick knacks, glass cases held costume jewelry inside and on the counter in spinning stands.

We passed a park where I saw people sleeping on the benches and in makeshift tents. It was the first sign of humanity I'd seen outside the farmhouse and the apartment complex. One man sat on a curb with a sign that read:

"Will swap tech for food."

Chris saw me looking. "He doesn't have any tech. He's lying to get money. Those Sweepers would have gotten him by now."

34

SARAH

AFTER TWO HOURS OF WALKING, my feet hurt even worse because I wore a too tight pair of shoes I found in the apartment. Blisters formed on my heels.

Chris saw me wincing every other step. "Hang in there, okay?"

I looked over and gave a smile. I didn't want him to worry. Devon stopped.

"Hey y'all. I think we're almost there. What you say, Chris? Does this look like your map said?"

"Yeah." Chris put a hand up to shield his eyes from the sun. I leaned down and put my hands on my knees. Time to kick the plan into action.

"Hey guys," I said. "I need to go to the bathroom. I think I'm gonna go behind that building over there and do it quick."

"Better be quick, woman," Devon said. "We don't got time to waste. Those Sweepers will be back."

I looked at Chris before I left. He gave a subtle wink. Despite the glaring sun, and his sweat-stained cheeks, the one thing that stood out were his blue eyes, my grounding force in all this chaos.

As soon as I rounded the corner into the alley, I launched into a sprint. My feet hurt so bad. I slowed down just enough to pop my shoes off. Now that the blisters on my ankles stopped rubbing against my shoes, I could run. The plan was for Chris to come after me, then meet up with me at the other entrance to the Garden. The alleyway opened to another empty street and a fork in the road.

I had to pull out the map. Standing out in the open made me nervous, so I ducked between a parked car and a wall. I saw a street sign that read Magnolia Avenue, traced my finger to it on the map, then realized I needed to go to the right of the fork. I hoped I had the map turned correctly. As soon as I made my way in that direction, a voice called out.

"Hey! Hey you!"

I didn't recognize it.

"Please stop, please!" the voice continued.

It reminded me of Lily, right before the Center.

Every fiber of my being told me not to stop, but the journalist in me told me to do it. When would I ever listen to my intuition?

I turned around to see a teenage boy looking out a second-story window. "What?" I yelled back. My tone was a blend between extreme annoyance and about to kill someone.

"Come on. They're right behind you! Come inside!" The boy yelled.

That could only be one person—Devon. Chris wouldn't have come with the group.

I scurried towards the door to the building and pushed it open. I climbed the wooden stairs. At the top of the landing, my left foot gave out, and I twisted my ankle. It took every part of my being not to yell out. A door opened, and the boy poked his head out.

"Come on!"

I ran into the open door and fell to the floor, wincing in pain. I heard him latch all the locks that sounded like at least six. Then he put a chair against the door. He crawled down on the floor next to me.

"Who are you?" he asked. "What movement do you subscribe to?"

Movement?

"What the hell are you talking about? How 'bout trading names first," I said, my tone still mixed with pain and anger.

"I'm Noah," he said in a flat voice. Noah looked to be about fifteen. He had short, curly brown hair and braces. His skin was pale, and he wore jeans and a green t-shirt. "Who are you?"

"Sarah." Finally, the pain subsided enough to let go of my knee. "Where are your parents? What are you doing here?"

"My parents got caught up in all the Go Back shit," Noah said. "Them and my older brother left a while back. They told me they'd come get me soon, but it's been at least eight weeks. I've been keeping track on a calendar."

This kid was all alone in this apartment!

"So, what are you waiting for? Have you gone out to find them?"

"Naw. I sit here and draw, mostly. I'm fine. Sometimes I get food from the guards."

"Wait. You get food from them?"

"Yeah, I got this special card that lets me do it. My parents gave me one before they left. Says I'm one of them or something. Truth is, I never really bought into any of that crap." Noah sat cross-legged, looking at his hands. After a minute, he continued. "Where you headed?"

"Well ... I was ... I'm really going to ... to the ..." I couldn't seem to get it out.

"The Garden, right?"

"Maybe" I said, stunned.

"Well, you're going the wrong way. It's back the other way."

Damn, I really need to figure out how to read a map.

"So, you've heard of the place? Is it really what we're thinking? Is it a place of resistance?" I asked.

"Kind of. I mean, it's gated, and you need an invitation to get in. The Backers are somewhere else, you know, where my parents went. They'll be back for me soon. Meanwhile, I'm gonna draw," Noah looked down. Something ain't right with this kid.

"Yeah. I hear that. Do you have any tech here? Any phones or tablets?"

Noah's face went from placid to outraged in two seconds flat.

"We don't believe in tech. We must go back to how it was before ... before this so-called Technopoly."

Okay ... now this kid scared me.

"Yes. Right." I said. "You're right. Technology is bad. So glad this Go Back thing worked out." I knew I had to get out of here, but how? "Noah, you mind if I look out the window really quick? I want to see if anyone's out there."

"I guess."

I went over to the window and peered out. Nothing. No Chris. Not anybody.

"Look Noah, my boyfriend is waiting for me."

"Oh ok, I see. Well. I wouldn't want to stop you." The edges of his mouth curled in disgust.

"Thanks. I knew you'd understand. Thanks for helping me out back there."

I turned to take my leave.

Noah's voice filled the air.

"Sarah, remember, once you go back, there's no going forward, okay?"

I bit my lower lip and pushed the hair out of my face. I stared into Noah's vacant eyes.

"Ok, Noah. Thanks for everything. Hope your parents come home soon."

I opened the door, darted down the stairs, and pushed the outside door open. I ran the opposite way, hoping to find the secret entrance to the Garden, and of course, Chris, who was due to meet me there.

35

SARAH

I COULD SEE I WAS HEADED in the right direction because I saw Saint Street and followed it for about half a mile. I ran shoeless, sticking to alleys, hoping to avoid the posse. Every so often a rock dug into the bottom of my foot.

Soon, I saw a cathedral to my right with a chain-link fence surrounding it. I climbed it and trekked through the overgrown grass around the back. My senses told me I was close. I could feel it. I pulled out the map and realized I was there—at the back entrance to the Garden.

I couldn't see Chris. Maybe he got lost?

I sat down in the tall grass behind a bench, waited, worried, and listened to every sound. A gentle breeze rustled the leaves of a tall tree in the middle of the overgrown courtyard. Beyond that, I heard a helicopter *buzz* above and rolled myself into a ball and hid under the bench.

After about an hour, fear crept over me. Chris should have been here by now. I knew I took too long with Noah. The sun had set, the few clouds in front of it opaque with a blazing magenta behind them.

I spotted an annex behind the church and went to the door to knock, but before I could, a male voice called out from a high up window.

"We thought you'd never come."

I felt like Dorothy in the Wizard of Oz, except I didn't have Toto. "Um, can I come in? I have an invitation ... or a map. Please. I know Olivia," I stammered.

I heard a buzz and pushed the door. Inside, I found myself in a dark entryway lit by a dim overhead light. Another door in front of me, turned the handle and stepped inside to find a long hallway with beige walls. The voice spoke again.

"Come on in, Sarah. We've been waiting for you."

My body shuddered.

The hall opened into a larger communal room with armchairs and a fireplace. People filled every seat. A man wearing a long brown cloak stood in the middle. Underneath the open cloak he wore a royal blue shirt and pants. He had short black hair. He looked white but had a slight accent, maybe German.

"Welcome to the Garden," he said.

"Thanks," I said. My voice sounded a mile away from my body. "I'm actually waiting for someone else to meet me. His name is—"

"Chris? Right? Olivia told us you'd come," the man said. I could tell he was someone of importance because he was the only one standing and talking. He wore an armband with an embroidered *G*.

Maybe it meant G for Garden?

"Yes. Chris," I said trying to stabilize my voice so he wouldn't suspect any form of hesitation on my end.

"I'm Gavin. We're the resistance you've been looking for. We are here to destroy the Backers. We believe they are flawed, and we want our tech back. Do you agree?"

I hesitated and decided I had to agree. "Yeah. I mean, yes. Of course. I want things to go back to normal, whatever that means."

I felt awkward looking at all the faces peering back at me. Most looked about my age, black, white and brown. They all wore the armbands. I wanted to reach for Chris's hand. His strength. I knew I'd have to gather my own now.

"Okay, Sarah. Well, we're glad you're here," Gavin said. "We have a lot to teach you."

"How did you know my name, and Chris's? Did Olivia tell you?" And even more, how do you have electricity I wanted to ask, but first things first.

Gavin looked down. He held up his left hand, palm facing the crowd.

The crowd stood up and said in unison, "Welcome, Sarah. We are glad you're here." Then, just like that, they got up. Some hugged me. Some paused for a brief conversation. I stood there, feeling like some sort of misplaced prophet.

A middle-aged woman with long grey hair approached. "What is it like out there? Dangerous?" She picked up my hands in hers.

"Yeah, it is. In fact, I am pretty worried about Chris. He was supposed to meet me here," I said not wanting to give too many details.

"It will be okay, Sarah. He is on his way." She stepped aside and three others stood behind her.

Each one held my hands.

"Where are you from?" A balding man shorter than me asked.

Next a girl younger than I asked, "Did you get rid of all your tech? Like, I cannot believe this is happening!"

Behind her a person with mohawk and two nose piercings in the left nostril said, "Name's Lucky. He/They. You excited to help?" They were the first to introduce themselves.

I hadn't thought about that. Things had moved so fast, in a blur.

"Not sure if eager is the word. Grateful to be here. Thanks." I felt tired. I saw Gavin leave a group and come over to me.

"Come on," Gavin said and motioned me to a tall blond woman. "There's someone I want you to meet. Darby, come here."

A woman that looked like a runway model with flawless tan skin and legs a mile long stepped forward. Darby said, "Hi Sarah. I'm here to show you around. We'll get you settled, okay?"

"Um, ok. But I need to find Chris. He was supposed to meet me at the gate. He's with me," I pleaded with a shaky voice.

"It's okay. We already have scouts out looking for him. Olivia told us you'd be here," Darby said. Gavin walked away and talked to another group. "She gave you the map. She's the reason you're here," Darby said. "Come on, let's go."

She turned and walked with me close behind. We left the common area and headed past what looked like an office break room, then past a conference room with an enormous oval table. A large map of the U.S. with lots of pins and markings hung in the hallway. People came in and out of rooms, waving to Darby. I nodded and gave a half smile. I just wanted to know where we were going.

We ended up at the end of the hall. Darby took me into a cramped room and closed the door. It looked like a makeshift library. Shelves in the middle of the room held plenty of books. They were thick and hardbound.

"Have a seat," Darby said pointing to a small desk. "Can I get you something to eat or drink?"

This was all so surreal. I wanted to run out of the room, screaming for Chris because I had left him behind with that psycho Devon and company! I could only hope he was still alive or not too far away.

"Some water would be good." I didn't want to be ungrateful, but I also didn't want to be too needy.

Darby left, I assumed to that break room. I figured I had five minutes to look at the books. The spines had titles like *Technopoly, NeoLuddism* and *Rebels Against the Future* ...

Mixed among them, I found some encyclopedias, a box full of maps;, and a box, of all things, cell phones; the box next to it full of tablets, and another held chargers.

The door rattled, and I returned to the desk and put my head down. Ten seconds later Darby called out.

"You okay, Sarah? Did you fall asleep?"

I lifted my head up and gave a fake yawn. "Yeah, I am kinda sleepy. It's been a crazy day, for that matter, a crazy few months," I chuckled.

Darby set down a plastic cup of water.

I chugged it down, forgetting to savor it. "What is this room?"

"This is our library. It's taken us months to put it together. See that poster?" Darby pointed to a print of a man in pantaloons, with a pained expression. "That's Ned Ludd, and he started all this bullshit."

I gave Darby a puzzled look. This guy looked like he lived a long time ago.

"Ned Ludd is the king of the Luddites, a movement that started hundreds of years ago, but never went away. The Luddites were against the modern world. They felt threatened by advances like machines. This turned into the Neo-Luddite movement that rejected all technology with leaders like the bat-shit-crazy Unabomber Ted Kaczynski."

She said all this so matter of fact, like a school project presentation or something. I felt she had given this speech before.

"This underground movement began, subtle at first, no one had any idea. No one took them seriously. They didn't even have a name. They were mostly bored hackers, hell bent on erasing everything society had become." Darby looked at me as if to ask if I had questions.

"Go on."

"So anyway, one thing led to another. No one suspected anything. Until three years ago, the group had no name, and through that technology they were so hell bent on destroying, they found each other. virtual meetups began around the globe, they used the so-called Deep Web to hide out and populate, and posted vague signs around cities with their logo—propaganda. People got curious and checked them out. They won city council seats, then Congress."

"But how? I never heard of the Go Back movement until I ended up at the Center." I asked, hoping she didn't know I knew everything.

"Easy. They ran under the guise of one of the two main political parties. They used fear to manipulate the general population. People voted for them because the backers are fucking brilliant at propaganda. It's not unheard of for this shit to happen in history. Think Hitler, hell think … George Orwell, 1984. Fiction becomes reality. As long as people believe it so."

I looked around at all the books and wondered, for the first time, which side did I belong on? Did I need tech to survive? I desired happiness and a normal life, but running away scared me. I needed to find Chris and fast.

Darby gazed at me. "We know who you are. We know why they are after you. Honesty from now on, okay? Now, let's go find Chris." She turned and left the room.

She didn't give me a chance to reply, only time to sit by myself and wonder if I'd ever be able to trust anyone again.

•   •   •

Darby returned after several minutes with the short, balding man who spoke to me earlier. Each wore a burlap backpack. She handed me a pair of shoes.

"Put these on," Darby said.

We left through the front of the Garden. Darby pulled a key from her pocket and unlocked the chain. We heard a low roar of thunder. The air hung thick with humidity.

"Why do you lock it if it's so easy to get around back?" I asked.

Darby swung around causing her hair to flip. "We hide in plain sight. The Backers don't take us seriously because of our appearance, but they should. The lock keeps them off our back." She nodded over at the balding man who said nothing.

I didn't know what to say to that. I wanted to prod, but finding Chris took precedence. "Come on, let's find Chris. Where should we head?"

"First we have to get the car." Darby let us to a maroon Honda CRV parked half a block away and opened the door.

"Take us to where you ran off and we'll look for clues there."

•   •   •

We drove past the empty storefronts.

"What happened to everyone?"

"They're either at Centers, working for GB or holed up somewhere like us trying to make it. Some people went to work on farms. They became big business after the collapse."

I spotted Magnolia Avenue, so I knew we were close. We drove to where I took off my shoes and they still sat there! Darby parked and we all got out.

"There! We're here."

We all walked around looking for any sign of Chris. Through the alley, we made our way into a parking lot next to a warehouse. Right before I wanted to give up, I spotted some white specks on the ground about twenty feet ahead of us. As I walked closer, I realized they were tiny balls of paper. I picked one up and unwrapped it. It was part of one of our handwritten maps. I could tell because I saw one of the symbols on it.

"Over here!" I yelled to Darby and the guy. "I found a trail!"

Darby ran over to me from the other side of the parking lot. "What, little pieces of paper? That could be anything."

"No, they have the symbols from the Garden on them. Chris and I had them on our maps."

"Well, that's great, but looks like the trail ends here. We're at a dead end."

The balding man pointed to the parking lot. "Is that more trail," he said.

Darby scoffed. "Well, you finally have something to say, Bill. Perfect timing."

We all walked to the paper. The trail continued, though more spaced out, into another alley and to an entryway to an apartment or condo building.

"This has got to be it. He's here, I can feel it!" I said.

Darby shrugged. "Alright, let's go. Good thing I brought supplies to barter with." She stretched her left hand back to pat the burlap bag.

We got to the top and found a landing with two doors. We heard talking behind the left one, so Darby knocked.

A man's voice bellowed from inside.

"Who's out there, man? We mean no harm. It's me and a couple of ladies. We aren't trying to hurt anyone, ok?"

"Just looking for a friend. No harm intended. We're from the Garden," Darby replied. I couldn't believe she identified us like that.

"Look, go away and we'll leave by the morning," the voice from inside said. "You don't have to worry about us. It's cool. Tech is not our friend, okay.".

"We just want our friend. We have stuff to trade. Now, open up," Darby said in a stern voice.

The door flung open and there stood a man who looked like a cross between a heroin addict and a mad scientist. His frizzy dirty blond hair stood every which way around his face. I looked behind him and my mouth fell open. Chris stood there looking right back at me!

The man stood between us like a human blockade.

"Dylan, this is my girlfriend Sarah," Chris said in the background.

"Wait, you two know each other?" Dylan put both his hands in his hair and scratched. He looked at me, then back at Chris and two women I saw sitting on a couch.

"Let him go and we'll be on our way," I said.

"Dylan. It's cool, okay. Sarah's who I've been looking for. I told you," Chris said.

Dylan shut the door so that we could only see him in the opening. "That's it. I'm supposed to let him go. What do I get out of it?"

"We brought you some gasoline. You can get out of town. We also brought rations. I know you need these, Dylan," Darby said.

Bill opened the bag and showed Dylan a tool. It looked like pliers, but the handles were twice as long, and the head twice as short.

"Wire cutters and gas, huh? That's enough of a trade for him?" Dylan looked back at Chris and two women on the couch.

Just as he did, Bill hit Dylan over the head with the tool and yelled for me to run. Dylan's body slumped on the carpet. His head bled. Chris grabbed our bag and we all ran down the stairs.

When we reached the bottom, we made our way back to the CRV and sped off back to the Garden.

36

SARAH

"WE'RE GOING A DIFFERENT WAY in case we're being tailed." Darby said. The CRV zigzagged through the brick streets causing a severe bounce in the backseat where Chris and I sat.

During the drive, my mind raced with all the information Darby had told me back at the Garden. The Luddites, Neo Luddites and Technophobes. I mean, why would anyone want to do away with technology?

Before the shit hit the fan, and they threw me in the Center, I loved all the social media sites. Tech was booming, but the industry could not keep up with demand. Apple couldn't churn their iPhones out quick enough. Then people turned their social media off because someone had hacked them, or they were fearful of a Russian influence on Facebook. People covered up their laptop cameras for fear that people were spying on them. Jeez, which side am I on? I thought I knew, but ...

Chris shifted his weight. His hair was damp with sweat.

Darby continued driving for a while, then the car slowed down and parked but not at the Garden. "Shit," Darby exclaimed. "Get out."

I shifted my body to get a look up front and saw the gas gauge on empty. "We're empty," I said to Chris. He leaned down to get his bag and got off the floorboards.

Bill put his hands on his hips and shook his head. "That's what we get for the government wanting to 'drill, baby drill' and getting rid of EVs."

"We walk from here," Darby said. "But not all together. The Garden is ten blocks southwest of here. We can't all get rounded up together. That would be a nightmare." Darby ran her fingers through her long, blonde hair. It's like she didn't even have to be beautiful.

Darby and Bill took their leave. They darted around a brick building across the main road. Chris and I remained behind, holding hands. Holding on to whatever we had left. We snaked around the alleyways to avoid the main road.

"How did you find me?" he asked half a block into our journey.

"We found your trail. Once we did, we came to get you, and I'm so glad we did."

Chris kicked a rock and tightened his grip on my hand. "Me, too. That guy Dylan was a son-of-a-bitch."

As we walked, my mind went back to Devon.

"So, what happened to Devon?"

Chris hung his head and stopped walking. I could feel the tension exuding from his body.

"After you left, he and the group took me to … Did you see that warehouse and the parking lot on the way to find me. Of course you did. That's where I left the trail. Anyway." Chris rambled. I'd not seen him this rattled before. He had been so stoic up to this moment.

I pulled him next to a dumpster that shielded us from the main street. Thankfully, it didn't smell at all. I put my hands on his shoulders. "What happened. Just tell me."

Chris paused for several seconds then began. "So, after you left, Devon and his posse took me to that warehouse and he uh. He uh," he stuttered.

"He what?"

"Not he. I. I killed him with a box cutter." Tears ran down his face and I wondered why he cried for someone like Devon. Then my nurturing side took over, and I hugged him close.

"I never wanted to kill anybody, not even him, Sarah," Chris said into my shirt.

I felt a physical pain, like a tightness throughout my whole body. It's then I saw some red spots on Chris's sleeve, likely from Devon's blood.

"Chris, we have to go. I am so sorry you went through that, but you're here, and you're not a bad person. Not at all."

He pulled away. "I had to do it. I tried to slip away but he followed me." Chris stood there sniffling.

"It's okay. Listen. We have to go to the Garden even though I don't really want to," I said.

"Wait? You don't want to?"

"There're some things I've been thinking of. That way, no matter what we decide, no one can ever find us." Chris looked at me with such trusting eyes. He didn't even say anything. He didn't have to.

We walked, our arms locked together. We crossed the main road and down some side streets. I knew it was about another eight blocks to the Garden, but I didn't want to go directly there. I wanted to make a pit stop first.

We walked without talking, not wanting anyone to notice. We passed row after row of empty shops. Finally, we came across one with guitars. I'd wanted to stop there before, but the Sweepers came.

"Chris, look," I said pointing inside.

Chris stopped and read the sign: "Rockin' Robin—We're here for all your music needs. Humph," Chris said then stepped forward in a trance. He tried the knob with no luck.

"Dammit," he said under his breath.

I felt this was a mistake. Darby would surely worry about us if we weren't back within a short time.

Chris broke a window with a rock and kicked in the glass then climbed in. I followed right behind, my heart pounding with anticipation.

The shop smelled of old wood and paper. Guitars hung from the ceiling in rows upon rows so far back you couldn't see the end. "Oh my God!" Chris looked up in awe. "Look at these Stratocasters and the Les Paul! Oh, and the Martin!"

"Martin?" I asked.

Chris lifted up a light brown acoustic guitar and cradled it like a baby. "A Martin D-28 1966 Brazilian Rosewood. This puppy'll set you back more than ten-grand!" Chris's eyes sparkled with tears, happy ones this time.

I smiled. "Okay, we'll take it," I said to an imaginary person behind the counter.

Chris started scouring around.

"What? You need sheet music?"

"No, looking for a strap or case or something to make it easier to carry."

I looked around frantically, then in a corner I saw what looked to be a heap of straps.

"There!" I said pointing. Chris went to the area and dug through, picking out a strap that looked like it would fit his new find. Sure enough it worked, and we left the shop grinning from ear to ear.

"I can't wait to play this for you soon."

"Chris. It's getting late. We have to hurry. I'll take us straight there now, okay?"

We wove between parked vehicles. As we approached the main road, I heard the whiz of moving cars, which made my heart sink. No way did we go through all of this just for Sweepers to catch us.

I saw a light from a row house to the right of us, but all the other buildings were dark. Chris went in front of me to form a human shield. His new guitar made a barrier between us.

I looked over at the house and saw three adult sized shadows in front of the window. The door opened and a young woman stepped outside. I turned to run, but Chris pulled me back. It was then I saw the strap around her shoulder and a muzzle of a weapon sagging behind her.

"Welcome you two. We have much to show you," she said. "Please enter and make yourself at home if you will?"

Her voice sounded like it was from another time or land. I took a step back and Chris moved to my side and grabbed my hand.

"Okay, but only for a minute," he said. "We have somewhere to be."

We stepped inside.

37

SARAH

I NTRICATE LACE AND NATURAL-LOOKING beeswax candles filled the rooms.

"Please place your items here." The girl who told us this looked about thirteen but talked in a way three times her age. She carried a long rifle.

Chris and I put our packs down and walked to the formal dining area. The girl did not look strong, and we probably could have taken her, but the savory scent of something cooking overpowered us. We were starving.

"Welcome, you two. I suspect you found your way," said a man about my mother's age who appeared in the doorway between the dining room and kitchen. He wore puffy pants, a tie, and a silky white top.

"We did." And that wasn't a lie. We had found our way here effortlessly, on our way to somewhere else.

"Please, have a seat. We have plenty to share. We have a leg of lamb, minced pie and spiced wine. I suspect you'll take to our menu well. My name is Richard."

Richard had a curly-haired mullet of sorts. I contained my laughter for fear he'd kill us with the large carving knife. The table was deep-grained rectangular wood. No tablecloth. The dishes were white with a gold trim.

Chris and I sat next to each other, across from Richard and a woman.

"May I introduce my wife, Sofia? She prepared this lovely meal for us," Richard said with a smile.

I felt so uncomfortable, but these people intoxicated me. "Good to meet you," I said. Chris nodded.

After that, the young girl entered the room bringing plates of food. She curtsied and left each time she set a plate down.

Chris and I waited, not wanting to be rude and eat before our hosts.

"Please, enjoy," Richard said. "It is so nice to meet our neighbors. We had attended the church regularly but seems like recently things have gotten quiet there."

"Yes, um … we have noticed the same thing," I said taking a bite of the lamb. It felt like jerky between my teeth.

"We're so pleased to hear about the recent acquisitions. This town had become so … oh, what do you call it, Richard?" Sofia asked.

"Industrial," He took several quick bites of food.

I realized these people were definitely Backers. How they could live so close to the Garden made no sense, but then I remembered what Darby said about hiding in plain sight, and Gavin's cloak. Chris and I continued eating and drinking. I noticed the sun was almost down.

"Thank you so much for the lovely dinner, but we must head out," I said.

Richard looked at me with furrowed brows.

"So soon? Please sit with us for dessert," he begged.

Chris and I looked at each other. He coughed and pushed his right knee into mine.

"Really, we must take our leave, sir," Chris said.

"Okay, if you must," Richard said, then stood. Sofia patted her mouth with a napkin and stood. The girl appeared in the doorway. "Say, you're wearing modern clothes. Have you not been … rehabilitated? We'd be glad to take you in, to help—"

"No, really, that's okay. We're fine. We've already been to the Center and are looking to meet up with some ..."

"Some, what? Some others like us?" Richard pried.

"You could say that," Chris said. "Say, why are you all the only ones here? We haven't seen many of you around. Seems like a ghost town."

"Yes. It is a pity." Richard looked over at Sofia. She looked down with eyes half closed as if in prayer. "Most took off when the drivers came. They didn't want to give up their ... their ..."

"Their tech?" Chris inserted.

"Yes. Tech. Technology of any form is the work of the devil, son. You know, though, right?"

Chris hesitated. I said, "Yes sir, we know. We have none. So where did the others like you go?"

"Well, many of them went to neighboring towns to spread the good word. Not everyone wanted to believe, and we never meant to resort to violence, so we set up places."

"You mean the Centers, institutions?" I added.

"Yes, you could call them that. It's for the best, you know? This technological world had gotten so out of hand. People became so addicted. Such a shame." Richard cut a sliver of lamb and placed it in his mouth.

"Papa," the girl in the doorways said.

"Quiet, Judith. Not now." Richard walked in our direction. Chris grabbed our stuff by the door and my hand. It all happened so quickly.

"We must take our leave. Don't worry, we have others," Chris said. "Thanks again."

Chris squeezed my hand and pulled me out the door and down the steps. Richard looked out at us through the curtains for a second, then disappeared.

"Let's go. Lead the way," Chris said.

I ran, as fast as I could. We zoomed around buildings and past street signs.

"I thought it was right here," I said out of breath.

"Sarah!" A voice called out in the darkness. It was Darby. "Come on, you two!"

We followed the voice and sure enough it was Darby with an angry expression. We followed and about four blocks away, I recognized things. The town felt like a maze! Soon, we were in front of the Garden. The door opened and Gavin stood inside.

"So, you took a little detour? How'd that go?"

"It was interesting," I said, my breath still heavy. Chris and I dropped our things. Two people quickly picked it all up and took it away.

"Wait," Chris said.

"Don't worry, Chris. We're taking them to your rooms," Gavin said. "Follow me. We've got important issues to talk about."

We went to the common area, Chris, me, Gavin, Darby and a handful of others I'd not met.

"What's going on?" I asked Gavin.

"Please, sit," he said pointing to one of the stuffed leather chairs. Each sat in a row of six, forming four groups that faced a square area for people to stand in. Gavin went to stand in that area. Chris sat to my left. Darby sat across from us in the other group of chairs. Bill and the others sat in the rows to the right of me.

"Well, that's what I was just about to ask you?" Gavin said facing Chris and me. "Why didn't you come straight back? Why did you visit Richard and Sofia?" Gavin asked. His face held no emotion.

We hadn't told him about Richard and Sofia. "We saw the light on and were ..."

"Curious. And you know where that'll get you? Dead! Or worse, captured and sent back to the Center."

"Sorry," I said. "But how did you know we were there? Who were they? Why are they still here?"

Gaving gripped his cloak in both hands. He tilted his head to his right and wiped away some of his black hair away from his eyes. "Richard and Sofia are long-time holdouts," Darby said. "They've scavenged the area for antiques. They've lived off the grid for some time now. Before, people just looked at them as crunchy-granola weirdos. But now they are part of the majority. They stay because they think they'll be the leaders of this town when people return, to restart society."

"Restart?" I asked.

"Yeah, that's what the backers want to do. They want to start all over again, wipe out tech and get back to how it was, like the 19th century and before." Darby faced Gavin expressionless. Her hair hung loose over her shoulders, her long legs cross, and her right foot bouncing up and down.

"So, how do you know all this about them?" Chris chimed in.

"We infiltrated them a while ago. It was easy. They don't go out often, only to gather their eggs and collect from their garden," Gavin sounded bored. "They travel about once a month to a nearby farm. A horse-drawn carriage picks them up. Crazy as shit I tell you. I'm the one that went in and pretended to want to join up. I pretended my parents left me to join the resistance movement. They felt sorry for me and took me in. There, I learned everything about them, then I left as quickly as I came. I wanted to kill them, but I figured I'd leave them there, to learn from them again, or … to use them as leverage if need be."

Chris and I looked at each other. He raised his brows and covered my hand with his.

"So, yeah," Gavin said. "Now, to get you two to your rooms."

Rooms?

"We'd prefer to be together," I said looking at Chris. This reminded me of that summer Mom split Liz and I up. Liz went to out of state summer camp, but I stayed home for whatever reason. When she came home, she seemed like a different person. We drifted apart. I could not drift apart from Chris.

"Yes. We figured that, but trust me, it's better this way. You two need time apart."

"No! I want to be with Chris. We need to be together," I cried.

"It's okay, Sarah, it's only temporary," Darby interjected. "We need to make sure you can stand on your own."

I tried to get up, but Chris pulled me back. "Stand on our own?! Are you kidding me? We can! We have!"

"Yeah, I know. But trust us, okay," Darby said.

"It's okay," Chris said. His voice brought me back down.

"Come on, you two. Follow me," Darby said.

We went down some steps into a hallway.

"You'll be here," Darby said to Chris. "Look, your rooms are right next to each other. No worries, okay."

They had everything planned out. And I didn't like it.

"Here you go," Darby pointed to the next room, and I went inside. I saw my burlap bag on the bed, but no guitar. It must be in

Chris's room. Darby left and I sat on the bed, but jumped up quickly and raced to the door, when I heard the lock rattle. I turned the knob several times and banged on the door until my fist burned. Then I slumped down to the carpeted floor, and I banged on the adjoining wall.

"Chris! Are you there?"

I heard nothing.

Oh my God, what did they do to him?

I crossed my legs and put my head in my hands. Just then I heard Chris's guitar. His voice rose above it. The tune sounded familiar and as soon as I heard his voice I cried.

"Won't you help please ... baby ... I need you next to me."

I put my hand to the wall, laid down right there, and fell asleep to the sound of Chris's voice.

38

SARAH

WOKE UP TO THE SOUND of a key in the lock. I raised my head to see Darby standing there with a tray of food.

"Mornin' sunshine."

"Hey ... I fell asleep here," I said in a fog. Darby placed the tray on the bed. Oatmeal and a cut up apple. Wow, they're healthy here. Where'd they get the fruit?

I ate without talking.

"So, not even a thank you, huh?" Darby seemed irritated. "You know, we risked our asses out there looking for you two. The least we could get is appreciation."

I swallowed my food, and a piece of apple scraped the back of my throat.

"Thanks, yeah, thanks. Now, when can I see Chris?"

"You can see him whenever you like, except for now. We've taken him for questioning." Darby stood and headed for the door. She seemed so cold, not like before. I couldn't tell if she felt fear or jealousy. "You know, we may have to take that guitar. All that racket's gonna get us found out."

"Darby," I said in a low voice trying to gain her trust. "What did you do before all of this?"

She adjusted her yellow short sleeved cotton shirt. I noticed the game band with a G on the right sleeve. "Before doesn't matter. All that matters is getting things back to normal, whatever that means."

I had hoped for a more detailed answer.

"Look. Just hang tight. Chris'll finish up soon. We're giving him the low-down, like we did with you. You know, the history and stuff. He's in the library." Darby turned to leave.

"Wait!" I said, "Can you stay for a bit? I want to know more."

"Know more about what?" Darby shuffled her feet.

"I don't know. For one, what is the plan? What are we doing here? Where is Olivia? Guess I have lots of questions."

"All right, Sarah, since you asked. There really isn't a plan per se. We know we can't stay here forever. We know you're in, but we're not sure about Chris. That's why we're talking to him, okay?" Darby said and left. I sat alone with my thoughts.

I remembered first meeting Chris. Such a contrast to where we found ourselves. We hadn't had a "normal" relationship. Hell, we hadn't even had time to stop and think or talk about things. We just kept going because we were all we had. And maybe that's the way it was supposed to be. Two people who only have each other, muddling through life like it's all brand new. I wanted to go to the library now, find Chris to tell him I wanted to leave this place.

The entire world had gone to shit, and we were going down with it.

The softness of the bed felt surreal beneath me. My head on the pillow felt like my last salvation.

A knock on the door shook me fully awake.

"Who is it?" I asked, hoping with all hope to hear Chris's voice.

"It's me," his voice sounded strange on the other side of the door.

I rushed to the door and opened it. Chris stood there looking like a shell of himself, like he did back at the Center.

"Chris, come in. What the hell happened? What did they say to you?"

He walked over to the bed and sat. I stood in front of him and leaned in, hoping for an embrace, but he sat there idly.

"Chris, what's wrong," I said putting my hand on his.

Chris's face tensed. His lips tightened and he rubbed the thick layer of scruff on his face. "Sarah, I don't know about this whole thing."

"Me either, Chris. Oh, my God! This is crazy! The Luddites sound crazy … and that's what the Go Back based their movement on." I grabbed onto Chris's waist and pulled in, pressing my lips into his hair and neck.

"Sarah, I gotta say I'm so glad you're here. I know things aren't normal for us. I know …"

"Yeah, I know. It's okay. I know we haven't really gotten to know each other. This world is so messed up right now. Don't worry," I said. I noticed his eyes seemed more green than blue at the moment. The edges were wet. I wiped them with my fingertip. "Chris, no matter what, we're gonna be okay." I paused. "Because we have each other."

"What makes you so sure, baby?"

I loved it when he called me that. "Because. I know." No matter how I felt, it was my turn to be strong.

We fell onto each other, giving into the passion of the moment, the uncertainty of it all still in front of us. But one thing was certain, we needed each other.

39

OLIVIA

I PEDALED FOR HOURS along the route to the Garden, hoping that Ed would escape and meet me there. Cars passed me every now and then, but never stopped. I guess they could tell I didn't have a drop of tech on me. I crossed the Colorado River near Marble Falls using Highway 281 and stopped to catch my breath and gawk at the wide river. Docks with boats lined either side. Never liked rivers or boats for that matter. Always got seasick. I pedaled on until I came to a building that read "Andice General Store" with Coca-Cola logos on either side of the words. The door was open, so what the heck, I hid my bike behind a bench on the porch and went inside.

There were unlit beer coolers to the right of the entrance. Metal racks that held cans of jam, apple butter, and any kind of hot sauce you'd want, sat in the middle of the store. Beyond that I saw a small counter and a cash register. An empty floor cooler sat to the right it. Looked like it once held ice cream. Before I could look around anymore, I heard a faint, "Hello," from behind the counter area and nearly fell backwards from shock.

A frail old man wearing jean overalls, and a red plaid long-sleeve shirt walked slowly to the register and put his hands on the counter. "What can I do ya fer, young … uh … lady is it?" He had a scratchy old man voice with a southern drawl.

Old people scared the piss out of me before, even more so now because they usually sided with the Backers, but this guy didn't seem harmful at all.

"Lady," I confirmed and came to the counter.

The man looked up at me. His eyelids hung so heavy I was surprised he could see anything. "'Fraid we just got non-perishables here since the lights don't work no more."

"I'd love some, but I would also like to rest a bit. Is that okay?" I asked. He placed his elbows on the counter and waved his left hand back and forth in a gesture for me to sit a spell. "Sure, miss. Ain't busy around here. Take yer time." He pulled a stool from the wall behind him, grunted and sat down.

I turned around and walked to a booth made of knotty pine and sat down, then pulled out the yellow and black Sat phone to will it to work. I picked it up and held it in my right hand and tried Ed again. This time a scratchy voice answered.

"Liv. Is … you? I … at … here."

"Ed!" I yelled into the receiver. The old man didn't stir. Maybe he couldn't hear me from over there. Still, I stood up and went to the door in case I needed to escape. "I'm here! It's Olivia! Where are you? Over."

"Here … when … come … to the … street …" he replied.

I couldn't make any of it out. I shook the Sat phone hoping that would somehow make the connection better.

"Ed, switch channels. Can't hear you."

I heard clicking.

"Liv … need … now … help."

"Ed. Come again? Over."

"Liv. I need … help. I'm … Garden," he said.

Had he said what I think I heard? I let out a quiet laugh. "You're at the Garden?"

"Met Sarah and Chris."

"Ed! I can hear you now. Chris and Sarah are there?" Never had I wanted to hear someone's voice so badly. Plus, hearing him meant we were within the 50-mile talk range.

"Are you ok? Are they? Over." I asked. I went outside and around the corner. The old man still sat behind the counter.

"Yeah. But." The connection broke up then came in clearer. "I made radio contact. Isobel told me about a change of plan with Sarah and her traveling companion. The Garden wants to ..." Ed's voice cut out.

"Wants to what? Over."

"... Get back tech ... Sarah ... Over." he said, breaking up.

"Dammit, Ed. Can't hear you. What do I do? Over."

"Go ... Galloway Ranch ... Go now."

"Ed? Ed? You want me to go to Galloway Ranch? Over."

Static.

"Ed! Over."

Again. And again.

Nothing.

40

SARAH

I'M BOUNCING UP AND DOWN to the music. Full throttle, the sound waves hit my chest like a wet towel. The guitar shreds, the singer's wail bounces off the ceiling and into my body. I scream along. The crowd roars. Beer splashes. Plastic cups crush underneath our stomping feet. Smoke rises. The singer jumps into the crowd to surf. He's heading my way. I lift my hands up, but right before he reaches me, he lands feet first. The band stops playing. The singer looks at me. He takes off his dark glasses to reveal hollow eye sockets.

"Did you get what you wanted?" he sings into the mic. "Is this what YOU wanted? Are you ready ...to go back? Go. Go. Go. Back!"

•   •   •

I shot up in bed, my body soaked with sweat from the nightmare. I wished Chris was still by my side. He went back to his room late last night. Alone in my bed, I felt a sense of unpleasant *déjà vu*, except the ceiling didn't have tiles, more like popcorn. I told Chris everything would be okay, but would it? What are we doing here? Are we waging war? If so, then where was the enemy? The door rattled and I jumped out of bed.

Gavin stood with a book in his hand.

"Good morning, Sarah. How did you sleep?"

"All right, I guess." I lied.

"Come on. Get breakfast."

"You mean, out there? I ..."

"Yes, out there. You are our guest, not our prisoner."

"Let me brush my hair," I said. They had provided us a general toiletry bag with toothpaste, toothbrush, a brush, sanitary napkins, and pain relievers.

Gavin nodded and stood in the doorway. I brushed my hair and put on my only other pair of pants.

I got to the main room with the stuffed leather chairs where people milled around. The welcome smell of food wafted from the kitchen. Chris sat at a little table next to the kitchen door. My face lit up in a smile the moment our eyes met. We all sat and ate, not talking. As we finished up, a woman came to our table.

"Hi, Sarah. I'm Isobel."

I put my fork down.

"Here, let me take this for you two." She took our plates to the kitchen then returned with a chair.

"Look, I know you're wondering what you're doing here. I know ..."

"You know, huh? How do you know my name?"

"You're famous, Sarah. Like, everyone knows how you broke outta that Center. You and Chris. We've been waiting for you ever since." Her voice lowered. "You're amazing, Sarah."

Her emerald eyes pierced mine. I had to look away. Chris took my hand and frowned.

"So ... you've been waiting for us? That doesn't freak me out at all." I drew out the last word to make my cynicism clear.

Isobel pressed her lips together and rubbed them with her index finger. She sat back in her chair.

"Look, I think what Sarah's trying to say is," Chris began, "ever since we got here, you've treated us like prisoners. You lock our doors, make us sleep in separate rooms."

"Yeah, I know." Isobel leaned in. "That's Gavin and Darby. They said we had to. They said ... Look. I shouldn't be talking to you right now. Wanted to welcome you two." Isobel stood and pushed her chair in. She gave a quick half wave and walked to the couch and sat down.

I felt a presence behind me and looked over my shoulder. Sure enough, Gavin stood there. Chris let go of my hand and sat back.

"So, I see you've eaten?" Gavin said. His smile revealed a cracked front tooth.

"Yeah, thanks, man," Chris said. Gavin looked at Chris, then right back to me.

"We're meeting about the next stages in a few minutes. Sit tight. We'll introduce you." Gavin walked away talking to several people on his way to what I presumed to be his office.

The vertical creases in-between Chris's eyebrows gave Chris's frustration away. I moved my chair to sit beside him. We held hands and waited. No one else came to talk to us, like we were invisible. Isobel and another woman on the couch argued about something. Not yelling, but Isobel kept shaking her head and looking away.

"I could cut the tension here with a knife," Chris whispered.

"Yeah, this is so weird. I wonder what the next steps are? Hopefully, one of them will allow us to sleep in the same room."

Chris chuckled then got quiet.

Gavin was back. He walked to the middle of the room and people gathered around in a circle. By my estimation, there were about forty of us.

"Good morning, everyone. I know you're all wondering what's next. The planning committee has been hard at work outlining each step," Gavin said.

Planning committee?

"Rest assured, the committee will launch our next phase over the course of three days. Now, I'd like to tell all of you what it entails, but as you know, that would be a mistake. I will only reveal this information on a need-to-know basis. If you need to know something, you will. I will leave no one in the dark. Someone will hold separate meetings over the course of these days. I have assigned everyone a committee." Gavin pulled a piece of paper out of his pocket that looked like a scroll. "Everyone's assignments are here."

Chris turned to look at me and whispered, "This is messed up."

I nodded ever so slightly as an affirmation then continued listening.

"The planning committee comprises Darby, me, John and Everett. The backbones are Sarah, Chris, Isobel and Edward. There are ten techies who stay behind to monitor. There are five housemates who will keep the Garden in order. The rest are armory, spies and as needed. The armory is what it sounds like. Still, we don't want to resort to violence like they have but we will," Gavin raised the scroll and people cheered. Chris squeezed my hand. I wondered what the backbones did, and why he choose us?

"The spies spread out into the towns and report back. They also infiltrate as needed."

Gavin handed Darby the scroll. He unraveled it and walked away to post it on the wall. A clamoring ensued to see who got which assignment.

Chris and I stay put because, well, we already knew. Darby walked over to us.

"Sarah and Chris. You'll be working with Isobel and Ed. I see you've already met Isobel. Ed just got here, but he's valuable. He was one of them, but he's promised to help us. He was at the same Center as you two."

But where was Olivia?

"How do you expect us to trust him?" I asked.

"It's exactly what it sounds like. You're the backbone of this operation. The Backers are looking for you. You're gonna set the trap, and we're gonna go in," Darby looked down. Her tapping combat boots grew louder on the linoleum floor.

"So, you're using us? You're just gonna use us to bait the backers and watch us die? Are you gonna save us when those freaks get ahold of us again? We risked so much ... so much to ..." Darby cut me off.

"Sarah, lower your voice. You need to be on our side if you want tech back, right? And things to return to normal? So, this is it. This is the plan. It's that or ..."

"Or what?" Chris chimed in. "Or we get captured again? Or die? For what? So we can get back our smart phones?"

Chris's brows furled in a way I'd never seen, and the lines between his eyebrows ran deeper than ever. He stood up.

"Come on, Sarah, we need to talk," he said. I stood up and pushed my hair from my eyes.

"Ok, Darby, we'll think about it. I mean, this is a lot to take in all now," I said.

"There's no thinking necessary. This is the plan and if you want to …"

"Want to, what? Stay here and go along with your crazy theory?" I scoffed.

"Well, yeah," Darby said. "I'm sorry, Sarah, but I told you about the Backers. They've been around for a while and it's only getting worse."

Chris and I walked to our rooms. I could hear Darby following us.

"Check out some books in the library. You'll see. Then you'll get fully behind this, okay?" she said.

Without turning around Chris yelled, "Oh yeah, Sarah and I will be in the same room tonight, and don't stop us."

He opened the door to my room; we went inside and slammed the door behind us.

41

SARAH

"I MEAN, WHO DO THEY THINK THEY ARE?" Chris asked as soon as the door shut.

"I don't know," I said, trying to stroke his arm. He pulled it away.

I sat on the edge of the bed, watching him pace.

"We can do this. We'll figure something out," I said, trying to believe myself. But maybe I was wrong this time. Maybe we wouldn't be able to get out of this. Maybe it was time to forge our own path. But how?

Chris continued pacing and huffing and puffing. "I mean, we do kind of need these people," he said.

"But do we, really? How do we know?" I asked. Chris's pacing made a trail in the pile of the brown carpet.

"We know because look at the people we've met along the way, Sarah. Devon and Dylan. I had to take out Devon and who knows if Dylan is alive." Chris stammered and sobbed. I'd never seen him like this. He was always my rock. I ran to him and held him. He tried to pull away, but I wouldn't let him. I spoke into his chest.

"Chris, you did what you had to."

I cried, too, but forced it down like I'd taught myself to do, especially since my dad died.

"I love you, Chris. No matter what. I love you unconditionally," I said. It's the first time I'd said those words to any man, or any other person. My family wasn't one to echo them. Chris's chest continued to rise and fall. His soft sobs stopped. I felt his fingers lift my chin up to stare at his eyes.

"I love you too my little Dandelion," he said.

"What do you mean by that?" I bit my lower lip.

"Dandelions are beautiful, but most people see them as weeds. They step on them or treat them with chemicals. Blow them too hard and their beauty disappears. You haven't let those strong winds or chemicals get to you. You're still beautiful and you're a work of art and strength in disguise, Sarah."

Our lips met. It felt different this time. I felt an inner strength I hadn't felt before now. Maybe Chris gave it to me, but I'd like to think I gave it to myself, too.

A knock on the door jolted us apart. Chris and I wiped our eyes and stood stoic.

"Come in," Chris said.

In stepped someone I hadn't seen before. He was about as tall as Chris and with curly short dark hair. He wore black boots, green pants, and a white, long-sleeve shirt. I couldn't believe he was interrupting our sweet moment.

"Hey guys," he said. He walked to the nightstand and sat down on it.

"Do you mind telling us who the hell you are?" Chris asked.

"So, you know who I am," the man said. Was he asking us? I couldn't tell.

"No. Not really, but I'm guessing you may be Ed," I said and sat on the bed. "So, we're supposed to just trust you, huh? Someone who used to work at the Center, or one of them." My chest tightened with every word.

"Yup, sucks, I know, but if I were you I would."

I looked over at Chris for confirmation, but he just paced.

"So, what are we gonna do? What's the plan? Personally, I dislike anyone using us as bait in some takeover plan," I said.

"You two really broke out of the Center, eh?"

"Maybe," Chris stepped in. "Look, we don't have to tell you anything ..."

"No, no, you don't, but I recommend you do." Ed stared Chris down.

"And why is that?" Chris asked.

"Because I'm the only person you can confide in." Ed chuckled. "Well, maybe not the only one." Ed's brown eyes softened. He rubbed them and wiped his hands on his pants.

He then told us the story of his and Oliva's escape from the Center, and how they worked together and got out and got separated. How they'd built the Garden intending to beat Go Back.

Chris squeezed my hand as we sat on the bed listening.

"How are we going to find Olivia?" I asked. "We've got to get out of here and find her. We need to—"

Ed stopped me.

"Yeah, I've thought about all that. And trust me, I want to get the hell out of here just as much as you do, maybe more. But we'll play along for now."

This didn't feel right, but then again not much had for so long it became the new normal.

"Ok. We will. We're trusting you, man," Chris said. "So, how'd you get wrapped up in this GB mess, anyway?"

"How long you got?"

"All night," Chris and I said in unison, then laughed.

"I was inside my apartment staring at my new iPhone. It had all the bells and whistles, facial recognition, holographic imaging, an energy dense battery that lasted for three days without charging. I'd been tinkering with this beauty for like three hours when I heard a knock at my door. I put the phone between the mattress and box spring, then headed to answer it.

"When I looked out the peephole, I saw three men, and when I opened the door, they nearly fell inside my apartment.

"They asked me who I was, and I told them. They told me they'd been looking for me. Then they came into my apartment and started tossing the place. When I asked about a warrant, they told me all about the president and supreme court, blah, blah."

At this point in the story, we all sat on the floor cross legged in a circle, close enough so no one outside the room would hear.

"Yep, we heard the same deal at the Center," I replied.

Ed continued. "So anyway, I gave him a fake smile while I watched him rummage through my stuff. I sat back like I don't have a care in the world, but then one of the dumb asses called out he had found something. He held my new iPhone like a trophy. He told me I was busted. I planned to fight it. It couldn't be for real, right?"

"We all thought that," I said. "I thought the same, when Lily approached me."

"Wait. Lily? Young girl? Purple hair?" Ed asks.

"Yeah," I say. "She's the one who got me. Tricked me into taking her back to my apartment. Then she and this brute captured me—"

"Shit, she was asking about you, back at the Center. She asked me and Liv about you, if you were, okay? Damn, we suspected little. Should have."

"It's okay. I get it. Go on," I said to Ed.

"The three guys lead me out of my apartment and read me my 'rights.' I said nothing as they led me away, down the same stairs I used every day after work, or when I went out for dinner, or to go take a walk to think. This was not like any other time I'd walked down these steps.

"I saw some of my neighbors coming home. My hands were locked behind me, and three men guided me down, I couldn't wave. That felt awkward. I hoped they would never feel the way I felt in that moment. We reached the exit and one of them stopped before we go out.

"He told me I was going to the Center. When I argued with them, told them I wanted to go back. Back to a time and a place where they were not in power. Back to a time when I had the freedom to surf the net and have the latest tech tools."

"And then what?" Chris asked.

"They laughed all the way to the police vehicle they had waiting for me. They told me there is no constitution anymore. President Gibson and the GB Unified clan have declared it invalid if you didn't know already then dragged me into the car.

"At the Center, they drugged and brainwashed me for months, then gave me the lovely choice of either working at the Center or being released with no job, since the tech industry collapsed. I worked for them. I saw no other way. Then I met Liv—I mean, Olivia—and we worked with each other, created the Garden and came up with a plan to get here. Looks like that plan is about to change. We're now going to a ranch called Galloway."

"Wow," is all I could say.

"Yeah, wow," Chris dittoed. "So, you got away, too. That must be why they want us so close to them."

"I guess." Ed snuffed out another cigarette out into a cup. I wish he'd stop doing that. We probably had at least one more night here. "Doesn't really matter, now, does it? Why they want us, I mean," he continued.

"So now what? How do we get Isobel alone? And how do we know we can really trust her?" I asked.

"Isobel told me she runs a daily meeting around three pm. I can catch her after that," Ed said.

"Well, it's a good start," Chris said. "I think we need to play along until nearly the end. We tell them we'll be the bait, then pull a switch and take off right before that."

"No. That's exactly what they'll plan for. We must do something totally unexpected," Ed said.

"Something crazy, huh?" I added.

"Yeah, something crazy," Ed said.

"Someone's gonna die." Chris looked down as he said this.

"Yeah, we got that, brother. We'll get to that when we get to that. First things first. I'm gonna go to talk to Isobel."

He walked to the door and turned.

"Hang tight guys. So glad you're here," he said and left.

"What the hell just happened," I asked Chris.

"We're finding our own path," is all he said, then laid on the bed and closed his eyes.

42

OLIVIA

I MISSED HIS HUMOR. I missed how he always patted my knee when I worried. I missed his stupid jokes. I felt lonely out here without Ed, but I had to carry on.

Figuring out the Garden was a "bust" was a major disappointment, but we couldn't let that us stop us.

We always had a Plan B, and ours was Galloway, a ranch, halfway between the Center and Moffat. It had everything you'd need: building structures, barns, animals, gates, a flowing stream. After I talked to Ed on the Sat phone, I changed course and headed due South.

I tried him again in an open area, and the Sat phone came in loud and clear.

"How is it coming along there with Sarah, Chris, the others? Over." I asked Ed.

"Good. I told them everything. Well, as much as they needed to know," Ed told me.

"They're on board? We need Sarah and Chris on board," I emphasized.

"They are. As much as they can be," I said.

"Okay, talk soon. Okay?"

What I wanted to say is I miss you. I needed you here, with me. But to admit that would be a grave mistake. Ed would come find me. He'd do anything for me, and I knew that. So, instead, I simply said goodbye. Over and out.

My job was to secure Galloway, and to make sure it was ready for us. Galloway was just far enough off the beaten path to remain unnoticed. Ed and I spotted it on satellite surveillance at the Center once. There are many ways in and out.

As I pulled up to the gates, it was clear I had my work cut out for myself. Thankfully, I found the place. My injured ankle felt so stiff, I could barely move it anymore. I almost fell and caught myself on the expansive stucco walls that lined the road leading up to the property.

A massive double-door iron gate with a 50-foot wall arching over it greeted me at the end of the driveway to Galloway. My feet crunched under the sand and rocks. The air was dry. I reached back for my long dreads as a nervous habit, only to find them gone.

The only thing I could see beyond the gate was a dusty, gravel road.

"Lower your pack!" a female voice yelled from behind.

Shit.

I didn't turn around.

"I'm not here for trouble. Please, I just want to talk," I said.

"I said, drop your pack, or I'll shoot," the voice said.

I wiggled my shoulders, and my pack fell to the ground.

"Atta girl. Now turn around, slowly."

I took a deep breath in through my nose and out like yoga. Then I turned around to see a woman pointing a small gun straight at me. I raised up my hands, fingers to the sky.

"Please, I have no weapons. I dropped my pack. I just want to talk."

"Step away from the pack," she said. "Slowly, or I'll shoot!"

I stepped to my left counting in my head 1, 2, 3, 4 …

The woman ran to my pack and grabbed it. She rifled through, then frisked me.

"You know, you should have done this first. What if I had a secret weapon in my clothes?" I said.

"Shut up. I didn't ask you anything. Name?"

"Olivia. Sergeant Olivia Parker."

"Shit," she paused. "Shut up and come with me," she said under her breath.

She led me not through the gates, but through a door with a coded entrance. She blindfolded me and tied my hands behind my back.

We walked in silence. Several times I stumbled over rocks or cacti, I couldn't be sure. I wished Ed were here right about now. We went through several doors. I heard them creak and squeak behind me. Finally, we stopped.

"Sit. Here," she said as she pushed my right shoulder hard. I landed on a hard surface. A bench perhaps. She took off my blindfold and untied my hands. I found myself in a very ornate Santa Fe style living room. Shiny Saltillo tiles lined the floor and painted beams lined the ceiling. There was a piano and a fireplace with a carved wooden mantle. Navajo rugs covered the stucco walls. I sat on a brick ledge in front of the fireplace.

I heard clicking and crossed my hands over my stomach.

I wanted to run. Could it really be her? No, not here. No. No.

The sound rounded the corner and another woman, thankfully not Allabaster, stared at me. Blond. Long, wavy hair. Medium build and wearing a red shawl.

"So, you found us?" the woman said.

"Yes," I said. I wanted to keep it short to let her guide the conversation, at least for now.

"When you made contact, I didn't figure you would come, since you had that other place. What's it called?

"The Garden, Ma'am."

"Yes, right. I also expected quite a bit more of you, you know, to help around here."

"There are others," I said. "They are making their way here and could contribute a lot if you would let them. Sorry, I didn't catch your name. We always knew you as your GPS coordinates," I said.

She stepped to the piano and sat down.

"You know, the Moonlight Sonata has always been my favorite. Such an excellent mix of sadness and light."

She played. I'd heard the song before, but this time seemed much more poignant. The melody flowed quietly then at certain points bellowed out. The acoustics of the stucco and Saltillo made the sound even more intricate.

As suddenly as she began, the woman stopped.

"Just a taste," she said. "I never give it all away the first time."

This woman's crazy, but just roll with it.

"I appreciate your talent. Now, if you'll just give me your name, I'd be happy to discuss what my people can offer you," I said.

"Grace. Grace Shaw. Lived here on Galloway since I was a girl. This is my home and I'll be damned if a bunch of strangers take it over," she said.

"Ms. Shaw. Never. Never would we ever do such a thing. Surely, you've heard of the Go Back movement, or GB as it's called. I was there! I saw everything they have planned, and it is not good. It's—"

"Please, call me Grace."

She came to sit next to me. "Yeah, I was there, too."

"What?" I said. "At the Center?"

"Well, not really. As a ranch owner, we kind of live off the grid, anyway. The GB came after us first, wanting to team up. Sounded good, to begin with."

"To begin with?"

"Yes. But it soon became clear that the partnership they were proposing was not a good deal for us." She signed.

"What did they propose?" I asked.

Grace twisted her mouth, like she tried to figure out what to say next. "They proposed complete takeover. They wanted Galloway as a headquarters, an example of what could be. Living off the land, etc. But I told them, no. We use tech tools to better our farming community. We rely on technology to an extent and were not willing to give it up."

"And they allowed this?" I asked.

"No. They forced us to turn in everything. The only reason they didn't round us up, was because we had negotiated with them. But they left us with nothing. We had to agree not to speak out about GB and to stay put right here in Galloway. Since then, we've only been out a handful of times."

"Wait? You've only been out a handful of times?"

"Yes. It has been difficult, but we have enough to sustain us here, a stream, cattle, chickens, houses, security ... So, you can see why we don't take so keen to visitors," she said.

"I see."

"I'm sure you'll also understand that we have no other choice but to hold you for a time to make sure your story checks out?"

"Hold me? But, what about my people? I need to talk to them. If this will not work out, then ..."

"Then nothing. We must hold you. Your people will understand. If we allow you here, then you must abide by our rules. And there are rules. The first of which is that we secure all outsiders."

Two women and three men, all dirty and dusty ranch hands came through a doorway next to the fireplace towards me, arms outstretched.

"Olivia don't make this harder than it has to be," Grace said.

I stood up and tried backing away, but ultimately held out my hands. The group lead me down a long corridor and locked me in a small bathroom with a cot, a sink and a toilet.

"You'll have everything you need. Tomorrow, we contact your people. Negotiations will begin and if you don't meet our terms, then negotiations end," I heard Grace say from the other side of the door.

I laid in a fetal position on the cot. The metal bar gnawed into my right side. What I wouldn't give to talk to Ed right now.

43

SARAH

W E HEARD NOTHING for several hours. My stomach growled for a meal, but I couldn't bear to leave the room. Chris offered to go out and I accepted. My body and mind felt like a paper weight pushing me into the bed. He returned several moments later with a folded piece of bread with peanut butter in it. He also brought a small bowl of popcorn.

"They were making it out there on the stove. I'm surprised we didn't smell it," Chris said.

I sat on the bed and ate. Chris ripped the sandwich apart and gave me my share, a jagged edge of bread staring back at me. I thrust as much as I could into my mouth and chewed. My cheeks filled up like a hamster. Now I wanted some cold milk or water to wash this down.

"Thanks, Chris. You're my hero," I said with a smile. "Let's go away together."

Chris tossed a popcorn kernel in his mouth, put his hand to his throat and coughed. "What? Um, okay. Where?"

"Enchanted Rock."

"Enchanted Rock. Really?"

I leaned over and kissed him. It must have caught him off guard because he threw his head back with wide eyes.

"Yep, Enchanted Rock. Nothing can stop us there." I stood and threw my arms in the air.

Chris signed. "I'd go anywhere with you, but you know we have to –"

I pushed out my palm in a stop gesture. "Nope." I put both hands over my ears and shook my head. "Forget about reality for a minute."

"Alright, we'll go. And we'll camp under the stars. I'll bring my hammock!"

"That's the spirit!"

We both laughed, one of the few things that kept us going at this point. We finished our food, sat and waited. Then there was a knock. Chris opened it. Isobel and Ed stood there. I felt my heart thumping. I pushed myself to the edge of the bed.

"Come on in, you two," Chris said, then closed the door.

Isobel crossed her arms in front of her body, shielding herself from a potential enemy—us.

"Hey Isobel," I said. "Good seeing you again."

Isobel sat across from Ed at the foot of the bed, Chris and I sat across from each other near the pillows.

"What's this all about?" she asked, her tone left a bitterness in my brain, like she couldn't stand us to bother her about any of this.

"We're making another plan," I said.

"What other plan? Gavin and Darby, they … they are …"

"Yeah, we know. And we're not having it. We will not sacrifice ourselves to the GB freaks. We're planning something else, and we want you to come along with us," I said.

Isobel wiped her brow. "I get that. I really do. Why trust us?"

"You could say that," I said.

"There's something you should know," Isobel said. "Gavin, Ed, Olivia and I have been working together for some time. We've been communicating, while Ed and Liv, I mean, Olivia worked at the Center."

Chris and I looked at each other. "Yeah, we already know that," I blurted out.

"You did?" Isobel mumbled and shook her head. She twirled her wispy hair in her right hand. Her small-framed body shook.

She rolled a cigarette back and forth between her fingers. "I got out of a Center, too."

"Really?"

"They got me in a coffee shop. It was one of those underground places that had an encrypted version of the Internet. It cost like a dollar a minute to use, but it was worth it. I was trying to gather all the physical contacts of my online friends. Up till that point I only had their social media handles. I wanted to know how to find them in case the net went dark."

"Lots of people there looked like me. I'm not sure what gave us all away, but before I knew it guards were at the door, with guns and bags. They demanded our tech. The employees were yelling at us to give it up. A guard grabbed one of them and told them to take them to their internet source. They said the power would go out in 60 minutes.

"People were throwing away their phones and tablets and running out the back door. Guards blockaded it. I sat there frozen, watching everything around me unfold like a bad movie. The sounds of electronic screens cracking, crying and guards yelling all blended together.

"I was having a panic attack. Before I know it, they strapped me down into an ambulance."

"A similar thing happened to me," I interrupted, "except they forced me into a windowless van."

Isobel nodded, "Yep, so I woke up in the hospital, my wrists and ankles tied to the bed. A nurse came in and checked my IV She told me to push a button for more meds. I didn't want more meds. I wanted to get out of there. I found out I wasn't in a normal hospital. I was in a center. They gave me a pamphlet about their new way of life. I pretended to read it. Days later they unhooked me from the bed, but I lay in and out of a drugged state."

I closed my eyes and shook my head.

Isobel continued, "Nurses came in and out, took vitals, gave me food, etc. One nurse seemed to take a liking to me. We'd talk sometimes.

"One day she came in and she got way too comfy with me. Whatever it was, I took advantage. I told her I'd give anything to feel the breeze on my face. Told her it would make me feel alive again. She assured me that day would come, but I'm not ready yet.

"So, I asked her to lay with me. She laid down and for a slight moment I wanted to love her, but I talked myself out of it. Shortly after that, I struck the lamp into the side of her head, knocking her out. I jumped out of the bed and piled all the sheets over her lifeless body. I put on her lab coat, hat and shoes, and slipped her keys into my pocket.

"I pushed open a door that led to a courtyard. It must have been the one she and I talked about all those times. A maze of sidewalk laid out before me. Different colored flowers lined each side.

"I ran to a locked gate on the opposite side of the yard. I tried a key and to my surprise it worked. The whole thing was easy, well except for the killing part, and even that was easy, physically. Emotionally, I'm not sure I'll ever get over it. And here I am."

Isobel put the cigarette to her mouth and pulled out a lighter. She breathed in the smoke and held it until her face turned red.

"Gavin and Darby took me in. I was on the side of the road, lost and hungry. They were scavenging for tech and food. I'm not sure why they picked me up. I mean, I looked like a lost dog. I don't know if I can go against them, ya know?"

"Yeah. I get that. And, I mean, you can only do what feels right for you." I said. "Please. Don't tell them our plans."

"I don't know. I can't promise anything." Isobel stomped her cigarette out on the floor and stood. "Sorry guys. I gotta think about this. There's strength in numbers ya know? See ya." She left.

Ed shrugged. "Well, we tried. I mean, what did you expect? Why do you think I hide out in my room all the time. These people are fucking sheep."

"I don't think we should give up. My primary worry is that she'll tell Gavin and Darby," I said.

"I don't think we have to worry about that. Isobel is one to keep her options open, if you know what I mean. Plus, she helped us out when we were at the Center," Ed chimed in. "Okay folks, well we'll reconvene tomorrow."

Chris still sat there, looking up at the ceiling.

"What is it," I asked.

"Nothing."

"Can't be nothing."

"Well, it's just this whole thing. We've all been so busy trying to get away from the Backers, that we've not looked at the Garden and what it stands for. I mean, they want to get our tech back, right? But how? Then what? And what good is all the tech for, anyway?"

"I don't know. Let's go to the library."

44

SARAH

CHRIS AND I STEPPED into the empty library. They must have packed the books away for the impending revolution. How forty of us were going to take on the GB movement and defeat them was beyond me.

I searched the books that were left behind. Chris stood on the other side of the room looking through boxes. Tossed aside on a bottom shelf, I found a pamphlet.

NOTES TOWARD A NEO-LUDDITE MANIFESTO

Skimming through I read:

The technologies created and disseminated by modern Western societies are out of control and desecrating the fragile fabric of life on Earth. Like the early Luddites, we too are a desperate people seeking to protect the livelihoods, communities, and families we love, which lie on the verge of destruction.

I kept reading to find out several principles of the Neo-Luddites.

- *They are not against technology, but are against any technology that destroy human lives and communities. Neo-Luddites believe technology is never neutral, and they can use it for good or evil depending on who's using them.*

- *All technologies are political. Someone has created them to reflect and serve powerful interests in historical situations.*

- *No Television. Television breaks down family communications and narrows people's experience of life by changing reality and lowering people's attention spans.*

The Neo-Luddites want people to criticize technology by examining its sociological, economic and political meaning. This involves asking not just what we gain by these technologies, but also what we lose and questioning their impact on living beings, natural systems and the environment.

These sounded okay, not too crazy or far off. So, why the need for these institutions or centers? Why the GB movement?

"Chris, hey, look at this." I handed him the pamphlet and he sat down to read.

I rummaged through the rest of the books and found very little. Also, someone took the tech and cords. This place was empty.

After a while, Chris put the pamphlet down.

"Wow. Sounds kinda crazy, but kinda ... kinda ..."

"Not too crazy," I finished.

"Yeah. I mean. This GB movement seems so extreme. I guess no one would give up their tech without a fight, huh?"

"I read another book earlier, and it said the Backers didn't like computers because, even though they help people do stuff, that they bring people further and further away from peace, honesty, stability and good work," I said.

Looking at Chris, I couldn't figure out what side I was on. I wasn't against tech, but I had come this far without it. Did we really need a war to get it back?

I leaned into Chris. I'd always wanted a love like this. We didn't have to say anything, just looked into each other's eyes. And it was not corny or annoying. The only problem was the world was blowing up around us. We were in this place. This unknown place, with an unknown future. But isn't that how it's always been? When had the future ever been clear?

Chris exhaled.

"We have to make a move, Sarah. There will be another meeting soon."

"Yeah, you're right. Maybe we should go into the common area. Try to find Ed and Isobel," I said. Chris stood then outstretched his hand.

"My lady," he said and smiled. His lips were red and full. What I wanted to do was pull him into this couch and lean into his chest and listen to his voice all night. I wanted his lips against mine. I wanted to run far away. Just us. But I knew that could not happen, so I took his hand and got up.

We walked into the common area where a few people milled about, chatting, waiting for dinner. Isobel spoke to Gavin. She looked at me, then glanced away. Then they walked our way.

"Follow my lead," Chris whispered.

"Hey, you two," Isobel said.

"Hi," I said. "How are you guys?"

"We're good," Gavin said. "We hope you're up to the task because the next meeting is tomorrow. Early."

"Yeah, we're ready. We see you've already packed things away. Are we moving to another headquarters?" Chris asked.

"That's on a, uh, need to know basis," Gavin said flashing his chipped tooth. I wondered if he got it before or after all of this went down.

"So, one thing I am curious about," Chris said. "How far has this GB movement infiltrated? How many of them are there? There aren't too many people here, so wondering if we're … ?"

"Outnumbered?" Gavin responded.

"Um, yeah," Chris said. I looked over at him then back at Gavin, trying to put on my best poker face.

"We don't know. But from what we've gathered from the encrypted web and by word of mouth, the Backers are strong. I mean, obviously, they've been able to shut down communication and technology as it stands," Gavin looked around the room. His eyes couldn't seem to focus on us.

"So, the plan stands as it is?" Chris asked.

"Yes," Isobel said.

"Where do we go from here? I mean, we're gonna lead them into a trap, right?" I asked, looking straight at Gavin. He didn't even flinch.

"Yep, that's right."

"But, like I said before, what about us?"

"You'll be okay. You're just our decoys."

"But how can you guarantee that?"

"We can't. You just have to believe. You know … like with the Bible and shit," Gavin laughed so hard he snorted. I disliked him even more if that could be possible.

The conversation continued into more mundane topics like what's for breakfast tomorrow and what items we should pack for our journey.

Gavin and Isobel walked away arm in arm to another room.

"Are they?"

"Maybe," Chris said. "Doesn't matter, besides. All we can do is hope she'll change her mind and come with us."

I thought about the manifesto I read and about the Center. I thought about Ed and Isobel, Chris and myself. Where do we all go from here? They had thrust us into this new world against our will. I thought about my sister, Liz, and my mom. Chris's former band mates. Everyone we left behind and had no way to contact now. I hadn't thought about them for a while, and that got me wondering where they were. What was going on in the rest of the world? I felt so disconnected. Was it because of the lack of technology?

45

SARAH

THE NEXT DAY, Chris lay in bed naked, physically and emotionally. I peeled my eyes open and looked at his body enveloping mine. His back rose and fell with every breath. I reached my arm around him to feel his thin, soft stomach. He stretched awake. I rubbed my hand against his chest, feeling the intermittent chest hairs between my fingers.

"Good morning," he whispered. Chris rolled over and faced me. I took one lock of his hair in between my fingers and rolled it around like a cigarette.

"Morning," I said back. My breath must have been terrible, but that hadn't gotten in our way lately.

For a moment our lives seemed perfect, like nothing could come between us. Like we could stay here forever, on these sheets, in this bed.

Then I heard a loud knock at the door that sounded more like a punch.

Chris and I sat up and reached for our clothes. We put them on quickly. We stood by the bed.

"Come in!" Chris yelled.

Two people entered I'd never seen before, a man about my age and a woman who looked to be nearly 70.

"Gavin and Darby are about to start," the woman said in a raspy voice.

"Be out there in ten, okay?" the man said. They both turned to leave.

"Wait!" Chris called out. "What do we bring? What can we expect?"

The man left, but the woman turned around to face us. Her head bobbed up and down, exaggerating the wrinkles on her face.

"Kid, I can't tell you that. Just bring yourself. We ain't leavin' till tomorrow or the next anyway, so get your asses out there in time."

"Yeah, we will. Okay, thanks."

After she left, Chris and I sat back on the bed.

"What the hell was that?" I asked. "I'm gonna pack up now."

"No."

"No? Why not?"

"Because we can't draw any attention to ourselves. We have to go along with the plan then take off."

I looked down at my shoes, which felt too tight. "I think we could wear layers, at least several pairs of underwear, you know?"

"Sounds good," Chris said looking over at me, then over at his guitar. "Guess we're not taking that, huh?"

"Oh, Chris," I looked over at him with sad eyes, knowing full well it wouldn't help anything.

"We can find another one," he said. He rummaged around our stuff. "We can only take a few items, you know. We should try to get as many powdered items as we can from the pantry."

"Yeah, I know. Look let's get out there. I'm getting anxious."

Chris took my hand and kissed my forehead. We walked out of the room stoic, two people with hardly a plan, but hardly a plan had gotten us this far. Several others had already gathered in the open space. Someone claimed the couch. I could see Isobel sitting there, twirling her hair. Gavin and Darby stood talking with others, presumably their team.

"Where's Ed?" Chris whispered.

I looked around. People leaned against the dark wooden pillars, talking. To my right, the kitchen hummed with people making dinner. Pots and pans clanged. I assumed we'd have soup again tonight.

Chris and I stood amongst the underlying hum of the others talking. It grew louder with every minute. Then, I felt a tap on my shoulder.

"Hey."

It was Ed. He smelled of soap and his hair was slicked back.

"Hey Ed. You ready?"

He nodded and took his place next to us. I saw him looking over at Isobel with folded arms. He carried no bag. Hard to tell if water or grease smoothed down his dark, curly hair. I saw him flex his biceps.

Gavin chimed in, "Hello, everyone. Thank you for all your hard work leading up to this next phase. I know many of you are still wondering what you're supposed to be doing or what you will come the day after tomorrow. But you'll ..."

"We'll what?" A lone voice rang out.

My breath nearly stopped at the sound. Someone is questioning it all.

"Oh, we have a dissenter in our ranks?" Gavin said. The crowd moaned.

"Yeah, what about it!?" The mystery voice yelled out. I still couldn't tell where it came from.

Gavin shifted his weight back and forth. He ran his hand through his silken curls and looked around without a care in the world. Chris and I looked at each other and gave a slight shrug.

Then a man appeared through the crowd. He was middle-aged and heavyset, his round belly flopped over the waist of his faded jeans. He was bald in the middle of his head, but his strands grew long on the sides, a homage to his younger years.

Gavin and he stared each other down, a bullfight amongst men.

"David, we've been through this."

"Yeah, yeah, Gavin. I know all your bullshit," David said with a southern drawl so thick, I could have sliced it with a butter knife. "But what about us?"

"What about you, Dave? You get to stay here with your lovely wife and guard the homestead. Isn't that what you wanted, Dave?" Gavin spoke the last sentence in staccato, each word drawn out for several seconds.

David wouldn't let him finish.

"No, Gavin. That's not what I want. I want ... well you know what I want. We want—"

Before I got uncomfortable enough to tug on Chris's shirt and suggest we leave, a group came forward and dragged Dave away, which was not a simple task. Dave wouldn't go down without a fight, but no one, not even his wife stepped forward to help him now. The group took Dave to the basement and threw him inside with a thud and slammed the door.

I shuddered and wondered why Dave got so mad about watching over the house.

"Now. I'll continue," Gavin says. He coughed to clear his throat. "As I was saying, many of you may still wonder what we will do in 48 hours. I will brief many of you after this meeting. Some of you, like David, are to stay behind and look after this place. It's a great ... He coughed again. ... great ... responsibility, you know." Gavin coughed more into his hand.

Darby appeared next to him. The crowd let out a long sigh, possibly of relief.

"So, as you all heard," she said. "You will all know what you'll be doing shortly. Now if there are no more questions, Gavin and I should go." Darby put her arm about Gavin, whose head hung. His hand covered his mouth, and he coughed every so often into it.

The crowd dispersed.

"What the hell was that?" Chris asked me.

I turned around and Ed had already gone. Part of me wondered if he's already planning his own separate exit strategy.

"I don't know," Chris said. "Let's go back to our room. Now."

•　　•　　•

Most of our belongings laid sprawled on top of any available surface. We had packed all we could into one backpack. We had stuffed it so full, it bulged out like an eight-month pregnant woman, ready to burst at any moment. Chris sat at the edge of the bed. He kept looking around, not saying anything. I paced the room, thinking of anything we may have forgotten.

"We should really go to the kitchen and get rations before we head out," Chris murmured.

Just as Chris said that the door opened, and Ed came in.

His eyes looked sunken like he'd been crying or not sleeping, or both. His dark hair stuck to his forehead either in sweat or because of a recent shower.

"So, I've been thinking."

Well, this could have gone either way. Did he not want to join up with us, or was he thinking he wanted to work with us, but he had to be in charge? Either way didn't sound great.

"I think we should go for it, even if Isobel won't," Ed said.

I nodded my head and looked over at Chris. His eyes told me everything I needed to know. He wanted in. I nodded to Edward. Without even saying so, we entered a pact. When the time came, we'd run.

46

OLIVIA

THE COT DUG IN UNDER MY STIFF BACK. I was tired of being here, in the dark. Grace left me in here a day ago, and already it felt like a prison. I had no way to know if I'd ever get out. The ten-by-ten room had a small nook with a toilet and sink. I felt truly in hell in this paradise of a house. I mean, I had found this huge ranch, only for them to toss me in the one room that they'd not updated in a hundred years.

I heard a knock on the door and my body rattled up.

"Yes! I'm here!" I shouted through the wood.

The lock rattled and the door opened. Grace hovered in the doorway.

"Why d'you even bother knocking, if you were just gonna come in anyway?"

"Just being polite, Olivia. Politeness still lives on, even in such extreme situations as ours, correct?"

"Uh, sure. So, did my story check out? Did you reach Ed? The Garden?"

"Yes. Ed was less than cooperative. Said they are already heading our way. That the Garden plan didn't work out. He assured me you are on our side, and we can all live and work together," she said.

I pressed my palm to my heart and sat back on the cot. The wooden bar dug into my quadriceps.

"So, can we stay?"

Grace leaned against the door frame and twirled her wavy hair into curly q's. If this had been "before," before all this, we probably never would have met. I'm a city girl. The whole concept of living on a ranch would never have appealed to me.

"I've got something, or rather someone, to show you before I answer that," she said.

Cryptic much.

"Any clues to who this person may be?" I asked, fearing it may be Allabaster.

"You'll just have to trust me. Come on," she motioned for me to follow her.

I followed her back through the living room and into the kitchen. The architectural details astounded me. More wooden beams lined the ceiling. There were stained glass cabinets, and the stove had eight burners, with double ovens beneath. A large spread of food sat on the counter.

"Please, may I?" I asked. I was so hungry, I could eat a horse. Probably shouldn't think that kind of thing here, though.

"Yes, of course. Help yourself, Olivia." Grace said.

I reached for a bunch of grapes, ripped them off the stems and thrust them into my mouth. I grabbed some cheese and shoved it in as well. Then I grabbed some crackers.

"Slow down, Olivia. There is plenty more where that came from. We grow our own grapes here at Galloway. And that's fresh goat cheese."

"Mmm hmmm," I replied with my mouth full of food. I heard voices from the outside of the kitchen getting louder. I swallowed. Wouldn't want to look like a pig in front of this special guest.

I looked around for a napkin to wipe my face and by the time I turned around to face forward, I saw her.

Kiwani.

She looked taller, more well groomed, but it was, in fact, her.

"Kiwi!" I cried out. "Is that really you?"

"Olivia. Oh my, God. Olivia!" she called out and ran to embrace me.

We hugged for a long time, then I pulled away.

"What are you—"

"Doing here?" she finished my question.

"Yeah."

"I've been here since … well … almost since the beginning."

Her soft eyes had grown hard, but still loving.

I saw Grace in the kitchen's corner watching us. I wasn't sure what to say, for fear of revealing too much.

"Well, that's great. Thank you, Grace, for taking her in. I really appreciate it," I said.

Grace nodded.

"So, anyway, I've been at Galloway for at least three years. I took off once the raids started. I was with a group. Most of them got rounded up, though. Taken to Centers. I was about to give up, when Grace and her group came along. Offered me shelter for work. I earned my keep, sis. I did. So, here I am and now, finally, I found you!"

Grace stepped forward. "So, yeah, your story checks out, I suppose. We had a community meeting, and I told them about you, and the others. Kiwani soon realized she was your sister. She vouched for you and we trust her, so …"

"So, we can stay?" I asked.

"So, you can stay. We need to get the others here, quickly. We cannot let the Center find you. If they do, it will be disastrous," Grace said.

I knew she was right.

"Okay, so give me the radio, so I can talk to Ed. If we have to meet halfway, we will," I said.

Grace tossed me the radio. I looked at Kiwani and smiled. No matter what, I knew it would be okay.

47

SARAH

T HE NEXT DAY, after cementing our plan with Ed, Chris looked over at me in bed and smiled. The lines on the bridge of his nose had grown deep; his hair long and shaggy. I looked back over at him and smiled. I'd given myself to him so much in these past months, today was no different.

We laid in bed just a little longer this morning, forgoing breakfast. We'd stashed a little something extra in our pack for such a moment.

"What are you thinking about," Chris asked.

"Thinking ... Thinking about what will happen when ..."

"When, what?"

"You know, when we try to escape." I closed my eyes and pictured Chris and me. In my daydream, we escaped easily from the Backers to an uninhabited island. We created our own society. No one told us how to live or what to do. We made love on the beach every morning and bathed in the rising tide, then scavenged for food. We laid together and made music, babies, a school. We found others like us, and it was perfect. Then my eyes opened, and I remembered where I was. The Garden was far from perfect, though Chris lay next to me. His scent drifted over me like a blanket, covering me in comfort until our next move.

"Yeah. Not try. We will."

"Yeah, we will," I said, trying to convince myself. Fear raced through my veins, though, that the Backers would catch us.

"If the sun rose no more, I would still love you ..." Chris sang.

I looked over at Chris. He looked at me. We said nothing, but said everything. A soft knock hit the door.

"You in there, guys?" a voice called out.

When I opened the door, Isobel was there. She looked pale.

"Come in," I said and closed the door behind her. Isobel dragged her heels along the carpet and sat down.

Her hair looked greasy and unkempt. She pulled her hair and twisted her fingers.

None of us said anything. I looked over at Chris and his brows raised up as if to tell me to wait.

I sat next to her and did just that. Chris stood.

She spoke up.

"Ok guys. I've thought about this a lot. I ... I really want to go with you, but I have one condition."

A condition?

Chris and I said nothing, but urged her on with questioning hand gestures.

"I ... want Gavin to come. I think ..."

"Wait, what?!" Chris said. "Gavin can't come! Why does he need to come?"

"He needs to come, trust me, okay," Isobel said.

"Why should we trust you, Isobel? Just give us one reason."

"I can't tell you why," she said. For a moment I thought she would cry, but then she shot up off the bed and stood tall. She ran a hand through her hair. "Gavin. He's a good guy. He wants what's best for this new world. I know this. I do. I've been with him since ... since ..."

"Oh my God, you're in love with him," I spurted out.

Isobel looked past me. She bit her lower lip and breathed out.

"No. I'm not. Not that should matter. I just know—"

"Know what?" Chris said.

"I know that Gavin will be an asset for us. He knows all the history. He knows how to get at the GB group. He knows. He knows." She sat back down.

I couldn't help but think Isobel might be a little crazy. Darby was the one that knew all the history. Why was Isobel so hell-bent on going along with Gavin? I'd never even had a real conversation with him.

"I don't know, Isobel. I mean, Darby is the one who seems to know everything. She basically runs the library," I said.

"Yeah, she runs it, but it's all a front. Darby doesn't know shit, Sarah. She knows nothing, literally."

I grew tired of this. The constant back and forth questioning, doubting. My journalism training taught me to be a skeptic, to pry at the root of the issue, to get to the truth. Well, maybe it wasn't possible now.

"So, how do we approach Gavin about going? Or have you already?"

"Yeah, I did. I didn't tell him that was what we were definitely doing."

Chris stood, arms crossed looking at me and Isobel talking like we're two aliens. I beckoned him to tell us what he thought.

"What does Ed have to say about all of this?" Chris asked.

"I don't know. I haven't talked to him," Isobel said.

"I call bullshit," Chris said.

"No, really. I haven't. I haven't had the time to."

"We should go now," I demanded.

Isobel looked at me then looked away. We all walked to the door, and I opened it. Outside we heard the usual rumblings, but the voices and people's movements seemed more frantic. There were lots of bags lining the walls, and no savory scents came from the kitchen. Gavin sat on the couch with his legs crossed. Isobel waved at him when he glanced this way, and he tilted his head as if to say he knew what we're up to. We walked to Ed's door, and I heard noises through the crack.

"Wait," I said.

I heard Ed's strained voice and another, lower, more forceful one that did most of the talking.

"Ed. We gotta go, dude," the deep voice said.

"Yeah. I know. I'm going. I'm going. Let me pack up, okay?" Ed said.

Two men left Ed's room and pushed past us without so much a backward glance.

Ed's room was a disaster zone, though I'd never seen it before. I could tell they tossed it. Books lined the floor like tossed tissues. Clothes everywhere. He sat on the bed, head in hands. He looked up and saw us, then looked back down.

"Oh, hey you guys. What's up?" he said giving a false chuckle.

"Who were those guys?" I asked.

"Nobody ... Uh. I gotta pack up, ya know ..." Ed sniffed and shuffled his stuff around into a bag on his unmade bed. Light tried to peek in through the saggy, white curtains. I wondered where he thought he was going instead of with us.

"You okay?" I asked.

"Yeah. Sure." He continued putting stuff into a maroon, carry-on suitcase.

"Ed. What the hell?" Chris said. "Where are you going? We thought you were ..."

"Yeah, you thought wrong," Ed snapped and sucked his teeth. He looked left and right and cinched the suitcase shut. He held it in his right hand, walked to the door, and Chris jumped in front of him.

"No fucking way are you leaving. Where are you going anyway!? You're supposed to be coming with us!"

I'd never seen Chris so mad. He and Ed stood face to face, eyes locked. I'm not sure who would win this battle, but I hoped it would be my guy.

"Something came up. I have to go do this ... this other thing."

"What other thing? This is bullshit," Chris said.

Isobel turned to leave. I grabbed her arm, and she shouted.

"Stop, Sarah. I'm going now, okay. It's better this way. You'll see," Isobel said and yanked her arm out of my grasp.

Before I could blink, she was gone. The only person who stood by my side this whole time was Chris. Ed and Isobel looked like afterthoughts, or better yet, just fair-weather friends who disappeared at the first sign of trouble. I'd had plenty of those in my life and I'd be damned if I cared about these types now.

Ed sat down on the bed.

"Close the door," he said. His voice was deep and different.

"Okay, so, the Garden folks have been pressuring me to turn you in. They say I need to pack my bags and come with them. That you two are on your own and that you are the only ones that can lead us to the Backers and the Sweepers and all that BS. I played into it, but I never really meant it."

"So, who left here before we came in?" Chris asked.

"That was Harry. Harry is Darby's little bitch. He does all her bidding, you know?" Ed looked over at his bag. I looked over at Chris, wondering, again, who the hell we could trust anymore.

"So, ok. You told Harry that you'd turn us in to the Backers, then what?" Chris asked.

"Nothing. Then he told me to pack up. That things were moving quicker than we thought. I didn't believe it."

I looked around Ed's room. There were no distinguishing features, like posters or belongings, only clothes and books strewn about. He could be anyone, but he had expressed an interest in coming with Chris and me. We had tons of reasons to distrust him, but my instincts told me to do so. He knew Olivia and she was our key. The only question was could she unlock the door to our futures?

48

SARAH

T HE NEXT DAY, Chris and I headed out to the common area for breakfast. We carried our small bags to seem sincere, like we wanted to sacrifice ourselves for the greater good and get our tech back.

The last meeting we attended about an hour ago was standard. Gavin stood in the middle of our group and laid out the day's plans. The Garden got a device that could scan and document all evidence of any tech. We learned that even though the Backers despised technology, they kept their friends close and enemies closer—so to speak. Therefore, they had all the tech we had given up, either voluntarily or by force and the Garden had a way to track it. The method used to only belong to police forces and government agents, but someone in our midst showed us the way for immunity. We would meet up with the GB group in three hours. Before that, we were to pack everything quickly, and only pack the most necessary items.

Gavin told us the plan was for Chris and me to approach the Backers and offer ourselves up for the Garden's freedom. The Garden wanted to become its own community, apart from any other. They wanted the Backers to "back off" so to speak.

But Chris and I wanted no part of this. Ed didn't either. As for Isobel, we hadn't seen her since she left Ed's room yesterday.

Chris and I sat in the common area contemplating our future

I rested my head on Chris's shoulder, breathed his comforting scent and thought about the guitar we about to leave behind, also my mom and Liz … and Chris's family.

"Chris," I whispered. He looked over, his blue eyes shimmering. "What do you think will happen to us?"

"I know we'll stay together, you and I. What happens after that is anyone's guess," Chris said. He stroked my arm. I closed my eyes and try to rest before the big moment.

I must have fallen asleep, because before I knew it, Chris jostled me awake and we were standing. Most of the Garden's members lined up at the door. Those chosen to stay behind milled about near the extremities, like the kitchen and bedroom areas.

Chris and I found each other's hands and walked to the front door as a united front.

Light streamed in from outside, and my body craved the warmth of the sun. Stepping out, I closed my eyes and reveled in it. Gavin said we'd have to walk at least a mile before the meet up point. Before our journey, I looked up at the church steeple. It had a gothic gold cross on top. The white paint on the spire peeled so much, I could see it from the ground.

"Where's Ed?" I mouthed to Chris. He shrugged. I looked around but saw no one I recognized, not even Isobel or Gavin or Darby. We stepped through the tall grass, our shoes getting wet from the morning dew. Once on the sidewalk we passed empty storefronts and warehouses. Discarded cars lined the one-way streets.

The group barely talked above a low mumble, but I could make out Gavin's voice behind me.

"Hey you two. How's it going?" he asked as he passed me and Chris on the left.

"Good," Chris said giving my hand a light squeeze.

"How much longer do you think?" I asked Gavin.

"Not much, but I wanted to talk to you before we get there. Isobel told me you don't trust me, and that's understandable."

Chris and I slowed to a shuffle. The clouds grew darker and hung low in the sky. A faint rumble of thunder filled the air.

"Oh, wow. Yeah, it's not that we don't trust you, we don't really know who to trust, you know?" Chris said.

Keep your friends close and your enemies closer. Our feet shuffled faster. Much of the group went around us, all carrying their packs and many smoking and chatting.

"We don't really want to sacrifice ourselves. I mean, what if we get shipped back to the Center? There's no guarantee we'll be able to get out again," I said.

Gavin stuck his right arm out to signal us to stop. He threw his cloak over his shoulders and put his hands on his hips. His eyes looked directly into mine.

"You won't get caught. In fact, you will not meet up with the Backers at all. Look, I knew you two were planning to take off beforehand anyway, and I don't blame you at all."

I jerked Chris's hand and pulled him closer to me. How did Gavin know this?

He went on. "Darby and the rest of these people think the Garden is, like, it. They think this is the beginning of a new society; that they'll get the Backers to give us our tech back and they'll leave us alone. But that's not gonna work at all."

Gavin reached into his pocket and pulled out a crushed up soft pack of Camel lights, pulled one out and lit it up. He dragged in deep while continuing to walk.

Chris looked at me. Our eyes met, our secret language in full force.

I was ready to take off right now. The group ahead slowed down. Through a gap, I saw we're nearing a town square of sorts. I spotted a water tower in the distance.

"We're in Moffat?" I asked Chris.

"Huh?"

"Moffat. Look at the water tower."

We continued walking. Gavin walked through an opening of people to get ahead. People stopped and lingered. We were right in the middle of the square now. Red brick apartments perched atop stores with different colored awnings, and a circle loop drive made up the middle.

People sat down, pulled out smokes, drinks and talked. Chris and I took a cue and sat on the sidewalk, our backs against the side of the building. Chris pulled out an apple to share. In the near distance, I saw Gavin, Isobel and Darby. I hadn't seen Darby in a while. I also still wondered where Ed went. This big plan of ours, or lack thereof, worried me.

Two squirrels chased each other around a maple tree. Black grackles surrounded us squawking for food. We ate our apple to the core and Chris tossed it far away. The birds flocked to it.

Chris leaned over and kissed my cheek, then leaned back against the wall.

"Be right back," I said. Chris looked at me in protest, but I took off before he could say anything. I walked in Gavin's direction. As soon I caught his eye, I nodded to the right and headed in that direction. Gavin stopped his conversation and headed my way. We stood under an awning in front of an antique shop. There was an old baby buggy in the window and lots of junk spread out on tables.

"Where the hell is everyone, Gavin?" I asked.

"Oh, so now you ask," Gavin said in a low voice. He reached into his pocket for another cigarette.

I blew out a deep breath. My patience was not even thin anymore, it dangled by a thin thread.

"Tell me now. You want us to trust you! Tell me now, motherfucker."

"Language, Sarah. My goodness. Okay, I'll tell you."

We sat down and Gavin talked. After only about a minute into his story, I swiped his cigarette and took a drag.

49

SARAH

AFTER TALKING WITH GAVIN, I couldn't get back to Chris fast enough. When I reached him, he was sleeping against the building.

"Wake up," I said.

He opened his eyes and rubbed his hand over his face.

"Yeah ..." he mumbled.

"Listen, I talked to Gavin, and Isobel is right. We need to go with him."

"What? Why? What happened?"

"Look, Gavin knows stuff, okay. He can get us out of here. Let me tell you what he told me.

"Okay, so what does this all mean, Sarah? What are we gonna do? The Backers will be here any minute, right? We're supposed to be the decoys, but we're getting out of here, right?"

"The Backers aren't coming. Gavin just created this as a distraction to keep everyone busy and not ask too many questions," I said. Chris looked at me like I had two heads.

"Chris, Gavin knows Olivia. He knows everything."

"What the hell!"

"Shh. Keep it down!"

"Oh, my God. What about everyone else, Sarah? We can't just leave them here."

I wanted to agree because I never wanted to hurt anyone, not even a fly before all of this, but that bubble had burst.

"They aren't buying what Gavin has to say. They think they can defeat the Backers with reasoning. They don't believe what's going on at the Centers, because, well, they've never been."

"But what about Ed?"

"I know. I want him to come, too, but … no telling where he is now. It's now or never."

I looked up and saw Gavin and Isobel heading over.

Isobel looked at me and smiled.

"You two in?"

"Yeah," I said, looking at her. "We are. Totally."

Isobel left and talked to others gathered around. Presumably, she told them the Backers will be here any minute.

She told them she convinced Chris and I to offer ourselves up.

She told them that this was the moment. This is what we'd planned for, but it was all a ruse. The world was blown to hell and gone, and we were still playing games.

The sunset created a vibrant pink sky behind the low stratus clouds. Our group gathered around. We all looked rugged. I hadn't showered in a few days but had at least sponged off. Both Chris and I, and most of the people who had longer hair just let it become matted tangles. Others cut their hair above the ears.

Off to our right I saw another couple. The guy held his girlfriend's hand and kissed it. She seemed to do all the talking. I then noticed that although she looked to weigh only 100 pounds soaking wet; she had a protruding belly. I recognized them as the man and woman from my GB van, and I knew then what I had to do. While I wanted to help Gavin and Isobel and get to Olivia, I couldn't leave the others behind.

"Ok everybody, listen up," I raised my voice so most people could hear.

"What are you doing, Sarah?" Gavin asked. His voice was low and deep.

I put my hand up and walked to the middle of the crowd.

"I know someone told us the Backers are coming."

The crowd cheered a simultaneous "yeah."

"Well. They're not."

The crowd mumbling raised to a roar.

"Now, hold on, hold on," Gavin yelled. The crowd calmed down, but people still talked. "I think what Sarah means to say is—"

"No. Gavin, stop! You and I know we can't keep lying to these people. We are not in communication with the Backers. We know they're at the Centers, but we …"

"What?" a man in the crowd said. "There is no such thing as Centers, right Gavin?" He turned to the crowd and most people nodded and gave verbal agreement. Gavin said nothing but turned to Chris and me. Isobel squeezed both her lips together so tightly they disappeared. She was freaking out I could tell. Chris looked at me and back at the crowd and urged me on.

"Look, everyone. Calm down. Chris and I came here with every intention of offering ourselves up. But that isn't going to happen. Gavin and Isobel know it. And so do Chris and I. We're going to a woman named Olivia. I met her at a Center. She got me out. Now she's getting others out. We can help people. We can fight the Backers from there."

"But what about our tech?" someone shouted out. More cheers.

"Tech is not the issue right now. The issue right now is making sure we're all safe and that we can create a real town or city again, find out where the others are."

The crowd murmured. Some people turned away and start talking amongst themselves.

"See, Sarah. I told you. They don't believe it. They don't believe in the Centers. They don't take this shit seriously," Gavin said.

I looked at the crowd then back at Chris.

"Ok everybody, listen up," I yelled. No one stopped talking. "Listen up!" I yelled again. "I know what happens at these Centers! They drug you! They make you sign contracts to never tell people the truth. We have to get people out of there! We have to!" Crowd mumbling continued. People shouted. The pink sky turned maroon; dark purple clouds loomed. I felt a raindrop on my cheek.

"You don't have to come if you don't want to. But I know some of us need doctors."

"Let's sleep on it. We need to find shelter, though, before the sweepers come, ok. Think about it." I turned to Chris, and he took my hand. Gavin and Isobel looked at me and shook their heads, but I knew I did the right thing. The crowd dispersed. I saw a group trying to pick a lock of one business. It worked and people went inside.

"Let's find some shelter," Isobel said, looking over at Gavin. "We'll find you in the morning."

"Shouldn't we stick together?" Chris asked.

"Naw, just stay close by, okay, and don't come out till first light."

Isobel and Gavin left. Chris tugged at my arm. We slept in an abandoned restaurant, both of us taking either side of a booth.

50

DUSTY LIGHT BEAMS STREAMED IN from a window of the restaurant. I lifted my head and right arm to peel it away like a band aid to an open wound from the plastic bench I called my bed all night. I looked around and couldn't see Chris, which sent me into a semi-state of shock.

I lurched up on the bench and look around, feeling a terrible crick in my neck.

"Over here, babe," Chris called. He was by the cash register.

"Any money in there?" I chuckled knowing cash money wasn't really good anymore, but who knew, right?

"Don't know. I can't get the damn thing open."

Chris banged on the thick, plastic casing, then pushed random buttons. There was a keyhole, but no key in sight.

"Come on, Chris. We should get moving. Did you find any food? I'm hungry!" I turned to look at him, but my neck cried out in pain. I walked over to the register. This must have been an old-time diner. It had black and white checkered tile. A vinyl couch sat against a wall fashioned like an old '67 Chevy. I didn't really know about old cars, but that was the first model that came to mind.

"Let's go to the kitchen. There's gotta be something we can take along," I said.

Chris and I headed that way. Behind the register were several black, squishy floor mats. They smelled of rubber. This must have been a new place. We pushed open some swinging doors and found ourselves in a walk-in pantry. Chris and I rummaged around, looking for any non-perishable food to take along. I scored a carton of oatmeal and dried fruit. Chris found trail mix and potato chips. We swiped a few water bottles from a cooler.

The air felt damp, and locusts buzzed. We saw no one and for a moment could forget about everything going on, our quest to find Olivia, dealings with everyone else. Chris and I held hands. He ran the other through my hair, but it got tangled, so we laughed.

"Hey you two lovebirds." Gavin and Isobel walked towards us.

"Hey, where's everyone else?" I asked.

"Not sure, but it they don't get here soon, we're leaving. That's the deal," Isobel said. She cocked her head to the right. She was chewing gum. Hadn't seen that in a while. Her moving jawline was so defined. I'd always envied people with defined jaw lines.

"Ok, well, what now?" Chris asked.

"We wait." Gavin said. He sat down on an elevated esplanade. A squirrel squatted below but darted straight up the planted tree.

It was like an hour until we saw any movement. I was almost ready to call it quits.

A crowd gathered around. Chris, Gavin, Isobel and I stood in the center. Gavin did most of the talking.

"We're heading out, everyone. We're gonna meet up with Olivia. I know some of you don't want to do that, and that's okay. I know some of you want to ..."

The crowd roared. Looking out, I saw the pregnant couple again and I walked over to them.

"Hey guys, remember me?"

The girl looked at me sideways. Her eyes darted between me and her man. Outside noises hummed. Locust noises filled the air, like a distant hum of my childhood. I remembered plucking their empty shells off the plants around my house. Their living body shed and flew away, leaving behind this crispy hull. I always wished I could do that. Peel off the outer layers and begin again. Perhaps now was the time.

"I'm Melissa and he's Rich. But what does it matter anyway?" she blurted, her eyes averting mine like the plague.

"It matters because we've been through shit, at the same time. I was there. I was there when ..."

"No! It doesn't matter. You couldn't stop it. You couldn't ..." The girl buried her face inside Rich's green Army jacket, her sobs muffled by the dense fabric.

I stepped closer and she pulled away, putting her hands on her stomach in protective Mama mode.

I stepped closer still, reaching my own arms out to her belly, perhaps seven months along. I don't know since I'd never had a child of my own.

"What's the baby's name?" I asked.

"What?"

"The baby's name ..." I asked again.

"Evan," she said. Her eyes met mine. Finally, we reached an understanding. Rich spoke up now, too.

"Look, we've had a rough time. Melissa and I ... we ... barely escaped with our lives from that damn place."

"I know. Chris and I, we ..."

Chris interjected suddenly. "Yeah, we know how it goes, okay. Are you with us or not?" His stance made it seem like he's not asking, more like demanding. His legs spread apart; his newly formed black matted tendrils had overtaken the hair I once loved to run my fingers through.

"I think so. What the hell else can we do?" Rich said.

Rich, Melissa and unborn Evan stood a little closer to me and Chris.

The rest of the crowd mumbled and dispersed, some sat, some stood up. A cool wind picked up. It picked up my heavy hair, my brown roots overtaking my auburn dye. A crow cawed from a nearby tree. My heart was restless in this new reality, whatever that meant. I could sense a change. But what? Slowly I turned to the crowd and announced in a loud voice, "Okay, who's with us?"

The crowd murmured.

I looked over at Chris, Gavin and Isobel. I didn't see Ed. I could only hope he was communicating with Olivia somehow. As my thoughts ran wild, another noise made me turn my head. That's when I saw her. The woman from the center.

"Allabaster!" Isobel called out.

Behind her I saw Ed with two guards, his hands behind his back.

My stomach dropped. The crowd dispersed in every direction screaming.

"Freeze!" The guards pointed guns our way.

We all put our hands in the air.

Allabaster stepped toward me.

"Gotcha. Thought you were pretty smart leaving the Center like that, but no one gets away!"

I stepped forward and looked her square in the eyes. In the distance I saw Rich and a group waiting to pounce. My heart pounded. I knew I had to stall her so they could make their move. Whatever it was.

"How did you find us," I stumbled out.

Allabaster licked her lips and gripped her gun in both hands, pointing it directly at me.

"Not that I should tell you, but that Garden place has been under our surveillance for some time. Plus, when we heard nothing from our scout near there, we found out that you had been there. It was only a matter of time."

Chris and I kept stepping backwards. "What you're doing to people is inhumane! You won't get away with this!"

"What we're doing, Ms. Grimes, will help humanity. We are cleansing the world of tech and addiction. Can't you see that, girl?" Allabaster clicked her tongue several times at me. She was so close, a flick of her saliva hit my cheek. It took all I had not to wipe it away. Didn't want to move my hands for fear of being shot.

"If that tech is so horrible, then why are you keeping it for yourselves? Olivia and I saw it with our own eyes!" Ed called out. One guard hit him in the back of the head with the gun. Ed fell to the ground.

"We only keep the tech we need we need to find people like you, who think they can get away without turning in their tech. That's how we found your precious 'Garden'. We're there now and we will round up anyone who returns …"

"You took the Garden! You bastards!" Isobel screamed and cried. Gavin shushed her.

I laughed harder than I could even remember. Harder than before all this mess even happened.

"I don't see what's so funny, Ms. Grimes."

"Sarah, what the hell?" Chris hissed.

The guards looked puzzled and lowered their weapons. My laughs grew even louder, until I screamed, "Now!"

Rich and a crew of about two dozen others stormed through the trees and jumped the guards. A gun went off, hitting one of them. He fell to the ground in pain. Looked to be his leg.

Gavin and Chris jumped Allabaster. They held her hands behind her and tied her to a tree with a bungee cord.

"You'll never get away with this," Allabaster screamed. One guard dropped his weapons and begged for his life, saying he never wanted to join GB. We tied him up, too.

Ed pointed a gun at the other guard, who dropped to his knees.

Isobel and I gathered all the GB surveillance tools like walkie talkies. We even scored several cell phones.

We took everything.

"Come on guys. They're probably chipped too. Not long before someone at the Center realizes they're missing," I said.

"What should we do with them?" Chris asked. By now we gagged and tied the other guards.

Several others tended to the gunshot victim. Someone found a branch to use as a makeshift crutch. I'm guessing at least twenty minutes had passed.

"We should kill them," Gavin said.

"Gavin!" Isobel retorted.

Allabaster sat stoic, not making a sound.

"It would send a very powerful message."

Chris looked down and I knew what he was thinking.

"No, we leave them here. Now let's go," I said.

Somehow, I had become the leader.

No one dissented, so we left them there, tied up and gagged. If they haven't been chipped, who knew if anyone would find them and their deaths would be on us.

51

SARAH

THERE WERE TWENTY-SEVEN OF US, Chris and I included. Rich and Melissa walked beside Chris and me. Gavin and Isobel straggled behind. Chris and I held hands here and there, not talking much.

"What made you come back for us, Rich," I asked.

"Had to. I mean, I've been resisting GB for all this time, then they locked us up, we got out. Shit, it was the least I could do. I couldn't let you guys go back there."

"Well, thanks. I know it's not enough, but thanks," Chris said. I nodded.

We kept walking. No more talk about what happened. No one talked about what may have become of the people who went back to the Garden, or anywhere else.

"How long do you think it'll take?" Chris asked me.

"Not sure. I'm hoping we reach there by sundown. Don't want to have to contend with the Sweepers, you know."

Ed told us the guards ambushed him when he left the group to call Olivia on the Sat phone. Before his capture, Olivia told him she'd found her sister, and that we were welcome there. The news was a huge relief. That made me think of my own family.

Outside Moffat we found vast plains filled with farmhouses. I saw people working the fields. Here and there we passed fruit and vegetable stands. They didn't take money.

"Can we trade?" I asked one, holding up salt and rice we found along the way.

"Si, Señora," the man said. I saw one of his suntanned index fingers was missing halfway. I tried not to stare as we exchanged bags.

"Where you go?" he asked. A ray of sun hit his face causing him to squint.

"Next town over," I said. I didn't want to reveal too much.

"You one of them?"

Chris and the others gathered on the other side of the road.

"Come on, Sar," I heard him call out.

"No," I said to the man. "I gotta go. Take care, okay." I turned away saying nothing else.

Gavin looked over at Isobel and Chris. Chris waved us on, and we walked. During the walk, I had plenty of time to think back to what my mom told me before all this shit went down. I wondered where she was. I wondered about all my family. I'd been so busy trying to survive and move on, I had thought little about them. Somehow, pressing on, I told myself that I'd be able to talk to them again soon. Olivia found her sister, so there was hope.

Chris squeezed my hand. Time ticked on. My footsteps felt heavy with each step. Melissa and Rich took a break on the side of the road. I wondered how and when she'd have baby Evan. Darkness fell. I saw the glow of light coming from the next town over. Must be it. We all paused for a brief respite in a grove of Oak trees. Long, protruding roots served as seats. The large canopy covered us like an umbrella.

"What are you thinking?" Chris asked.

"I'm thinking about what's next," I said. I looked over at him, his handsome chiseled features hiding beneath sinking cheekbones, his blue eyes seem to glow in the setting sun, cascading a warm feeling through my whole body. "I love you, Chris."

His whole face relaxed.

"I love you too, Sarah."

We camped out beneath the trees, figuring if the Sweepers found us, we'd outnumber them. I fell asleep next to Chris. The next morning, we awoke to the sound of a rooster crowing.

"So, what are you hoping to find?" Ed asked me the next day.

"Hope," I said.

"Hope?"

"Yeah, a little, I guess."

"But what about our tech? What about the sweepers and GB and all that?" Ed asked. I could see Chris out of the corner of my eye talking to some other people. Others gathered their stuff, preparing for the last stretch of the walk.

"Doesn't matter," I said. "We have each other, and we'll figure it out."

"Hmm. Yeah." Ed turned away and looked around. "Galloway about two-and-a-half miles away. All right folks!" Ed yelled. "Gather up and let's go. We're all in this together now."

About an hour into our trip, we reached the metal gate surrounded by a tall stucco fence.

A sign read, "Welcome to Galloway."

"We're here," I said. The road beyond the gates was quiet though.

A door along the wall opened, and a dog and a woman stepped out. She had long, blonde hair and a red shawl.

"Can I help you?" she asked me.

"Well, not sure," I said. "We're looking for Olivia."

The woman looked at me and squished her face up.

"I see. You must be Sarah."

"Um. Yes," I said and looked over at Chris.

The woman mumbled something, then took off quickly, pulling her small, yapping dog behind her.

"What the hell?" I said to Chris.

"I think we should divide and conquer. Let me look at the map," Ed said. He studied it for a moment, then pulled out a pad of paper and made several copies. He handed them out to groups and instructed them to spread out and meet up there in thirty-minute increments.

But the woman in the shawl turned around and stopped.

"I'm Grace and you are welcome here. Please, come in."

The metal gates opened, and she beckoned for us to walk through. Chris and I lead, the others followed.

As we walked down the sidewalk to the entrance of the main house, my whole body felt a familiar vibration that made my arm hairs stand on end. It was the low hum of music. I couldn't make out the lyrics, but they sent me right back to that night before the world blew to bits; the night I met Chris.

At that moment, in simultaneous thought, I was equally glad and filled with regret that I had written that article.

But we couldn't really go back, even though GB would like us to think so. They could take all our tech, but no matter how much they took, they couldn't force us to go back. We could only look forward.

ABOUT THE AUTHOR

Emily Wagner is a writer, educator, and former journalist who always questions the "what if?"s of this world, hence her preference for speculative fiction. She is an alumna of the Taos Toolbox writing workshop and two-time honorable mention in the *Writers of the Future* contest. She lives in Baltimore with her husband and two children.

YOU MIGHT ALSO ENJOY

THE CERES ILLUSION
by Sue Eaton

Something is definitely rotten in the experimental settlement on Ceres.

THE CREDO OF COMRADE JANUARY
by Robert Bagnall

Solar explosions known as "The Pulse" have rendered all electronics useless and sent Mankind back to a pre-digital age.

O2
by Kellyn Solvera

Restored to life in a future world where access to the very air he breathes is rationed, a man attempts to break free from the governmental restraints, only to discover why the government now regulates everything.

Available from Water Dragon Publishing in
hardcover, trade paperback, and digital editions
waterdragonpublishing.com

9 781967 547173